A BRIMSTONE FILES NOVEL

HEX-RATED

JASON RIDLER

NIGHT
SHADE
BOOKS

Night Shade books may be purchased in bulk at special discounts for sales promotion, corporate
gifts, fund-raising, or educational purposes. Special editions can also be created to specifications. For
details, contact the Special Sales Department, Night Shade Books, 307 West 36th Street, 11th Floor,
New York, NY 10018 or info'skyhorsepublishing.com.

Night Shade Books™ is a trademark of Skyhorse Publishing, Inc.®, a Delaware corporation.

Visit our website at www.nightshadebooks.com.

10 9 8 7 6 5 4 3 2 1

Library of Congress Cataloging-in-Publication Data

Names: Ridler, Jason Sean, 1975- author.
Title: Hex-rated : a Brimstone files novel / Jason Ridler.
Description: New York : Night Shade Books, [2017] | Series: The Brimstone
    files ; 1
Identifiers: LCCN 2017006571 | ISBN 9781597809030 (softcover : acid-free
    paper)
Subjects: LCSH: Private investigators--California--Los Angeles--Fiction. |
    BISAC: FICTION / Fantasy / Urban Life. | FICTION / Fantasy / Paranormal. |
    FICTION / Fantasy / Contemporary. | GSAFD: Mysery fiction. | Occult
    fiction.
Classification: LCC PS3618.I39225 H49 2017 | DDC 813/.6--dc23
LC record available at https://lccn.loc.gov/2017006571

Cover artwork by John Stanko
Cover design by Claudia Noble

Printed in the United States of America

Thanks to Nick Mamatas for connecting the dots, Kate Marshall for her vigilant eye, Jeremy Lassen and Cory Allyn at Night Shade Books for taking the chance, and to all y'all reading this right now. Cheers!

This novel is dedicated to Inta Mezgailis Ridler (1938-2013).

From a black and white TV in the laundry room, she'd feed my heart and brain doses of Star Trek, Rockford Files, Kolchak, Mike Hammer, and the Twilight Zone while she chain-smoked Viscounts and folded clothes.

When I started writing, she sent me a bunch of second-hand Mickey Spillane novels. She'd enjoyed them more than the acclaimed work of Hammett and Chandler. When I asked why, she laughed. "Oh, way more sex and violence! Good stuff!"

Thanks for the inspiration, Mum. Here's to the good stuff.

"In this city a person can hide from God for a long time."
—Steven Erickson, *Zeroville*

"The so-called glamour queens are short lived.
Where are they now? Take out your old movie magazines
and trace the queens of yesterday. There are a lot of
yesterdays for them but no tomorrows . . ."
—Ed Wood, Jr., *The Hollywood Rat Race*

HEX-RATED

CHAPTER 1

I RAN A CROOKED PATH THROUGH THE HEADSTONES AS IF CHASED BY A drunk minotaur, my ancient oxblood wingtips kicking up forgotten trinkets left for long-departed souls. As I was leaping over a burial mound, my shoe slipped on something round.

I smacked a tombstone with my shoulder, spun like a top, then crashed back down to earth chest-first, just a bee's wing away from a foundation stone that would have cut my head open.

"OW!"

If Edgar could see me, late to his funeral, he'd be furious.

At eye level was the dirty culprit: a fat 8-ball, twice the size of the kind you'd find in any billiard hall. A stray parting gift for a lost loved one.

I couldn't resist. Running late and elbows in grave dirt, I picked it up, shook it twice and asked, "All right, Magic 8-Ball, will today's adventure turn out in my favor?"

I turned it over. The murky glass bottom swirled with a blue liquid before a white message rose to the top. *"Outlook not so good."*

I smirked. "Everyone's a critic."

I tossed the toy to the ground and sprang back to life, on down the dusty green alley of the cemetery until I saw the two members of the work crew I'd met yesterday. They pointed to my left, and I ran through the stones to find the small funeral procession gathered around a fresh grave.

I hit the brakes to avoid crashing into anyone, and dusted the dirt off of my freshly rented duds. I coughed, but all eyes were on me like white on rice. "Very sorry, everyone." I switched to a wary smile and heavy eyes. "Had car trouble en route. I guess the only funeral you should be late for is your own." I mimicked a "rim-shot" in the air, complete with sound effects a la Buddy Rich. The half-truth-and-joke combo usually worked to charm folks out of distress.

Here? The crowd in black glared. Not at me, or my patter, but at my outfit. A baby-blue tuxedo, last year's prom sensation, was all I could afford on my own dime. This funeral had sucked my reserves down to the marrow. The lapels flared as sharp and wide as the bellbottom trousers, which hugged me a little too snug for such a somber occasion. Grave-dirt skids no doubt made the whole ensemble filthy in the eyes of my social betters. The small gathering's disdain was cold for July in L.A., but the funeral was my responsibility, and they held their tongues. They could release their nastiness beyond my earshot. Though I reckoned they'd be of familiar vintages:

"Can you believe James Brimstone came to a funeral dressed for a high school prom?"

"He must be forty and he's showing off his . . . you-know-what?"

"Smudges? On his funeral outfit? Edgar would be disgusted."

I nodded at Father Creedy, who began his sermon while I squirmed in the sun. What I wouldn't do for a Dubonnet on the rocks and the darkness of my office, but there was work to do, parts to play, and promises to keep.

The cemetery grunts had done a fine job of digging a hole for Edgar's funeral, a deep, tight six-by-three frame. Above the hole, a cherry wood coffin was mounted, wrapped in chains and padlocks upon Edgar's wishes and courtesy of my bone-dry checkbook. My mentor was many things, but generous with lucre wasn't even last on the list. On tour with the Electric Magic Circus, I once joked with Jane Tarzan, our unbeatable wrestling angel, that Edgar's nickname ought to be "Frugal the Ungenerous," whose change purse could only be opened by Hercules himself. When Edgar found out about the gag, as he always did, he had me cleaning outhouses and digging holes for elephant dung instead of learning how to execute a Paris drop, escape from a locked safe, or use a deck of cards like a weapon. It was worth it to make Jane laugh, though I suspect she only laughed because she knew that no one but the first god of lies could keep a secret from my mentor.

L.A.'s merciless three o'clock sun scorched Inglewood Park Cemetery as it sidled up close to watch the Amazing Edgar Vance's very last public appearance. Proving to an intimate audience that even he could not escape the grave. My tux baked the sweat out of me like a rotisserie chicken, inking the powder blue into ugly sweat spots, as if my tux hid leaking bullet wounds.

Father Creedy moaned on.

My smile was at half-mast, but I wanted them to look at me, the cheap, lousy fellow who'd done such a crap job. I was human flash for their scorn. Not the casket and its locks and chains . . . which I could taste. One of the worst things about being Edgar's whipping boy was this delicious side-effect of his training in the actual arcane, the disturbing and nightmarish world of sorcery, magic, and dark arts older than the blood of dead gods. I could taste real magic. And it never tasted good. Just a thousand different flavors of awful. Those chains and locks had enough mojo on them that my mouth felt like it had been sucking dirt for the past hour, but I kept it shut.

Promises to keep, and all that jazz.

Father Creedy's whistling voice cut through the heat. ". . . and so we consecrate Edgar William Vance to the ground, so that he may find his place in eternity at the righteous side of God." Across the hole, his sad eyes perked without joy.

My half-smile froze. I'd told Creedy, whose real name was Chip Toledo, if that was a real name anywhere but L.A., to cut the "righteous" out of his sermon. Actors always make big words sound threatening. Bad actors give them menace. And Chip was no Olivier.

I twisted the plastic ring on my left pinky, a faded green toy I'd held onto from the very first dint I'd made in the world of crime: stealing from a vending machine with a penny I'd gimmicked with a kite string. It also served as a signal to "Father" Creedy to shut his piehole because he was making an ass of himself, and that further attempts would result in his commission being cut *another* fifteen percent.

"And now," Father Creedy said, "is there anyone who would like to say a few final words?"

Smoothly, my hands dropped in front of my privates because the sweat stain was starting to leak downward. But just as I opened my mouth—

"I'd like to speak." Mick Fletcher walked close to the grave, dressed in a dire combo of tie, jacket, shirt and pants, a human black hole. His vulture neck protruded from his collar, and his stare cut across the casket's surface, aimed straight for my heart, fuzzy eyebrows set on "arch." My balls itched.

"Edgar was the greatest performer I ever saw." Everyone nodded, dutifully, myself included, but that didn't break Mick's glare. "Greatest escape artist since Houdini. Better magician than Blackstone. And he cared, you know? He cared about magic and those that loved it." More nods. More glare. "Even if some of us didn't love it as much as we should."

Mick stepped back, and I enjoyed the image of him surrounded by headstones. He was Edgar's greatest fan, and a royal pain in the ass. Edgar did love magic. It was all he loved. Mick would try and impress Edgar with a new card trick or pigeon gimmick. Edgar would study him seriously, give him backhanded advice that would have been an insult if Mick hadn't been so enamored, and after the poor guy was led out of Vance Mansion, I'd have to endure Edgar's cackles and snide shots about "Poor old Mick the Mark." Edgar held him beneath contempt, but enjoyed using him for free labor at shows, the devoted disciple who never knew he was, in fact, the master's pet rube.

But it took one to know one, so I couldn't hate Mick as much as Edgar. Hell, I'd been just like Mick, just the professional variety. At least until I quit Edgar's schemes. This funeral was the last.

A stunning, bottle-blonde thirty-year-old in horn-rimmed glasses and baby-doll good looks approached next, the kind of beauty that worked in B films until she was old enough to play a mother and had to find a different vocation for beauty and presence. She wore a starched plaid skirt, pink blouse and mascara melted into her blush. Good old Debbie Faye.

"On behalf of Mayor Yorty," Debbie said with the commanding tone of stage performances from yesteryear, "I would like to thank the late Edgar Vance for his charity work with the city, especially at the Children's Hospital of Los Angeles." Debbie stopped there, since she knew the truth and kept it quiet: Edgar's charity work had largely been doing balloon animals for publicity shots. Then his "trusted manservant KipKip," me dressed in banana leaves and a mask like some stray character from *The Jungle Book*, would spend all day doing "Pick for Me" and "Is this Your Card?" for a dozen bald-headed kids and burned teens while Edgar and Suitcase Sam Yorty had afternoon delights at The Hairy Tarantula. I missed those kids.

The mayor's klaxon stepped back, and Father Creedy coughed. "Anyone else?" His New York accent had begun to creep through his faux-Irish brogue, so I nodded and stepped to the edge of the grave.

"I'm glad you're all here," I said, and there were a handful of snorts and more daggered silences. "I'm James Brimstone, and I worked with Edgar back when I was eye level to a slug. I apologize for my tardiness, but my Dodge Dart doesn't run on magic. If it did, I'd have stray coin for a better suit. As I'm sure you know, Edgar Vance was among the greatest magicians of his age. He performed around the world and entertained millions of people for over forty years." Gentle nods. "I could regale you with stories and legends of Edgar's past, but I'd be breaking the magician's code of honor, and the last thing we need is for Edgar's ghost coming back to harass anyone." One lady sniffled, then laughed. "Now, about the chains and locks."

Their attention was mine.

"I'm sure I don't have to tell you they come from Edgar's own private collection. The locks were crafted by Theo Fabergé, of the famous eggs, and Edgar spent his life trying to pick them. The chains are the very same worn by Houdini during his very last and near-fatal performance. They were the only restrictions he never bested. Edgar thought such gear would be fitting on his final day above the soil. Should you ever see Edgar, in dreams or passing on the street, you will know that he not only beat death, but outdid the great Houdini, too."

Mild laughter. Time for the hammer to fall.

I cranked my smile to 1000 watts. "You'll also notice the cherry wood coffin, also part of Edgar's instructions. Now, Edgar had no family except his millions of fans. And his estate is now property of the good folks at the Magic Castle . . . but I was made executor of his will."

No one breathed.

"You can imagine that the cemetery would like to be paid for all their hard work."

The crowd squirmed.

"Don't worry, I'm not asking for donations at a funeral. That would be crass. But I wanted to let you know that I recently opened up my own business. As of today, James Brimstone is a fully licensed private investigator in the state of California, and sole proprietor of the Odd Job Squad Investigative Services. I'm sure you saw the ad in this month's *Los Angeles Free Press*?"

Their glares would have melted tombstones.

"Having trouble with a neighbor's dog? Ex-husband being a dope with alimony? The Odd Job Squad can handle it. That's the James Brimstone guarantee!"

Muttered curses swelled while angry grievers tossed flowers into the grave. "You're a no good, dirty shill, James Brimstone!" one of them said. I didn't look up to verify who, since whoever it was spoke for all. "But wait, there's more! Today you get the Friends of Edgar Vance discount!"

Hisses and swears hit me like rotten tomatoes. Shamefaced, I just stared at the coffin as they walked away from the horrible man who would ruin a funeral with a sales pitch. "Damn you, Brimstone!" some old lady cried. My eyes were down in full hang-dog routine.

In short, everything was coming up aces. That Magic 8-Ball could suck a lemon.

Then it was just me and Father Creedy, AKA Chip Toledo.

"That was some pitch, man," Chip said. "You really want those squares to hate you."

No, I just need them to leave thinking I'm a rotten son of a bitch and Edgar is dead. "I had to distract them from your amazing acting, Chip," I said. "You were stealing the show from a dead man."

"Really?" he said, full Bronx accent now assaulting my ears. Now he was just Chip Toledo, out-of-work actor on his hour off from slinging coffee at the Starlight Diner. "Could you put that in writing, man? See, there's an audition for this musical called Godsweet, and they need a priest who's kinda groovy and—"

The crowd shuffled away through the stones, past the gravediggers. "I'll make sure to send it with your last payment." A dusty taste in my mouth, sour and bright and strong . . . a taste of magic.

Chip clapped his hands. "Out of sight. Acting is my freak, you know, James?"

No one was looking back, but I needed to be sure. "Chip, please keep up the act a little longer—"

"Hey, I didn't mean no disrespect."

"Just stand here and be still until we can say one last goodbye."

Still was not Chip's strong suit. While sweat trickled, seeking new crevasses in my neck and groin, he fussed with his collar, cracked his knuckles, and scratched the back of his head like a stray mutt with ticks. "You got a cigarette?"

The sourness came from no direction I could sense. It was a presence, like the coming of a storm before the first raindrop. Then it was gone.

I exhaled. "Does this look like the venue for a smoke break?"

"Hell, sorry, James. But I could really use one."

"You may find it hard to believe, 'Father Creedy,' but I never enjoyed the taste of my lungs being barbecued."

"Just asking."

I could hear the 405 hum in the distance like a second pulse. The rest of the day loomed. It would be nice to stay in a cemetery. I always found them peaceful. Even been known to take a date to them when there wasn't a horror film on at the local theater. But Edgar's funeral soured me on the idea that they were sanctuaries. Edgar had that effect on people.

I waved over the graveyard crew.

Then the flavor of magic filled my mouth like a fist.

When they moved, I saw her, a witch in black and white, wild silver hair sparkling like the Pacific at noon, a cane she didn't need in one well-manicured talon of a hand, sunglasses too big for her head, giving her the countenance of an aristocratic bug. Alicia Price walked toward us, and I steeled myself for a contest of wills no one had ever won.

"Hello, James," she said, voice as clear as spring water and hard as a concrete bunker. "I think you know why I'm here."

I did.

But she was not going to leave this cemetery with the skull of Edgar Vance.

CHAPTER 2

ALICIA PRICE'S BUG STARE CUT MY ABILITY TO SPEAK, AND THE TASTE of her sour magic presence was like a mouthful of dusty prunes.

"James," Alicia said, "you look . . . the same as always." She paused. "Terrible."

My smile firmed as I wet my lips, the grave crew muttering to each other in courtly Spanish. "Well, we independent men of action can't spend our precious coin on finery like those born of vintage pedigree. Maybe if my family line traced back to Alexander of Macedon—or is that just a rumor?"

She raised her chin and for a split second you could see the razor beauty she must have been between eighteen and fifty, the kind of pretty that cuts you to the quick and leaves you dripping. "They're always true when they're about me."

I nodded. "Glad you could make it to Edgar's funeral." I turned to Chip, who was back in the Father Creedy role, his expression confused but austere, as if the last page of his sermon had vanished. Goddamn modern actors can't improv a thing to save their lives, or mine. "Father Creedy, your work is done. Best you run along home."

"No," Alicia said. "Please stay." She turned to the grave crew and spoke low in their mother tongue. *"Gentlemen, I apologize for the delay, but I am an old lady and every step is a hard one, especially in a place I don't wish to visit too soon."* They laughed. The old gal was charming as ever.

Her cane tapped the coffin. "Hello, Edgar. About time you gave up, you old crow." She perked an eyebrow at me. "Is it true? He actually—"

"—Slipped on a bar of soap in the shower." I crossed my heart. "Scout's honor." Not that I'd ever set foot in the Scouts. By the time I was old enough to join, I'd been with the Electric Magic Circus for four years and would have had badges in knife throwing, fire eating, and playing doctor with a bearded lady.

Her face rumpled. "Landed on his head?"

"On the edge of the grand Belgian tub in Vance Manor. Might as well have been hit with an anvil."

"You don't sound despondent, James."

"There is no one path through grief, Alicia, though we meet at the same destination."

Her lips pursed. "The *Lost Passage* of Virgil? Well, I'm almost impressed, coming from a commoner."

I chuckled. "I have a great local library."

She voided the breath from her nose so curtly I half-expected the grass to blacken at her sandaled feet. "I am already tired of you, James. I will take what's my due. You will bear witness, and we will all walk away thinking this was a wonderful time." Her rictus made Father Creedy grunt.

"No," I said. "You won't."

"Spare me the empty heroics. They fit you worse than this ridiculous outfit."

"Not heroics, Alicia. Just facts. Go ahead. Take your due. If you can." I cupped my hands in front of my balls. "I'll wait."

She grimaced, tapped her cane once, and a shudder ran through the desiccated grass.

I coughed. "Did you pass gas? I thought people of your uncommon heritage were classier than that."

She sneered. "So, Edgar wasn't bragging. He managed to train a stray from the common heap to resist being charmed."

"By magic, anyway," I said. "Now, if you want to grab dinner and try buttering me up with kind words and stories, I might be moved." My smiled dropped. "But even you don't have the goods to make me move."

She sighed as Father Creedy and the two grave diggers stiffened and their eyes went white. Alicia spoke in the tongue of ancient Macedon, and all three men walked with determination to the casket. They rattled and shook and tried to crack open Edgar's coffin.

"That's a hell of a racket for a sanctuary," I said.

Alicia shushed me. "Unless you wish to join him."

"Not at all," I said, hands still across my balls. "It's just that there's a four o'clock funeral and the procession is heading toward us. And Edgar's locks and chains are charmed to be stronger than a cooler in a casino. He knew you'd be coming, Alicia. Because once Edgar's in the hole, covered in sacred ground, even you don't have the mojo to rip out his skull."

Creedy's hand clasped my throat, cutting off my soliloquy.

"Silence, dilettante," Alicia said, cane across her shoulder, about to slug my head into left field. As the marionette formerly known as Father Creedy lifted me off the ground, I pointed to the distance. In a cul-de-sac, a procession of limos were circling the parking area.

My knees hit grass, adding another stain to my already tortured suit, and I sucked in air. The rattling of chains stopped. All three marionettes went on standby. The handle of the cane caught my chin and dragged up until I stood. She stared me down.

The black shades had fallen down her nose, and there were the wild black eyes of Alicia Price, one of the most dangerous sorcerers still living on the Coast. "You were always a pretender in our world, James. Low trash brought into the Louvre because Edgar had a sense of humor. But I must admit a grudging sense of pride that you tendered your master this well. And that you could resist my charms."

Her backhanded compliment didn't register, but one word did.

Master.

My short-and-curlies bristled at the word. "He's not my master. Not anymore. I quit of my own volition. I'm just doing a dead man a favor. My life is mine, all mine, and no one else's."

"Of course it is, dearie." She laughed, then lifted my chin higher. "I heard about your new occupation. Rooting through trash, solving tiny problems for tiny people. It would be adorable if you weren't so pathetic."

"I'll take that as a compliment."

"And I know Edgar left you nothing. Which is exactly how he found you. A pure piece of American nothing."

I smiled. "I'd be happy to waive my retainer if you'd like me to help you hunt for your lost sense of decency."

The cane jabbed my sternum hard enough to shut my yap. "You're a hack, James Brimstone. I'm glad to know you'll die in obscurity, a failed heir to a grand magician." She tapped the cane again. There was the same "whoosh" of power, and the three men stood by me, eyes back to normal as they watched me fall on my ass. She turned her back on me and strutted off through the headstones. "Next time we meet, it will take more than sacred ground to stop me from sending you into Oblivion."

I rubbed my chin. The coffin's padlocks at eye level were black as a dead witch's heart.

The grave hands spoke in worried Spanish.

"Whoa, man," Chip said, all pretense of Irishness gone, rubbing his right wrist. "Whoa, man, I think I just had a déjà vu or something."

"Probably sunstroke, Chip. Might as well scram. I'll drop off your cut next time I'm at the diner."

Chip thanked me, reminded me of his need for a rec letter, and started stripping out of his priest uniform even as he walked away. Actors, heads, and freaks might as well come from the same tribe.

Chip out of sight, I nodded to the grave crew. They lowered the casket into the hole, filled and packed it hard enough that it would take the act of an Elder God to drag that casket from the ground.

To the world, Edgar Vance was dead.

Just as Edgar wanted it to be.

I waited, relieved and terrified that he'd be watching, ready to give me notes and correct my awful failures and mistakes. But Edgar wasn't under the L.A. sun. He wasn't in the ground. And if he stuck to his promise, in exchange for this sting, I would never, ever see him again. The price of freedom from his backhand, his temper, his abuse, his nightmare tutelage, was this last lie. I'd done my part. I was free.

When they were done patting the earth over that mannequin-filled coffin, I said *ciao* and headed for the parking lot.

Lilith, my electric-blue Dodge Dart Sedan, my pride and joy for a decade, had carted me through thick and thin. An ex-girlfriend had named her Lilith because I apparently enjoyed that car more than her company.

When I saw her, my heart sank.

Lilith had been punched in the face.

Two cracks in the windshield looked like an orgy of swastikas drawn by speed freaks with a switchblade. A parting gift from Alicia Price.

I slinked into the front seat, closed the door, and rolled down the window. The ghostly aroma of old Chesterfields made my lungs hunger for something I'd quit, so I hit the ignition and revved her up.

"Don't worry," I said to Lilith, "I'll get you fixed up good as new, just as soon as I get a case . . . to pay off this funeral . . . and rent . . . and . . ." I took one look in the rearview mirror at my powder blue tuxedo, stained brown, green and wet. "And it looks like this one's a keeper."

I stuck my head out the window, drove onto the main drag, and headed home, afternoon air running through my hair and cooling off my mind. My smile grew.

After all, things could always be worse.

Thirty minutes later, I drove down Alameda Street and proved myself right. Queen Bee was waiting for me outside the Thump & Grind Burlesque Club, dressed up like a debutante stepping out at fifty-five, mighty arms crossed across her moderate bosom, every ounce of her looking like well-manicured trouble.

She scowled at the state of Lilith, then one fingernail curled her intent.

We were having a landlord/tenant meeting in the parking lot, it seemed. That gave me hope. A public space meant she wouldn't kill me.

CHAPTER 3

"LATE, BRIMSTONE."

Bee's accent is what we call a Mid-Atlantic, a phony regional cadence that American actors and actresses affected to sound like an affluent and well-read Yankee from Connecticut that had gone to boarding school in Oxford. It was meant to convey authority, but it reminded me of Vaudeville barkers who joined the Electric Magic Circus. Both had the timbre of immediacy, but nine out of ten folks used it with all the authenticity of a three-dollar-bill.

Bee was not one of them.

I closed Lilith's door and kept my head low in deference to the woman who controlled my living affairs. "Now, Bee, you know I had a funeral to arrange."

"Then why are you dressed like some longhair kid about to lose his innocence in the back of his daddy's Ford?"

"Best I could afford, under the duress of circumstance."

"The plight of the cheap bastard again?"

Behind Bee, the Thump & Grind Burlesque Club appeared a giant square bunker of sin, decked out in circus colors and a thousand blinking lights that created the art deco outline of two ample burlesque dancers bumping their grinds alone and with each other. Or at least that would be the scene once the sun dropped and provided a canvas of darkness. "Thanks, Bee." I walked on as if exchanging pleasantries with a neighbor.

She sidestepped until she blocked my way and poked my chest, and I realized just how much residual pain Alicia and her marionettes had delivered. "OW!"

"You know the deal, Brimstone. Rent for space. No rent. No space. I'm not running some communist charity center."

My dirty fingers massaged knots in my chest. "God, Bee, I just buried a friend today. Any chance for a respite on account of grief?"

She laughed, hard and sharp. "You want mercy, Brimstone, find a church. You said weekly payments would be forthcoming for the office and cot."

"I did."

"That was four weeks ago, without a single payment—"

"How about complimentary bouncer services for tonight?"

She snickered. "You look about as threatening as a deserter from the Salvation Army."

"How about tomorrow?"

"How about you pay me."

Down the trash-filled gutters of Alameda, a thin shadow walked toward us, then turned hard to the right, heading towards the back entrance of the Thump & Grind. I watched it from the periphery of my vision, with dead-set eyes on Bee. I sighed. "You're right, Bee. Tonight is fair. Let me just scrounge what I can from my couch."

She crossed her arms and tilted her head, one pink heel stabbing the concrete. "Two dollars."

"You went in without my permission?"

"My house, my rules. You need real money, and it ain't there. Unless you got collateral?"

The shadowy figure reached the edge of the building, then vanished.

Shoot.

I angled around her, an angel's hair of distance between my neck and her reach. I tossed Lilith's keys in the air and Bee caught them like a bullet. "Of course I do. I just need to talk to my new client."

"Client?"

"Just you wait here with Lilith a minute." I pivoted on my heels like a dancing fool, just to be out of her reach. "I will be back before you can blink."

"Good luck, Brimstone," she said as I ran toward some stranger and prayed to God that it was, in fact, a client. More than likely it was more trouble. Maybe Alicia Price, back to take *my* brain, or one of her henchmen, or any number of freaked-out kids on a bad trip, wandering away from the strip and into Huntington Park. I just hoped they weren't black, for their own sake. The worst of L.A. was on display lately. Since the Watts Riots five years ago, the segregation lines of Alameda Street and Slauson Avenue were defended angrily by the residents of this mostly white working class 'hood. I'd found myself in two fights in the last two months, pulling some hicks or freaked out white trash off a black kid who had done nothing wrong. Each time, the victim ran, not knowing if I was friend or foe, and good God I couldn't blame him. Didn't we fight a war against Aryan shithooks? Sometimes this country's love of self-delusion and double-standards was enough to make me spit.

Whoever it was, they were heading for my office door. I hustled faster, hoping Lilith wouldn't be sold for parts before I was done, each step making me wish I could tear off this blue nightmare suit and have Levis or chinos or anything else on that didn't stink of grave dirt and desperation.

I turned the corner. Two dancers, Lace and Magenta, were in their street clothes, hair long and straight down their backs, beautiful without the lashes and curls, each hugging books to their bosom.

"You're not listening. I'm telling you, the Vietnam War isn't meant to end. It's just meant to distract us," Magenta said, tapping her cigarette ash. "Keep us glued to the TV screen so we don't see that the fix is in."

Lace laughed, then pushed her auburn locks behind one ear. "You think everything is a conspiracy, Genta. What's next, the Pyramids were built by aliens?"

"Don't laugh! There's a great book on it—Hey, James."

I tipped an imaginary hat, then looked around. The stranger who was buying me time was nowhere. "Ladies, did you see somebody back here?"

"You're the detective," Lace said, cocking her head to the side. "You tell us."

I smiled. "Thin, possibly ninety pounds of fast-moving darkness, hood on despite the burning sun. The kind of hustle you find with the desperate and the damned."

Lace gave me a golf clap. "Bravo. Look out, Hollywood, a new private dick is in town."

Tension eased from the neck muscles I hadn't noticed were flexed. Alicia Price would have used these two to rip out my ribs, if she was here. "Where'd our shadow go?"

Magenta took a drag, pointed at the rear service door, a battleship gray stain on the back of baked red bricks. "She's a slip of a thing, some scrawny runaway who probably dreams of being the next Raquel Welch."

"Or maybe your first client, Sherlock," Lace said.

Bidding the two adieu, I strode to the back door.

Inside, the hi-fi at the front of the Thump & Grind was blasting loud enough that I could hear Merle Haggard singing about a prisoner wanting one last song before he sat on old Sparky. The cooking crew had already started the deep fryers bubbling, and the sticky air was dusted with the powdery aroma of facial makeup and artificial flowers that made the lady's dressing room springtime fresh all year long.

The shadow sat on the floor, back to my office door, hugging knees no bigger than a McIntosh. The door closed behind me and my night eyes snapped on quicker than a hiccup. In the dark of the hall, I saw her.

Rail-thin designer jeans, new sandals with manicured toes. No wafting stink of sleeping in filthy shacks or groovy quarters. No Indian beads or headband. Just the faux-floral bouquet of ladies' shampoo. This was no wayward Merry Prankster abandoned by her guru, needing to be deprogrammed from life on the commune. The hood was so low I couldn't make out her face, a well-worn jersey from someone three-times her size, the kind Midwest kids wear to college football games. So she wasn't local. Nor was whoever had either accompanied or dragged her to L.A.

"Ma'am?"

She didn't dart down the hall, which is just as well. Bee always wiped the floors to collect the loose change people drop as they were handing over their wages for a private dance. She'd skid herself into a coma.

"Ma'am? Can I help you?"

She gripped herself tighter, then a voice sang out that was honey and broken glass. "I'm looking for a place."

There's a difference between walking slow, and walking safe. I walked on my heels, approaching her until I tapped that invisible line created by our old ape ancestors to demarcate a safe distance to run. She shivered, and I stepped back, slid my body down the opposite side of the wall so that I was eye level with the darkness of her hood. "Well, this is certainly a place."

She unclenched the grip she had on her thin, tanned wrist. Tremors caused her fingers to dance as she reached into the kangaroo pocket of her sweatshirt. My ape brain screamed to get distance, but if she'd come armed and dangerous, at least I'd go out demonstrating I truly could do Edgar's greatest feat: catching a bullet. She drew her hand back into the darkness of the corridor. Something rumpled, like a hastily made Christmas gift, sat in her lap.

She held the crumpled newspaper before her like a shield. *The L.A. Free Press* shook as if she were hit with polio. Her voice was soft and scared. "Is this the Odd Job Squad?"

Behind her was the door to my office, a plain brown number with no identifying marks to let you know the former janitor's closet and shower was the headquarters for L.A.'s new detective, the fresh smell of ammonia provided for free.

A padlock clutched the knob. Thanks, Bee.

I needed a shower, a shave, a shine, a shit, and a better set of clothes . . . but that required a client.

"Indeed it is." I sat with my legs crossed and on the floor. She shuddered a little at the closeness of my wingtips, but didn't recoil. Good. Bad trips are hard to deal with, and for all I knew she was a Laguna princess who'd taken some Grateful Dead acid and was convinced red ants were in her bloodstream, or that her mouth was made of silver and she could only drink mercury. "I take it you need a hand?"

She gripped herself and the paper. "The police won't believe me."

Well, that was a bit of good luck. L.A.'s finest had never been friends of mine, and among my few policies was not dealing with cases that brought them out of their Crown Vics or doughnut shops. "That's just fine by me. Do you have a name?"

"Nico." The name fell from the darkness just as soft as flower petals. Given her accent, I bet her real name was Betsy or Amy or Linda, probably Minneapolis by way of Chicago, the "oh" sound having softened some in her transition to L.A., where accents are either dead or ridiculous.

"Nico, I'm James. How can I help you?"

Slowly, her hands unclasped her knees and rose to the edge of her hood. Spidery fingers pulled back the fabric as she leaned her head forward.

I killed my wince before it could reach my face.

Scars crisscrossed her face, as if she'd tried to kiss a rabid wolverine. Wild patterns. Not by a knife, nails, or talon. A beautiful face curtained by long dirty blond hair, marred with an attack of something not of this world. I tasted the dirty magic like a bad allergy, then swallowed the itchy flavor.

"Find who did this to me."

CHAPTER 4

SHE WAS TROUBLE, AND NOT THE FUN KIND.

My interest in Nico evaporated the second I thought past her woe and considered my own. Alicia Price had nearly tanned my hide, and my survival depended on staying out of anything that tasted like magic. Because the more you start dipping back into the world of the strange, the unnatural, and the realm between reality and mystery, the more you're playing with napalm and pretending it's silly putty.

And yet that face . . .

"You said the police weren't interested," I said, playing with the little green ring on my left pinky. "Did you call them?"

Nico's knees locked. "Found one in a car. He said . . . I had it coming." She sniffed, and I could hear the wetness of her cheeks grow as the tears fled down her face and tapped on her lip. "Just because I'm an actress."

Now, everyone in L.A. is an actress. Or an actor. Or former actor. Or a deluded soul who can't understand why the studios haven't found them yet, despite going to "The Julliard." I'm the rarest of birds around Hollywood, since I did my performing on the road after I ran away from home to literally join the circus. Having seen the Carney side of success, tasted the spotlight of the three-ring and ten-in-one, I was never pulled into the black hole of the movie business like others in this town. My dream was just to get the hell away from my father and make enough money to return to Oakland bigger and badder, but I ran into the infinite labyrinth of the arcane. I knew everyone in the City of Angels said they were one thing, but were actually another.

Worse, Nico and her face full of feral scars had me curious. Which was an invitation to danger. "What kind of actress, if I might ask?"

"One with a dead career!" she cried.

Indeed. In L.A., beauty was the first requirement of just about any job, and the most important quality. Crimson-tinged tears dripped off her chin. God, I just wanted to have that Dubonnet on ice, locked in my office like a Pharaoh's treasure. I drove my fingers through my sweat-soaked hair, hoping to regain a modicum of composure. "I'm sorry, Nico."

Her voice was hollow and reedy, the cadence one of desperation. "No one believes me!"

Her cry was the subtext of my ad. I wanted what cops wouldn't touch. Now my first client was crying at my door, Bee was waiting outside for rent, and the one thing I swore I'd never do once I was free of Edgar was to get anywhere near spitting distance of the world of magic . . .

. . . But the scars . . . like slashes. Grooves in rows of two. Not claws. No tiny weasel had ripped her flesh. Too wild to be a weapon in the hand of a junkie or head or drunk with the DTs. The attacker had gotten close. Already had her trust. My words fell gentle. "A friend did this to you."

Her hands shook in front of her face, quiet blue eyes holding on to the delicate connection I'd made. "Yes."

"Someone intimate."

Her hands dropped to cover her mouth, her wounded beauty a relief map of suffering. "Yes."

The scars didn't retreat from my mind, but I'd always had an expansive view of beauty and found blemishes to be nature's way of instilling charm. Without the scars, Nico was what my mother would call "a hell of a specimen." Gorgeous. The looks to hang a career on before the crow's feet and lifelines attacked. Thin, sharp nose; thick, soft lips in a gasping pout; bright blue eyes with angled eyebrows so that she looks either game or scared; and rich blond hair that had started to curl in the day's heat and sweat. She'd fallen out of the pretty tree and hit every branch on the way down, a kid who'd just grown into svelte but buxom curves that would make her twenties the happiest time of her life.

A life ruined in a day of violence.

"How did it happen?"

Her lips pursed into a sour puss. "You won't believe it."

She was my only client and if she walked away, Bee would be driving Lilith to bingo as collateral until I had a dime. "Try me."

Nico pulled her knees to her perfect bosom, then inhaled hard. "We were on set. Today was the final day of shooting. And everyone was so good to us, made us feel so comfortable." She blinked as if re-calculating her thoughts, then looked at me hard, the kind of stare that doesn't want judgment but whose tone is so thin it can't help but demand it. "It's an art film." Then the normal look of a kid at someone who's seen more than forty winters. "It's like Andy Warhol. You wouldn't get it."

I smiled. "I'm familiar with Mr. Soup Can."

She exhaled a dismissive sigh. Her painted toes flexed in and out of her sandals. "Octavia wanted us to shoot at dawn, because of the light, but it was so cold it reminded me of Kansas."

"Hometown?" Nico nodded. Which meant her real name sure as hell wasn't Nico, not in real life. "And Octavia was the director?"

"No, producer."

I nodded as if this was normal. But producers in this town never go on set unless there's a fire, a starlet locked in her trailer, or as a PR stunt because the media is coming. And they sure as shit don't touch "art" films. "Nico, you were shooting in the San Fernando valley this morning."

Weak tears plied down her face. "It's an art film."

"Easy, Nico. I don't care if you make space movies with Ed Wood, but I need to know the truth. You were in the Valley. The producer was there, and she wanted the dawn's early light."

She nodded. "It was going to be Maxine's big moment."

"Maxine . . ."

"Maxine Graham."

"She was your co-star."

Nico looked at me as if I'd said the ocean was in the sky. "She is *the* star."

If Nico wasn't the star before these scars, it made me wonder what kind of specimen Maxine was . . . And the thought dropped from my mind when I saw the horror blooming like tiny mushroom clouds in Nico's deep blue eyes.

And part of me screamed *Run, you idiot! Who cares about your tomfool detective agency? You know what you taste here. A whiff of the dark stuff. You wanted lame duck cases, guys cheating on their wives, insurance scams, petty junk you could outthink in a heartbeat and make spare coin and a nice bottle of Dubonnet at the end of the night . . . This kid . . . this case . . . everything says "Danger, James Brimstone!" and you don't want to be dragged down again into Edgar's world of true magic and charms and hexes and demons and nightmares. You owe no one anything now. You're a free man. Don't go back to prison for some lost girl from Kansas—*

I ground my teeth. Nico's eyes spelled ruin, and I knew it. The next thing uttered from my mush would either sink me or save me. Releasing the lock from my jaw, the words fell out.

"What happened to Maxine?"

Enjoy being late to your own funeral, idiot.

She buried her head in her hands. "She . . . she did this to me."

The backdoor opened and sunlight turned our shadows into long stalks. As Nico drew her hood, Lace and Magenta strode down the hall, platform shoes thudding, Virginia tobacco and something sweeter in the air. Bee didn't allow reefer in the club, but Lace wasn't much for rules and Magenta thought they were safer than cigarettes controlled by a vast conspiracy of power that traced its roots to Atlantis.

I didn't have the heart to tell her how right she was.

"Hard times, James?" Lace said. "Didn't realize the hallway was your office."

"Temporary arrangements. Now, ladies, if you don't mind, I'd like a little privacy."

"You don't control the hallways," Magenta said. "Hey, girl, what are *you* trying to hide?"

Nico winced at the hint of conflict. This was a fight or flight moment.

"Easy," I said, sliding my back up the wall to standing position and taking their soft and stoned eyes off of Nico. "I just want a quiet moment—"

"You won't keep me quiet," Magenta said, then poked my already sore chest. "I'm so tired of your voice around here, sounding sweet and doing nothing. You don't think I know this whole detective thing is a front?" Nico's hood faced Magenta. "That you're probably spying on us for the FBI, or CIA, or the monsters at the RAND corporation down in Santa Monica." Lace was no help, laughing at Magenta's tirade. "I take orders from nobody, especially not some covert freak!"

Before I could utter a word, Nico was on her feet, running down the hall into the main showroom of the Thump & Grind. She ran with the speed of the terrified, past the dressing rooms, the kitchen, and private bathroom, straight for a beaded door.

Behind that door was the three-hundred-pound monster known as Jonah, so big you would have thought he'd been the one who swallowed a whale. But the last thing I wanted was Nico grabbed and subdued by our resident monster.

"Nico!" I said, dashing after her. "Stop!"

The screen of beads jangled as she drove through into the freshly polished dance floor, though she turned halfway too late. She was in the main room. Where I wasn't to bring clients. Ever.

I cut through the curtain and found Nico in Jonah's arms, mouth covered. Merle Haggard still blasted from the stereo about how "Momma Tried."

"Staff only," Jonah said, high and loud. Jonah had a speech impediment on account that he was partially deaf. I pitied anyone who chose to make fun of him, a six-foot-seven, chunky three hundred pounds of muscle stuffed into a tight blue *Carpenters* t-shirt, denim jeans, and shit-kicking engineer boots. Nico was too scared to move.

"She's not staff, Jonah," I said. "She's scared. I'll help her back into the hallway."

"You broke the rules," Jonah said, as Nico trembled.

"Relax, Jonah. She didn't know the rules. And it's not fair to punish someone for something they didn't know, right?"

He thought about it.

"I'm sorry she came out here, okay? She's my responsibility. You really want Bee coming in here and seeing you strangling a girl?"

Jonah tipped his head down. "I'm just holding her."

"She doesn't want to be held, Jonah. That can feel like being strangled. And the last thing Bee needs is a clown car of L.A.'s finest coming in here because a young lady wished to use the bathroom and got accosted by Hercules."

I would not say Jonah was slow. He was a fair sight smarter than many gave him credit. And he was not rash.

So it damn near flipped my wig when Nico bit his hand.

The giant screamed. Nico ducked out of his raised mitts, darted past the main stage and headed toward the Gentlemen's Booths: the alley of sad men and strong memories. And, go figure, it was a cul-de-sac.

I ran after her, Jonah's long legs on my tail, and slid across the polished floor. Jonah, thank God, followed suit. He shuffled like a tap-dancing spider and slipped so hard he landed on his side. It bought breathing space and a sliver of hope as I caught up with Nico while she gunned it down the hall.

Nico ran to the last door on the right, opened it, and slammed it closed on my wingtip. Pain snapped up my spine, like I'd become a one-man Tesla coil, but I managed to wedge myself in and shut the door behind me. She ran to the corner and retook the fetal position. I yanked one of the plush chairs and jammed it under the door handle. Then I cut the distance between us in half. "Look, Jonah's going to rip open that door like a TV dinner in seconds." I kneeled, putting the weight on the balls of my feet. "Nico, listen. Something happened to you. Something you can't explain. Something that isn't a bad trip. Something attacked your face. Bit it. Repeatedly. Right?"

Her wet eyes glared at me from the maw of her hood. The doorknob shook. Jonah's shoulder hammered the door and cracked the frame.

"I'll take your case."

The chair skidded a few steps.

"But I'll need a retainer."

Jonah grunted as his shoulder tackles started to push the chair. Nico's hand emerged from the kangaroo pocket. Ten hundred-dollar bills were scrunched in her fist. "Is this enough?"

"Bah!" The door sprang open and Jonah was in.

I yanked the cash, pushed it in my lapel like a greenback handkerchief. "Indeed."

Then I turned to subdue the giant.

CHAPTER 5

"JONAH, SHE'S MY CLIENT," WERE THE LAST WORDS I SPAT before I was ducking and weaving his giant soup-bone fists.

He was fast for a big man, but all offense, so I kept drawing him into the room so his long reach was extended. My back hit the wall.

Damn.

"Hit the lights!" I told Nico.

Jonah charged. "Rah!"

He jabbed left, and my left palm blocked it as if it were a sparring match; the sting from impact shot through me like moonshine. Then a right cross forged its way through the air with a bull's eye painted on my jaw, just before the room went dark.

Everything slowed.

I move a tad faster in the dark, as if it were my natural element, courtesy of a dozen wrestlers, prize fighters, and street shooters who would teach me in pre-dawn, when they began their insane training regimes.

My night eyes snapped to life. Nico's form was gently illuminated, but the scratches on her face were a supernatural pox of scars. I hate violence more than anything. It's the lowest form of entertainment. But it also happens to be ridiculously popular with young angry men, including the one whose right cross was cruising at me like an ICBM.

I ducked under the blow and heard the crunch of bone against wall. Jonah's aura was frazzled white, innocent but damaged and manipulated. He was no monster. Which is why I wouldn't hurt him bad. The big man was just doing his job, playing his part, and didn't really mean any harm.

Shoulder to his gut, I hooked both tree-trunk legs for a double takedown any beginning wrestler would know, but I was willing to bet the fresh paycheck in my fine attire that this gentle giant had never worked the mats.

Jonah's back slapped ground, and he turned to his right to get up, exposing his neck. Viper-quick, I snaked my arms around his neck, locked my bicep under his chin, and hooked my right hand on my left forearm as my left hand cupped the back of his head. Everything cinched in what Dr. Fuji had called a "blood choke": Do it right, and it's *good night, sweet prince*. Do it wrong, and it's ninety-nine-to-life.

Jonah railed against the growing pressure and deepening darkness. He yanked himself to his knees, me riding him like an afterschool piggyback. He tried tossing, flinging, and ditching me with the intent of a career bull who hated the rodeo. Then his chest sagged as the carbon dioxide slipped out of his lungs but no air snuck back in. He tried flipping me forward but I just hung there, a knot on a giant's back. Meaty digits dug into my forearm, but his strength dipped, and his nails scratched my skin, pulse fading fast.

"Nico! Lights!"

The world snapped back as I released myself from Jonah and slid off his back.

The giant dropped to his knees, rolled on his back, and lay there exposed, right hand swelling into an even bigger, uglier fist.

I exhaled with a whistle, then looked at Nico. "Well, I hope that gives you some faith that I know what I'm doing."

Nico's hood nodded, then she shirked away from the door as Queen Bee stood there, a blackjack in her fist and two cooks behind her. "Now what is the meaning of all this!"

"Easy," I said. "Bee, I told you I had a client."

She came forward. The cooks, Hector and Ramiro, flanked her with a rolling pin and a butcher knife apiece. "You mean you weren't abusing a private booth and Jonah caught you?" said Bee.

I motioned Nico to my side and, thank Zeus and Co., she followed. "No. Nico's in a bit of trouble and I'm going to help her out. She just signed on with the Odd Job Squad and thought she could leave through the front door, not knowing our special arrangement. Jonah was doing the right thing for the wrong reason, and now I really must get on to the case. Oh, and I've got your rent. So I'd like my car." I took out eight of the ten bills from my pocket.

Bee grinned. "Plus interest."

I took out another and waited. Bee could suck me dry of my last Benjamin if she wanted to for the hassles I'd caused.

She laid out her palm and I crossed it with the greenbacks. Her pink talons closed around them. "Wake up my giant, please?" she ordered her two culinary bodyguards.

"Now that we're jake," I said, "I need to take my client to my office so there won't be any more confusion."

She snorted. "You've paid your abode rental, not your office rental."

"What?" I said. "That's shooting dirty pool!"

"And the house always wins. Hundred dollars, Brimstone," she said. "Or it doubles."

One Ben Franklin left. And you can't run a case on charm and empty gas tanks alone.

I inhaled hard and turned to Nico. "I gave you all I had," she said.

I turned back to Bee. My anger cools quickly, which is one reason I've survived forty goddamn years. The logic of my next action fell out pretty simply: it was better to take a case with a hundred dollars and no office than the reverse. I turned with a smile. "I'll get it to you tomorrow. Right now? I need Lilith."

Bee dug into her purse, tossed the silver key.

I escorted Nico past Bee. "Tell Jonah I'm sorry for the bad dreams. If he wants, I'll teach him how to get out of that sleeper."

We walked down the hall, Merle Haggard singing about Folsom Prison. Bee exclaimed, "When Jonah wakes up he's going to dance a jig on your head."

"Then I look forward to our next dance."

"Be careful, girl," Bee said as we strode down the hall. "Don't let the fancy duds fool you. You're rolling dice with a snake."

Nico's body bristled at the word.

And now I knew what it was that had maimed her.

THE STARLIGHT WAS WHAT A KIND SOUL MIGHT SAY IS "NOSTALGIC" for people ten years my junior who prefer to think of the Fifties as the era of pretty innocence. In layman's terms, it's a sack of comfortable lies.

Red vinyl seats. Lime green counter tops. Tiny juke boxes in every booth with Chuck and Elvis and the Killer at the ready, and currently playing a sad Sinatra song about how lonely a Saturday night could be . . . if you were as handsome, rich, and powerful as Ol' Blue Eyes. The aroma of the Starlight was working man's sweat and burned coffee grounds, coupled with Comet dust and deep-fried everything. The magic bubble of the fifties was as much an illusion as anything else in L.A. Race riots. Freedom Riders showing as much courage as Marines at Iwo Jima. Those Japanese Americans who'd been fresh out of the barbed wire hell we'd shoved them in since Pearl Harbor coming home to find themselves treated like enemies, their homes sold and their neighbors rich off the spoils. When L.A. burned under the Watts riots I volunteered with a Red Cross unit, patching up black, white, Latino, and Asian Americans caught in the crossfire of hate and degradation.

The only ones who talked about the "Good Old Days" were folks of one flavor: vanilla. These myopic twits wished all those blacks would go back to where they'd come from before they helped us win the war by doing dangerous munitions and navy work, and that kind of racist amnesia also fed the battle cry for all the Asians to go back home, even though most of them had been here long before the current set of whites who'd fled the dust-bowl came to California and proclaimed it their white Shangri La. So the pseudo Fifties that I heard too many moaning about had started to rise like a lost Utopia, wiped clean of the ugliness that was alive and well on the streets and in the alleys when Johnny America went to sleep.

It wasn't the bullshit ambience that had me coming back. The Starlight offered coffee, biscuits, and what they called "steak" for two bucks. The biscuits and steak were tougher than I was, but the coffee wasn't strong enough to defend itself.

I dunked the biscuit into the mug. All the while, the jukebox ended the glory days of Sinatra the Hairpiece and played songs that upset no one but annoyed the hell out of me. The current rotation was some "invented" rock and roll band that dressed like Archie comics and sang about women as if they were condiments and candy, saccharine-sweet Don Kershner junk that was slowly starting to edge out the fuzzy guitars of long-haired kids who seem to have given up on whatever rebellion they'd believed in back in last year. I pined for the haunting notes of Django Reinhardt, the Gypsy jazz wunderkind with only two fully-functional fingers who played as if he had five hands. Music made against the odds, no matter how loud or quiet, always made me feel hopeful. But "Sugar, Sugar" was giving my soul diabetes, if I even had a soul left.

A murky green plastic cup of water sat before Nico, exterior abrasive, the kind you give children who are learning to grasp things without handles. Her hood was still up, but I saw her plain as day. Sparkling blue eyes, heavy lids, and the bite marks across her face like scars on the Mona Lisa. Every other woman in L.A. was a beauty queen or movie star in waiting, but Nico held your attention without trying, even while marred. She'd been silent during the ride over, and she seemed jumpy enough to dash out of Lilith if our conversation got too tough.

But I was on the clock and burning daylight. "Snake, huh?"

Her hands became talons, gripping her cup.

"Something tells me it wasn't slipped into your bed."

Her eyes darted from the glass. "How did you know?"

Two fingers on my right hand became crooked. "The gashes. Their angle of attack wasn't crooked. They came down from above." My fingers relaxed. Her grip didn't. "Why don't you start an hour before anything happened. We'll go forward from there."

She brought the glass to her mouth. Sipped. Swallowed hard. "It was the last scene. Octavia wanted natural moonlight, so it was so late it felt like morning might break. We were on set for the final . . . scene." I nodded, even though I knew we were talking about a skin flick and not the latest slice of genius from Billy Wilder. "My script didn't tell me what would happen, just the blocking. I was awakening from a dream into a night full of stars, tied to a stake."

I hated this film already.

"All I knew was that I'd be working with Maxine."

Now I was confused, then interested, then ashamed of myself. "The one who—"

"Yes, and a friend." Her innocence was endearing, but heart-breaking. Actresses had few female friends. They had rivals. And one wondered how deep Maxine's desire for the spotlight was if she'd ravage Nico's face. "She was the priestess of Hades, and I was to be her sacrifice. But she was supposed to fall in love with me and we'd . . ."

My hand rose. "I can fill in the blanks."

She sniffed. "Maxine's whole body was covered in glitter. She looked regal, like a queen." A single fingernail did figure-eights on the cup's abrasive surface. "I was so proud of her, you know? She was scared to do this scene, but I told it would just be nice. Sweet, even. But as she walked toward me, her gait got stiff, as if trying to reclaim her balance on a beam. I was so mad because I thought she'd gotten high. And here we were, and we had to shoot, and just make the best of it. And, of course, Fulton wanted the dawn so he didn't stop."

"Fulton? He the director?"

Nico nodded, but her lips pursed and part of her ease retreated.

"Not a fan?" I asked.

"Fulton is . . . he was in Vietnam."

"Okay."

"At Tet."

I exhaled. Reading about that horror show in the papers, I knew it was three times as bad as anything printed in the *L.A. Times*. And that particular horror movie was barely two years old. "He went from combat soldier to director?"

"He jokes that it's a better way to shoot people."

Black humor is far less dangerous than black magic, but no less unnerving. "So he's trouble, huh?"

The crazy eights she was tracing seemed almost like a comical way to write the sigil for infinity. "He's proud of being a soldier. Still wears his fatigue shirt. But he's . . . intense. His eyes . . ."

A roustabout with the Electric Magic Circus, Flash Harrison, worked as a stunt man in westerns during the 1950s. Tough guy. Served in New Guinea during the war. Quiet fella but great at gin rummy and certainly no slouch at protecting himself. He worked on set with Audie Murphy, America's most decorated killing machine. Like everyone else, I read *To Hell and Back*, but while others saw a role model, I'd felt I'd read the memoir of a broken man. On set, some nitwit actor from New York started to give Murphy grief about his line reading. Murphy, all five-foot-five of Kentucky rage, grabbed the guy by the throat. "And I saw it, James," Flash told me after a few high balls of Old Crow and winning most of the tips I'd earned as the dreaded "Man Eating Chicken." "That thousand-yard-stare. I'd seen it. Guys who looked at everything around them as a threat to their survival. Zombies of war, like in old monster movies. They lived in the haze of battle and there was nothing precious to life. The eyes saw through you."

I took a long sip of tepid coffee. "Is Fulton the one who—"

"James?" The voice came from across the counter, barely a whisper but also clear enough that it irked me into the moment.

I had assumed Chip "Father Creedy" Toledo would take the day off after the shenanigans at the cemetery. I would not underestimate his work ethic or need for rent again. I smiled big and friendly as he sauntered up with his scratch pad, apron, and freshly scrubbed face. "Well, hello Chip. And here I thought you'd be starring in *Easy Rider II*."

He snickered. "Not yet, man. Guess working funerals makes me an off-Broadway kind of guy." Nico stared at her cup, body in full wince.

"Why are you still wearing that outfit?" Chip said.

I had no desire to share my funeral story with anyone, but especially not in a public place with a new client. "Chip, I happen to like this outfit and won't return back to the shop until I've plum near worn it out. But then again, I was born when the Depression was eating families for breakfast and spitting them out as dust, so if you don't mind I'd rather not drag up my hardscrabble past, as me and my friend here have business."

Chip's face contorted as if he was trying to decode my words with his dimples. He blinked and said, "So, are you ready to order?"

"Positively poised," I said, then looked at Nico. "The food's lousy but the portions are grand. Would you like to help me split a steak and eggs with fries?" I'd been around actresses my whole life, and the only thing they cared more about than their face was their figure. It led to some bizarre behavior that I'd seen with the circus, diets and traditions rooted in vanity and forcing them into cultish behavior, from bathrooms becoming vomitoriums to living off of Pall Malls and a stick of gum for two days. The result was skin deep pretty and three inches of sad. But if I bought the meal, perhaps she'd eat it, get a fistful of calories in her guts so she didn't pass out once the adrenaline she'd been pumping finally ran dry.

Nico shrugged.

"And two coffees."

Chip left, looking back at the hooded beauty once more because he was a man and there are few things more intriguing than a mysterious woman. "Sorry for the interruption. You were talking about Fulton." I settled my face so it had the impression of my full attention. But outside, a blue Ford Thunderbird was parked in front of Lilith. The driver was working on a project in his lap, though far too precisely for a dirty masher who enjoyed an audience while he committed self-abuse on his sex. I kept my peripherals on him while Nico continued. "Was he the one who—"

"No, not Fulton." The timber in her voice was serrated. She wasn't lying. She was just scared of Fulton as much as the truth. She shook, grabbed a napkin, and sniffed. "This is the part where you think I'm crazy and toss me out."

My voice lowered to the tone my mother called "serious business." You didn't use it for gags. You never used it unless you meant it. You used it to be a life preserver for those who were flailing, to help keep alive the connection between the distraught and the helpful. I only wished it had worked on the loon who I called father before I got the hell out of Oakland.

"Nico, we've just met. You don't have much reason to trust me. But I don't think you're crazy. And I won't toss you out. You're my client. I'm here to serve you." I cupped my hands and leaned forward. "If not Fulton, then who?"

Tears slid down her cheeks, following detours created by the fresh scars, and winding their way down to two launching points: her delicate nose and soft but angular chin. In the track lighting of the diner, her set makeup was a melted version of its former glory, and yet didn't look garish, just a different tone of beautiful. "Maxine. She . . . she kissed me." She waited a heartbeat or two to see if I would cast judgment or make a rotten joke. Her eyelashes released a hanging teardrop. "At first it was nice, like when we'd practiced, but then . . . her tongue." Her shaking hand covered her mouth. "I pushed her off, but her arms were so strong . . . and that's when—"

Chip Toledo arrived with the timing of a hack comedian, and did his best imitation of a waiter who gave a damn. "Steak and eggs, as you like it, and a cup of our finest roasted coffee." The pile of greasy meat sat before me, the coffee smelling like roasted ashes, all the while I tried to figure what in the hell Chip's game was.

The obvious smacked me so hard I almost fell out of my wingtips.

He'd heard the words "producer" and "director," and now he was auditioning for a possible connection to the film industry. None of which bought him a single glance from Nico, just many winces. It could only get worse from here. I took out the last hundred, held it between two fingers. "Thanks. Just the bill and give us some time before you return."

The mental math Chip did about continuing his patter or taking a hundred and getting a tip probably broke a few circuits in this half-baked brain.

He pulled the hundred from my fingers. "You got it, James! Anything for my favorite customer."

"Bye, Chip." I sighed as he walked away. "Sorry, the service here is downright Shakespearean, at least when it comes to tragic characters." I picked up the mug, which didn't have a lick of heat. "Maxine pulled back, and?"

Nico's lips pursed as she exhaled. "Maxine threw back her head, and it crawled out of her mouth, tasting the air, wiggling above me." She kept tracing the eight on the cup, then gave me a hard stare. "A snake."

I sipped what I soon discovered were the dregs of the day's filter. "What color?"

Now I had her attention. "Huh? Why?"

"So I know what kind of snake." An impetuous look cut across her wounded countenance. "Nico, I'm not laughing at you and I'm not being a schmuck. What color was the snake?"

Her nails tapped the glass in her hand. "It was like . . . striped. Red, white . . . and black."

I shoveled in eggs so overcooked they were hard as Legos. "Are you sure?"

She winced, shaking her head. "I knew it. You don't—"

"Your friend's possessed." That steadied her focus like a gunshot. I spoke lowly through the chewy eggs, keeping Chip out of earshot. "Someone on that set, or involved with her, or that had it in for you, worked some pretty serious . . ." I hated using the word "magic" to describe the real stuff. The *Heka* badness of this world, primordial forces both malign and benign. Magic was fun. Magic was safe. Magic wasn't real, it was a trick, an effect, an illumination, a joke, a gag . . . but the scars on Nico's face were no punch line. "This was no accident, Nico. And you're right. It wasn't Maxine's fault. No one would do this to themselves. Someone did this to her." Someone who knew *how* to use a human vessel to raise some kind of demon, letting them incubate within them until the right time to strike. "Someone pretty bad."

Sweat crept down my back, and it wasn't because of the eggs and coffee. I'd just buried a body to keep all of this mojo out of my life for good. Just because I hated Edgar did not mean that I wished to skulk around in the embers and ash of supernatural power on my own. But incubating a demon with a living host? On some porno set? I was throat-deep back into the mana of the fantastic.

"And here's your bill," Chip said. "Thanks so much!" Then he walked off, quick as a gunshot.

No change from my last hundred dollars lay in the dish.

"Stay put," I said to Nico. "If you have the guts, enjoy the biscuit." The kitchen door had fluttered closed as I stood. "I'll be right back."

I walked at the speed between annoyed and "bladder about to implode." Maureen, the blue-haired head waitress, who was reading the *L.A. Times* with almost the foot-long ash tip of her cigarette about to cascade to the floor, took no notice. Through the door, waves of greasy heat stuck to my skin as the line cook, a bearded Greek Civil War veteran named Ares, flipped thin, sizzling burgers in his stained brown apron and gave me a dirty glare.

"The waiter ran off with my check," I said.

Ares tskd. The dripping spatula pointed at the back door.

"Ευχαριστώ," I said.

"Whatever," he groaned back. "Just make sure he's not getting ηλίθιος." I assumed in this context "ηλίθιος" meant "stoned," nodded, and dashed out the back.

Chip held a pretty intense bike chain with an open lock. "Little shits!" he said to two kids with overgrown bowl cuts, driving down Rugby Ave. on his green ten-speed.

"About to say the same thing, minus the plural."

Chip's shoulders hunched, chain rattling like a novice Hell's Angel. "Oh, come on, James!" He turned, big smile on his face. "I just thought you'd finally gotten around to paying me for that cemetery gig."

"Then why the getaway bike? And don't tell me you have an audition because everyone has an audition and you have yet to become 'everyone' in this town." Watching his brain stall to improvise a new script was painful and seemed to be giving him a mild stroke. "Chip, take your cut and give me the fifty that remains. Or I'll tell the young lady you're someone who can't be worked with because they're always stealing on set."

"I *knew* she was an actress." Chip dug into his ass pocket, and took out the money clip he'd obviously been given by someone far classier within his family tree. He shaved off two twenties, two fives, and handed them over in a fist. I plucked them from his grip as if taking tissues.

"Thanks, Chip. When I need someone to play a horse's ass, I'll be in touch."

"Count me out, James," he said to my backside. "Your gigs are too weird."

"Chip, old boy, I do believe you're—"

Shattering glass echoed from the restaurant's main room. I ran and slid across on the greasy tiles, and Ares hustled as if the ground was concrete and got to the main room as I tripped once before righting myself and getting back into locomotion.

I shouldered my way through the kitchen doors.

A Latino teen in a green soccer jersey stood between the booth and the countertop. So did Nico. He held a .38 Special to her hooded head.

CHAPTER 6

ARES WAS FOCUSED LIKE A SHARK, HANDS AT HIS SIDES AND ready for action. He must have been a terror in the hills of Olympos. Maureen slowly chewed bubble gum, hands in the air. The gunman flexed his feet, shifting weight from side to side before the wreckage of my uneaten breakfast. The splattered guts of eggs and biscuit swimming on the dirty tiles had an aroma that pierced my gut. "Whatever you want, friend," I said, "She hasn't got it."

The man in the soccer jersey shook the pistol. "What I want is my job back! But that bastard fired me! And don't call me friend!"

My hands reached for the sky. "Easy, sir, I didn't mean to agitate an already aggravated situation. You said you were fired?"

"By that fat bastard."

Ares spoke dark and guttural, using a swear that doesn't have an English equivalent, unless you count the phrase "man who masturbates himself into stupidity."

"Shut up! You fired me because you think I'm stupid, some dumb Mexican, and hired a white idiot who you can push around."

Ares's voice was a low grumbling made of scorched lungs and fresh nicotine. "You stole, Juan. That's why I fired you."

"I didn't steal anything!"

"Juan?" I said, taking a short step forward to steal focus from Nico or Ares, and tried not to wet myself. "Can I call you Juan?" The stares I received confirmed that both men thought I was an idiot who masturbated himself into stupidity. "You have every right to be angry. Finding work is hard these days. Hell, the new waiter stole from me."

"You see!" Juan said to Ares, pistol still shaking against Nico's hooded ear. "You hire a thief, after firing me? All I did was work hard!" Nico's body shook. Good God, the kid had been through enough.

"No one said you didn't work hard," I said, stepping forward.

Juan focused on me. "Who are you to tell me about hard work? You're some rich man dressed for the prom."

I smiled, awkwardly. "Juan, this is a rental. And given how many stains are on it I suspect it's going to be an eternal rental." I brought my next step up a little closer than the last one. "I'm what my pop called rat's ass poor, though I know that don't mean I've walked in your shoes. The way you're shuffling? That's because you've got cardboard in your soles to cover up a hole. You needed this job like a fish needs water and without it you're drowning. Right?"

"I didn't steal anything."

"I believe you."

Sliding my right foot forward, I inched my way closer to what I call the circle of trust: where a human being starts to worry that you can nab, tag, and grab them. "Stay back!"

The muzzle snapped from kissing Nico's hood to brandishing its maw at me. My heart punched my chest fast enough to remind me I was now dancing at the very edge of my existence. Blinking, I caught sight of Nico, but her eyes were down, face placid, as if this was normal. Strange, likely because she'd seen too much trauma.

"I said stay back!" screamed a new voice.

The ugly click of a hammer being cocked crept from behind Juan.

Down the counter, one of the hunchies, the counter-top lifers at bars and diners, had drawn his own piece, a Heckler and Koch, preferred souvenir handgun of American MPs in West Berlin, the kind you brag about at the Legion because you underpaid the Kraut who sold it to you on the black market. The man had too much flesh under a strong chin and was salt-and-pepper gray, with the same haircut he'd had since he was a recruit, shaved down to a crisp edge. But his eyes were sharp, like Ares, that generation who'd learned to kill for five years, then go to work the next day. He wore a black shirt under a green vest that hid the holster on his left.

My nose crinkled. Fucking guns. For what good they've done in the world, they'd multiplied death via stupidity by a factor of ten. Two trained killers, one scared kid, and my client were all nestled into a confined space with the chance for maximum casualties increasing as the sweat beads collected down my spine.

"Drop the weapon," said the former MP in annoying command voice, somewhere between football coach and kindergarten teacher. "Now, spic. Nice and easy."

Juan's glare went atomic, so I stepped forward again and all the rage drew down on me. "One more step and I'll kill you!"

"I know," I said, the worry in my voice pure and honest. "You're mad, Juan. You have every right to be. It's hard to get work. And losing a job, hell, it feels like the end of the world. But something tells me you're a survivor, Juan. You don't give up. And you were raised to think life was fair, and when L.A. proved that theory wrong, you were scrambling for scraps. Busing tables, well, it's a great way to stay fed when the tips are weaker than the coffee. No offense, Ares." Ares shrugged. "I'm sorry you lost your job, but I bet this day isn't turning out like you planned, so I want to offer you a choice." The old MP was giving me the worst case of Sour Puss and Stink Eye I'd seen since I flubbed my first magic trick in front of Edgar. "Now, the old man drawing down on you has you dead-center. He could puncture your spine, put you in a wheel chair.

"But I tell you what, if he does that or worse, I'll testify to say he started it."

"Fuck you, faggot!" the former MP said, gun still trained on Juan. "I'm saving that lady."

"No," I said. "You increased the likelihood of carnage in here by a factor of stupid."

"Watch your mouth, asshole, or I'll—"

"Both of you, shut up!" Juan said, pushing Nico forward but the gun still trained on me. "A couple of *gringo idiotos* bragging at each other. You're worse than my uncles. Ares, I want my job!"

"Move closer to that asshole," the MP said, "and I'll paint the walls with you."

I shuffled my feet so slow it looked like I was grinding my heels into the tiled floor. But I moved slower than Juan could perceive. "Gentleman," I said, using the timbre from the long-lost art of carnival barking, "I would ask you both to cool your jets and take into consideration the opportunity that is before us. Amazingly, you happen to be drawing down on the inheritor of the singularly most dangerous magic trick of all kind. Can you tell, by our situation, what that might be?"

Juan and the MP shared a glance, then returned their hate-stares to me.

"Why, I thought it would be obvious, but we're all under a lot of stress." I spread my arms wide. "Catching a bullet."

Juan sneered and the MP snickered. "Now, I'm not pretending I'm the greatest at it, but I've caught bullets in three countries, so I am no stranger to this danger. Truth is, Juan, I'm very good at this trick. Which means the next play seals things tight.

You could walk out of here now, before L.A.'s finest arrive to give you grief, or you can take your shot, and end up with attempted murder." The last word hung in the air like a haze. "Because I will catch that bullet."

Juan's sneer abated. "*Estas loco*, gringo." The pistol stayed on me as he shook his head at Ares. "You ain't going to give me my job back."

Ares, cool as ever, shrugged. "Could be someone else stole. If you leave now, maybe. You hurt anyone, and no."

Rage filled the MP's eyes, his glory moment vanishing. My feet slid forward as I lowered my hands to draw attention back. "Sounds like a deal, Juan. Tomorrow, come back and start new, without a thirty-eight. They just have an opening because a real thief no longer works here." My aching feet had brought me to within striking distance. Between two fingers, I held out the fifty that Chip had given me. "Here's some cash that he stole. Consider this a severance package if things don't work out. And, Juan, I'm sorry. It's all I got." Juan stepped closer, leaving Nico behind.

I stepped back. "The pistol's worth less, but that's my trade. We exchange on three. It's my final offer. Otherwise, you'll see a trick that will blow your mind, not mine. One," I lifted the cash so it was level with the gun barrel now two feet from my head. "Two . . ." I leaned closer as the pistol shook. "Three."

The money vanished from my left hand, and the pistol hung, pointed at Juan, hooked on his finger . . . but with the hammer clocked. My heartbeat doubled. Mess up the next move, and it was manslaughter.

I breathed through my nose, and moved with alacrity as my mind recounted the poem Edgar had forced me to memorize while working on card tricks and palming. *Don't imitate me; it's as boring as the two halves of a melon.*

I grabbed the gun. The barrel was upside down and in my palm, my thumb jamming the hammer and a finger blocking the trigger.

But the gag was sprung as soon as I gauged the pistol's weight. It wasn't loaded.

A smile curled upon my face, even with the MP ready to blow us both away.

Juan ran for the back door, cutting past me, then Ares, but my focus was on the MP, whose automatic pistol tracked Juan's back, looking for the most cowardly shot in history. I flipped the pistol in the air, caught it right-side up with my right hand, and held the house's attention. "Hey, Pat Garrett. Let Billy run."

The MP shook his head, holstered his gun, then grunted. "You're a coward."

I smiled. "Will have to learn to live with that, I guess."

Nico stood rigid, lips tightly shut. But the look upon her face was no longer placid. Tight, upset, frustrated.

"Nico?"

Then she was on me, arms wrapped tight, face buried into my lapels. Her tiny arms were strengthened by terror. "Come on," I said. "Cops actually like this neighborhood, so we should bolt before snake time." She broke her bear hug, then stared at the floor. I kneeled, grabbed the biscuit covered in greasy splatter and a few stray pieces of glass. "Ares, I'm taking a doggie bag. Call this an IOU?"

"Fine," he said. "But is it true?"

Nico was at the door. I blew off the glass. "What?" I asked.

"Can you catch a bullet?"

I smiled, pocketed the pistol and took a bite. "Ares," I said, all moisture vanishing from my mouth. "I'm ashamed you'd even ask." Biscuit bits flew off my words. I hacked and coughed away the dryness as I left the Starlight and followed Nico into the brutal afternoon heat. Adrenaline was fading like meat under the mouths of maggots.

"Faggot!" screamed the MP as the door closed behind me. Of all the things he could have shot into my back, I took his misdirected hate as a sign that things were going my way.

We sat in Lilith, and I asked Nico the usual questions to make sure she wasn't hurt or catatonic from the second trauma in twenty-four hours. "Sorry about all that," I said, rolling down the window. "Huntington Park used to be working class WASP, and they haven't exactly embraced the Latinos and Blacks who are working the jobs the former working poor see as beneath them now." I tossed the biscuit out into the street, and a parade of seagulls landed to tear it to shreds. I exhaled. "So, when last we talked, there was a snake coming out of Maxine's mouth."

CHAPTER 7

"HOW?" THE WORD WEIGHED NO MORE THAN A BREATH.

I'd sucked a chunk of biscuit from between my canines that was sharp enough to cut glass, and then crushed it with my molars. "How did I get this tux? Sad story. I was running late—"

The hood shook. "How did you convince him to give up his gun? How did you get him to do what you wanted?" Beneath the fear was a sliver of desperation. "*How?*"

The dusty remains of crumb tickled my throat. I coughed once, then swallowed the ricochets. "Most people don't want to hurt others. They're trained to do it. Juan was hungry, angry, and slighted. That can boil anyone's blood, especially in this neighborhood, where guys like Juan keep getting pushed down by the last of the red-blooded WASPs. But he didn't want to kill you, or me, or even Ares. He wanted to be heard." I watched the cars gunning down Florence, crossing Pacific Ave wanting a way out. "I listened. Then, I gave a choice between the ridiculous and the profitable. Most people need cash more than jail time."

"And if he hadn't?" Desperation had hardened, but then again, her hood still held the circular kiss from Juan's revolver. "Would you have . . ."

"Caught a bullet? Maybe two?"

She nodded.

"Well, sadly, I can't say. Magician's code, and what not."

"You were a magician?"

"Oh, just a childhood fancy, nothing more, all grown up and now." I swung the keys to Lilith around my finger, making a not-so-subtle point that I needed to know where to go. "You were telling me about Maxine, and your psycho director Fulton." Had to put the spotlight back on Nico, but not too hard, just enough to share a little and return to the job at hand. "Did he hurt you?"

"No, not one bit," Nico said, lying right to my eyes, the doughy "oh" of the "no"s sounding pure Minnesota before she tried to sound as smooth as a voice over actor on a serious documentary. "Never." Of her other "tells," rubbing her wrists beneath the safety of her sweater was the most egregious. She faced me, the legion of scars on display. "In fact, he was the one who tore Maxine off of me so I could pull myself off the stake . . . but Maxine shoved him hard. Fulton was tossed like Raggedy Ann, and landed in the pool. All the while that . . . snake had snapped back into Maxine . . . The crew must've seen it, but they did nothing and, God, I don't care. When Maxine ran, Fulton ran after. I've never seen such a look, James. It was downright—"

I caught my keys in my fist. "Feral?"

She gasped. "Was he . . . was he like the snake?"

I sighed. "No. What you saw from him was all too human. Just think, two years ago he was in a sweaty Mekong delta, killing in someone else's back yard, with the entire neighborhood out to murder him . . . and then he came back to America and a year later he was making 'art pictures.'" I whistled. "Hell of a jump."

She gripped her knees. "That's why I came. James, I don't know what's happened to Maxine, but I know she doesn't mean it. There's . . . something wrong with her."

Snake coming out of her mouth? "I'd agree."

"And Fulton . . . he'll either kill her—"

"Or die trying."

"I think so."

"And you want me to find the lady with the snake tongue before he does."

"And help her, before anyone else gets hurt." She sniffed, then came the tears down the broken river-scape of her once-flawless visage. "Can you help her?"

Selfless. That wasn't in most actresses' purse of attributes. I'd smelled revenge in her tone, but it melted into fear for a friend, the woman who ruined her, and desperation to stop the killing machine who was out to get her.

Killing machines I understood. It's the snake angle that was like Silly Putty in my brain. Human anchors for old demons wasn't the usual, even for me. It was older magic. Darker. And the taste of the damn thing didn't ring any bells. But I'd taken the retainer, and I wouldn't see another dime until I'd solved a case that, thus far, was pure mystery. "Okay, here's how we're going to run." I opened the glove compartment, and pulled out a spiral notepad with a ballpoint in the grooves. I dropped it on her lap. "You're going to write down the address of the studio that's in the valley."

She looked aghast, even though I'd guessed it before. "It's not what it sounds like."

"Of course not. Then you're going to write down everything you can remember about the snake. Use your senses. Taste, touch, feel, sounds, and appearance."

I jammed the key in the ignition, unrolled the window, then turned. Lilith's engine coughed twice before the engine settled on her everyday wheeze.

"Why can't I just tell you?" For the first time, Nico's voice wasn't terrified. Annoyance laced with frustration colored her words.

I hit the turn signal. "Because you're translating something fantastic into the mundane world. You won't be looking at me. You won't be expecting a reaction from the pad. Your mind will be making the straightest line it can between memory and now. Close your eyes first, then let the scene roll back. Trust me. I learned this from a very wise old man." Who would snap a whip across my back if I forgot specifics about filing of incantations, precise measurements for spells, or the names of demons he'd send in my dreams to test me. I shook. "Just try it."

Nico pouted, a new look that didn't scream of shock, and then I stuck my head out the window and pulled out onto Pacific Boulevard.

Nico's eyes flashed open. "Where are we going?"

The fuel tank's needle hovered above the E.

"Somewhere safe. Close your eyes, get writing."

Pacific Boulevard was a straight shot into Vernon. Only locals really know when they've crossed from Huntington Park in the south, and Bell on the southeast. Most people just jet through it to get to downtown, and don't look on the sides, don't see the stories etched on the faces. Vernon was a city of violence. We were riding across old battlefields and boxing rings. Tires cut across the marching grounds of the American army as it crushed José Maria Flores's Mexican forces at the Battle of Rio San Gabriel, the last embers of Mexican power in California being snuffed by Uncle Sam. But as the boxing capital of the world at the turn of the century, Vernon killed more in the ring.

On tour with Electric Magic, we had a palooka who lost regularly to make our little boxing contests look legit, an old codger named Stanley whose brain had been jumbled so bad he only spoke boxing. For Stan the Man, the greatest match ever was at the Vernon Coliseum. An eleven-round slogging match in which Jess Willard, future champ of the world, killed Bull Young at the eleventh hour. "It was death poetry in motion," Stanley would say, repeatedly, as if he couldn't help it, proud of the limited poetic vocabulary he'd assimilated. "Willard's hands were registered as lethal weapons. Never allowed to fight longer than four rounds or else they had to hire a gravedigger." All the while Stanley's gnarled knuckles pumped like angry hearts.

Driving past the dry cleaning shops, abandoned Chinese restaurants, and vacant department stores, Vernon was a ghost town that wouldn't die. The buses still ran for those grasping jobs in the glass and plastics works, but there was one employer in Vernon who ran his business like an enlightened despot. While Nico scribbled, I drifted through a yellow light toward a sign that told you in no uncertain terms who ruled the meat market:

A fat man with jowls and mutton chops kneeled with a bloodhound at his side, a giant brat in his corpulent hand.

SAUSAGE KING! MEATS AND TREATS FOR YOUR FAMILY TODAY!

The Sausage King of Vernon was Willie Mutts, of the Mutts Food dynasty. His fiefdom was the West Coast, and his signature brand was Sausage King Brats, perennial favorite of Forth of July celebrations. Locals laughed at his success from the gutters. Given his last name, rumor had it that the old Sausage King was filling his orders with L.A.'s finest stray dogs. Yet they remain the most popular meats in the region.

We passed the billboard, Mutt's pearly whites as bright as golden rings, big as his tombstones, and damn if I wasn't hungry all over again, despite the quick joy of Ares's floor biscuit.

Lilith coasted as much as I could let her past the Vernon Police HQ passing by on my side, then followed the gentle right to Santa Fe, headed toward 38th, just outside the industrial sector. On Nico's side we edged up on a neon jouster sitting high atop a pillar. As Lilith gurgled to a stop I hoped I had enough gas to roll out and find a station where I might scrounge the bread to get me to the Valley. But first, Nico had to be safe.

I wasn't going to drag her back to the nightmare she'd barely escaped. I'd find her demon-riddled friend, make my wage, and get back to my office and that Dubonnet on ice.

We parked in front of the offices for Happy Knight Motel, a nice stucco number on the ground floor below the walk-up apartments. "Why are we here?" Her tone screamed "flight."

Damn it. She was worried I was some kinda Creepzilla, dragging her to a motel for a bit of strange.

"I want to get you somewhere safe where you can rest while I go to the studio."

"The sign under the knight says no vacancy."

"That means hardball. Sit tight."

She gripped the door handle. "I'm not staying here alone."

Juan's gun show was still fresh off the griddle in her mind. "Absolutely. Just let me handle the talking, okay? This guy owes me a favor."

Happy Knight's office smelled of bargain-basement cleaning products with exotic knockoff names like Mrs. Cleaner, Spac and Span, and Cometz, but the master odor that punctured all was a lime-scented aftershave. The desk was empty, but the ghostly tang of lime meant he was around. A black-and-white TV sat in the top left corner, sound off, image of some Dodger's game rotating like a flipbook that might cause seizures. Nico stayed on my right, and I told her to keep writing things down as I rang the bell three times and kept my eye on the door on the right.

"Hot dog, we have a wiener!" came a voice only a mother could stand. The door opened and out popped Morris. Buried within that six-foot-three, three-hundred-pound frame was a former bodybuilder and Mr. America contestant, all muscle and vein and hard curves. But that was before a Chinese soldier had chewed his leg apart with a burp gun stolen from Morris's own regiment during the Chosin Reservoir retreat in Korea, leaving his leg behind, an abandoned popsicle in weather so cold even God would have worn a blanket. Coming home, the muscles soon met their end against an avalanche of beer, TV dinners, and Skippy peanut butter.

Before us now, Morris was still gigantic in a sweat-stained, short-sleeved, blue-and-red-striped dress shirt that would have given a test pattern a headache. But his build was akin to garbage bags filled with used clothes. Given his swagger you'd hardly believe he was swinging a wooden leg. His hair was slicked back with an ocean of Vitalis, and was as full and luxurious as mine. "Well, look what the dog dragged in."

"Good to see you, Big Man Morris," I said.

"Damn right, Private Brimstone. And I'll thank you to call me sir."

Nico glared at me.

"We spent some time together in Korea."

"Ha!" Morris said, slapping the desk hard enough to ring the bell without touching it. "I barely saw this cat in Korea. Damn near disappeared into the night half the time when you said his name. You Scout Rats might as well have been made of smoke." He smiled and the halitosis coming off of his rotting gums was almost strong enough to burn my eyebrows. "Now how did you two young lovers meet?"

Nico cringed, stopped writing on her pad.

"I'm working a case, Morris. My client needs a room."

That closed his rotting mouth. "Wait a minute. The guy who stole more weapons from the Chinks and Koreans than anyone else was given a P.I. license? Tell me, Private, did you fill out the forms under your own name, or John E. Public?"

"Thank God for correspondence courses," I said, then took out my provisional license from the great State of California. "Just graduated."

Morris raised his giant hands in mock submission. "Say no more, Detective Brimstone."

"I'm not with the police, Morris."

"Some things never change."

Before the world filled with a thousand and one awful army stories, I said, clear and strong, "Morris, we need a room."

"Hate to tell you, but my sign works and doesn't lie." He draped his hand over the empty key hooks. "As you can see, Detective, nothing up my sleeve."

I smiled. "Special occasion, Morris. I just need a room for the night. And not for your usual needs. I'd appreciate it if the dirty jokes were kept to a minimum in front of my client. She's had a rough day."

Morris's wide face crooked at the hooded Nico, and his jowls went pure hangdog. "I do apologize, ma'am. I did not mean to suggest anything dirty." Then his glare focused on me. "But unless you have a serious deposit, I'm afraid I can't—"

I had half a mind to knock him on his ass, considering I'd dragged his million-dollar physique out of the line of fire that tore off his leg, had come back that night to kill the Chinese soldier who'd removed said appendage and get back our guns on a day colder than hell's heart . . .

Nico dropped her hood and I tried not to move my face.

"Please, sir." Her voice caressed the air like a rose petal. "The . . . person who did this is still out there. I just want to hide. Just for tonight. I promise to be gone in the morning."

Morris's countenance froze.

Morris, it seemed, couldn't take the macabre. One look at Nico's ruined visage and I bet he was back in the Casualty Clearing Station, hearing the screams of men with their organs slipping through their fingers, doctors stabbing morphine to silence the blind, crippled, and insane. Seeing the horror narrow his pupils, I bet to myself he was back in that room right now, strapped to a gurney, unable to run . . . and maybe that's what triggered his five-thousand-calorie-a-day diet, to make it impossible for him to ever have his number called.

Quicker than a hiccup, he yanked a key from his pocket. "Room 211. I use it in emergencies. Very basic. Please, take it."

I plucked it from fingers the size of Snickers bars. "You're a good man, Morris. C'mon, Nico."

Outside the office, my feet dragged across the pavement. The day's adrenaline was gone. And now fatigue punched my gut with a haymaker. Nico's painted toes rushed up the steps and hung a right, going to the far end of the walkway. I followed with a dying light inside. Two life-and-death fights on a near empty stomach would do that. But there was also a hangnail of fear pulling me forward.

Whatever aggravations I'd had today, from Alicia to Bee, Jonah to Juan to Morris, there was a fresh hell waiting for me when Nico told me everything about the snake in Maxine's mouth.

CHAPTER 8

I WAS WORRIED WHAT MORRIS' "SPECIAL" ROOM WOULD BE LIKE. I turned the key. When I hit the light, the worries vanished.

No trash. No stink of day-old sex or thirty years of smoke imbedded in the walls. No taste of magic. Just a little mildew and lemon. Not one trace of lime stained the one-bedroom affair. Brown walls and a single bed with a worn but thick comforter. A pillow was tucked next to the coin accepter for "Magic Fingers," which was also the nickname of a guy with the circus that I'd rather forget. Considering my day, this was the Hotel Shangri La.

Brown drapes thick as my fingers shielded us from the late afternoon sun and I almost didn't want to look at my watch to know how late it was, because no matter the time it was going to be a late night echo. But I stretched my right arm to pull back my sleeves. The cheap Hong Kong knockoff Montine wristwatch appeared, silent as the hand ticked towards 5:09.

"Okay, Nico, let's see the details on the snake."

She sat on the bed, back to me, ass barely making a crease on the sheets. Hood still down, she held out the pad to no one in particular. I grabbed it while walking to the tiny orange plastic chair with the tiny wooden desk built for stray Munchkins writing the Wizard of Oz. I didn't want to know where Morris stole this hodgepodge lodge material, but I had a sneaky feeling a Sunday school was missing some of its furniture. When I turned, she'd dropped the hood. Her scared face rested in shadow.

"What sticks out most?" I said, voice clear and strong. Fawning and softness would eat up time we didn't have. Dawn was broke, daylight was bleeding, and a girl with a snake in her mouth was loose.

Nico's golden hair sucked in what little light dropped from the exposed 40-watt bulb. "Everything seemed so blurry."

I nodded, but that was strange. Trauma is many things. Blurry?

I flipped through the pages. Nico's handwriting was uniform, sharp, and clear: the product of finishing school, private lessons, or a privileged public school. Each word was centered, small letters, and dark ink. Perfectionist, strong emotion, but controlled. Someone had trained her hard and well to write this nice.

A handful of words worried me: a python, hissed like gas, smelled like dirty ashtray, air tasted foul, fangs like . . . "You say here that the fangs were like iron."

She blinked, put me in focus, and it was hard to see her scars. "It smelled like iron."

I gave a reassuring nod, though she seemed now far less the frightened girl at my door than a troubled girl thinking her way out of a crisis. Flipping through the book, I held my poker face while my mind back-flipped . . . iron serpents . . . ashes . . . gas . . . a demon snake anchored to a human host was bad enough, but serpents weren't that . . . modern. Abyzou was as old as the Jews, but fed on the misery of women . . . but asking Nico if she was a few trimesters short of a baby didn't seem kosher. This sucker was also clearly a serpent with a mouth and teeth, and not a tentacle, so I could cross a gaggle of Eldritch nightmares off of my list. And that only made things worse.

The attributes were modern, industrial: gas, ash, iron. Heaven help us if Union-Carbide had a new dark arts division.

Damn it. I'd need to consult my goddamn library, which was trapped behind a goddamn padlock, furious goddamn Jonah, and goddamn Bee—

Nico's doe eyes flashed hopelessness dead center at my face. "You okay?"

"I just . . . I feel useless. This sounds so stupid, especially as a modern woman, but I used . . . I was good at . . ."

"Getting men to notice and do what you want?"

The slightest of smiles peeked from her lips.

"And you still were. Morris isn't easy to sway. He's so cheap he'd sell you a cigarette he was about to crush out. Nice work."

"Guess I'm picking some things up from you."

I smiled. "You're a quick study, that's for sure." Then I flashed the book. "This wasn't easy, either. Thank you."

She looked at the slender hand that braced her on the bed. "Those were the details that I could pull out. Talking about it seems harder."

"And they're pointing me in the right direction."

"What direction is that? Toward Maxine?" Her little fists curled the bed sheet.

"Not so fast. Finding a girl with a snake in her mouth will likely be easier than finding how to help her. If she's going to have any chance of living through what's been done to her, I need to prepare some materials to get the snake out of the lady."

"So there really is one in her?" She crossed her thin legs on the bed, then hugged her knees in some hippie variation of the fetal position.

"You're surprised that I believe you?"

"I hoped, maybe, that it was all a nightmare. Maybe you'd say it was a dream and I'd wake up. It's so bizarre. How does a woman get a snake inside her?"

"She doesn't." Nico's eyes held me. "Someone puts it in her." Her voice softened. "How?"

Nico's adrenal glands were spent, fatigue stamped her face, and I had no idea what she was like on a good day. But the softness of her voice was . . . unnerving. So delicate. Vulnerable.

"It ain't easy," I said, shifting in the Munchkin throne. "So I want you to tell me who else was on set. Anyone who might have had it out for you."

"You don't think Maxine is to blame?"

"I don't think anything, other than someone is tinkering with some pretty powerful stuff, and if I'm going to help Maxine, I better know who I'm up against."

Nico tapped her thin, manicured fingers as she listed people involved in the "art" film, while I got a handful of tissues and tried to clean the dirt off every spot of my shoes, shirt, and lapels.

She'd mentioned Octavia Bliss, the producer and director of Nero Studios, so there was a clear Roman fetish in the house. That could mean dabbling in the old snake Cult of Glycon, the one Lucian had proclaimed was a hoax, but those rigged religions had made Alexander of Abonoteichus a pantload of cash . . . and they had never been revived outside of a crackpot magician in Northampton who, thankfully, was mostly harmless.

Then there was Fulton, the insane director who'd been at Tet. But outside of mutton chop side burns and two fists that were perennially clenched, Fulton remained a violent enigma in this puzzle.

Nico also told me of Shane Wyndham, Maxine's boyfriend who was on set, which made him the kind of boyfriend nicknamed a suitcase pimp, dragging his lady's heels, lipstick, and hairspray to and from sets, ordering her around, and making sure she gets paid. Nico swore he was a real nice guy, and I nodded, knowing he was a particular kind of shithook who preys on women, promises them stardom, and uses them until beauty or body runs out, then dumps them at the Greyhound Station at 7th and Santa Fe. Then he picks up the next star-eyed gal lost in L.A., promising she'll just need to do a few blue pictures to get experience and then, by God, MGM and Warner Brothers would be knocking down her door to be the next Twiggy or Mia Farrow. And she, starved of self-confidence on a diet of self-hate that men manipulated like clay, would be clay for each bastard Pygmalion.

But the strangest duck that Nico described was the screenwriter, TV Smite, who Nico said was four feet and not an inch taller. A bald dwarf, with big glasses, who chain-smoked unfiltered Camels and seemed to hate everyone on set except Octavia, who had hired him because he'd written a dirty book series she'd liked, all set in Rome. "Do you think he's to blame?" Nico asked. The hope in her tone had a flicker of malice. Beautiful women often dislike the imps and ugs of this world. Guess I'd hoped too much that her beauty wasn't just skin deep.

I scrunched up the soggy paper towel and launched it at a wastebasket. It ricocheted between the wall and the lip of the basket and tipped the damn thing over. I sighed. "I try not to judge people on their appearances."

"But he's a little creep."

"How was TV creepy?"

"He grunted at everyone. He hated the movie. He said Fulton had ruined his script."

I supposed even a skin flick world had its share of angry artists with pure visions that get trampled on by commerce. He must be from out of town, because that's just how L.A. works. "I grunt. Ares grunts. Dogs grunt. That doesn't make him a creep." So far, the midget was only a suspect due to his hating the film, so maybe he tapped a dark root to ruin it. The handful of writers I'd known took so much pride in their research you'd think they had a PhD in boring facts. Maybe TV knew more about Rome and magic and chose to pull a Phantom of the Blue Film and ruin the stars for shitting on his play. But I kept speculations in my head. No need to feed Nico's knee-jerk ideas and give them credence. "That's hardly a reason to saddle someone with demon possession."

"But he loved that stuff on set."

"What stuff?"

"All the Greek and Roman symbols."

Worry bit my nerves. I handed back the pad, and the stationary pen on the desk. "Show me what they looked like."

Her hands slammed down on the bed. "I can't remember! I just see that snake!" Nico rolled on the bed, back to me, exposing the small of her back, golden tanned above and below the panty line. "You have to get that thing out of Maxine. Please. Oh God, she was the only nice person there. She worked so hard. Please, Mr. Brimstone, she's out there, somewhere, and if Fulton gets her, or if that snake comes back—"

Then she was gargling tears and I was staring at the magic fingers, wondering how rich the inventor must now be. She needed food, rest, quiet, and I needed to start putting together a means to protect myself as I prepared to hunt down a woman possessed by some kind of snake demon raised by someone in a skin flick, likely to ruin Nico's star-bound face.

I walked around the bed, kneeled, and looked. Tears pursed out of her shut eyes. Her breath was hitched. "I'm going to hunt for Maxine. I'll call you every two hours. Don't open that door for maid service, Morris, or the girl scouts. No one knows you're here. No one followed us. You're safe. Grab a shower and rest. I'll be back soon."

She sat up. "Don't leave. Don't leave me."

I stood. "You need rest."

Her eyes pleaded. "Then I'm coming with you."

"No."

"Why?"

And then, my head kept screaming *What are you going to tell her, Jimmy? That you're going to crash course your research into this snake and try and find the means to protect yourself because there's a real foul taste in your mouth when you think of someone "updating" demon casting, a level of magic that is way above your pay grade, and there's no one in the magic community willing to help because no doubt word of your awful cemetery performance and general idiocy have made you persona non grata with the big leagues and now you're living with your choices as a grown-ass man in a prom suit covered in grave dirt, facing the unknown with no money, no resources, and no help except for a scarred girl who rolls into baby states when the horror swells, like she's seen the face of an Ancient One.*

Instead, I grinned. "I need you as the cavalry. I may need you to pull my ass out of the fire. Better to have you out here rather than where I'm going."

Nico stood on the bed so that she was looking down at me with pure intent. "I don't want to be alone. Stay!" It was as if she was talking to a dog that always did what it was told.

I turned my back, walked toward the door. "Don't answer the door unless someone says the code word." I turned to face Nico.

Those blue eyes shone like diamonds in the darkened light. Then, her lips were on mine and I was pulled in two directions. My hands went on automatic, securing a cup of her ass and neck while my two parts of my mind had a slugging match in my skull.

"She's a client." JAB!

"Then do what she wants." COUNTER PUNCH!

"That's not what we do." BODY BLOW!

"We help those who need it." TIED UP IN THE CORNER!

"This is helping ourselves to trouble." GUARD UP!

"She's hurt!" BODY BLOW! "She's scared!" BODY BLOW! "She thinks she's ugly as shit!" JAB, STRAIGHT RIGHT, JAB. "If you don't ..." DANCING BACK.

"If I don't . . ." STUMBLE FORWARD, GUARD DOWN.

"Then you'll make her feel worse!" STRAIGHT RIGHT, LEFT CROSS, UPPERCUT, KO!

Our mouths locked, and she gripped my face. She tasted of sunlight and fresh dew, and even the faint magic of her scars could not spit in the flavor. I pulled her ass with both hands and mashed against her as she gasped, still mouth to mouth, tongue wild and darting, her mouth on mine like she needed me to breathe. Legs wrapped, arms around my neck, she hung off me like a resplendent necklace, grinding her hips and bucking so hard the back of my knees smacked the bed and she tumbled on top of me, driving her mouth deeper onto mine. Before I could twist positions, she pulled back and sucked in air. "Stay." It was a command. I was about to say something when she muttered, sad, dripping. "Please."

I leaned up, and she gasped, expecting another kiss. "Okay," I said, almost as soft as her. "Just for now."

Lips locked, she tore at my belt and trousers while my fingers unhooked her button and pulled down her zipper. Urgency drove her motions, like a starved animal, needing something so desperately that to deny it would be to deny its survival. Before my hands could reach up her sweater, she had secured herself above me and slid down wet, working me until the friction eased and she opened deeper to receive all. Her hands lay on my chest as she rocked back and forth. "Stay," she whispered, grinding with her legs hugging my sides. I looked up at her hooded visage as she rocked back and forth, warmth swelling through me and reaching for my heart. "Stay."

Normally, I'd have twisted us into new configurations, surprise and mystery flooding her as I took control, changing the dance, shifting who followed and led. But Nico's day had been nothing but hell, other people pushing their will, so whatever she needed here was more important than me.

I laced my fingers in hers and she pressed my hands on my side, then lifted herself. She shook, riding me up, riding me down, and her eyes locked close, but the bliss pumping through us was growing.

"Oh God," she said, but her voice was shaking.

"Nico? Are you?"

"Shhh!" she hissed, as she ground down on me, and I reciprocated with thrusts aimed where I could feel her rough spot, that abrasive button that most men couldn't find with a spyglass and a map.

Her hands shivered as if she'd kissed a light socket. Her elbows locked as her head twisted. "Stay," she said, but weaker. I kept my rhythm. Her mouth gasped, then her back arched and she grasped my lapels like she was a cowboy riding a bronco before my thoughts bled into ecstasy—

We thrummed in simpatico like two rushing streams who become one river, and rich currents rippled from and to us, fast as a flash flood swelling a creek, a feeling I'd never known, a depth of connection never dreamed, but without her lips on mine I was drowning for air, and so was she, head back, hair swinging shadows across the walls, as if refusing to come closer until we reached the precipice of grinding pleasure and I yanked her sweater and shot her down to me. We kissed, came and screamed as one.

Ten silent minutes later, Nico slid off me, pulled up her jeans, then used the washroom. When she came out, I was zipping up my fly.

She pulled on the strings of her hood as if were her hair. "I . . . I said—"

"I won't be long. And I will save your friend, and keep you safe. I promise. Oh, and don't forget the code, should anyone come to the door. It's Blueberry Pancakes."

I got to the door before that hope died.

"Where are you going?"

I opened the door. "To find someone who can help me fight a demon."

Which sounded a lot more reassuring than "I'm going to the library."

SCRUNCHED YELLOW BURGER WRAPPERS DANCED IN THE AIR above the cars shooting north on 38th and brown paper bags with greasy spots lined the curb like the gutter of a bowling alley. Across the street was a Shell station with the ungodly announcement that today gas was eighty-six cents a gallon. Beside it was Magic 8-Ball Billiards and Brazier. "Serendipity," I said, then considered the prophecy of the toy I'd stumbled over in the cemetery.

"Outlook not so good."

I shrugged off the prophecy until I saw the handful of hogs parked outside, detailed with a skull with bat wings.

Hell's Angels.

I grinned. This would be fun.

CHAPTER 9

LILITH HAD COASTED ON FUMES TO HAPPY KNIGHT. NOW, SHE WAS empty, and I needed enough gas in a can to at least cash in for a quarter-full tank. Only hope was a pit stop for the lousiest sacks of shit ever to ride across California. Some will tell you the Angels were born in San Bernardino, that the Berdos were the decedents of rogue veterans who had bombed Berlin and were now too jazzed by high octane travel and violence to settle down with a wife and kids and GI loan.

But I'm from Oakland. I knew the seeds that became Sonny Barger's weeds when I was doing card tricks for lunch money in Temescal. And whenever I'd end up back in Cali with the circus, these fuckers would keep growing, sucking in the lost souls they could turn into tools. And within that gang, there was an inner circle so vile and secret that it reminded me hell is always one bad decision away from being made on this earth.

I unclenched my coiled fists.

A can and stretch of hose sat in Lilith's trunk, waiting for an emergency. The sun was high and merciless, but in L.A. traffic it might be dawn before I found what I needed if I didn't get going now. Say what you will about old wives tales and street myths, but the truth? Night is its own world, and with a modern demon hiding in the streets I didn't much fancy getting a serpent's kiss in the dark. But if I had to sweet talk my way onto a dirty picture set, best not do it with gas on my breath or looking like a baby blue nightmare in a sex-stained suit that was five o'clock funky.

No. I needed cash. Time to dust off the old Brimstone charm.

With Lilith sleeping behind me, I ran across 38th and headed for the Magic 8-Ball, hoping I could do what I needed quickly, easily, and without resorting to the lowest form of entertainment. I dodged the dancing garbage and avoided my own funeral as Chevys honked at my transgression. And damn if I didn't reach the other side wanting a Big Mac.

The Magic 8-Ball was a bunker-shack that shook with music. Garage bands I vaguely remembered pumped out from a poor speaker system inside a wooden door with a chicken-wire window. The hogs were all Harley Davidson originals. These were no new patches. These were established vets.

And I thought of that poor black man at Altamont. A man I couldn't save.

The press had said he was dangerous, higher than the Empire state, and had a gun.

That the Angel had to stop him before he killed a lot of people.

None saw what happened.

That poor man had been hexed. A sigil was branded on his face from a punch he'd received earlier, one laced with a ring whose face bore the plate of a dead Viking god that some of these Angels worshipped. The leader of this inner ring had the oh-so-clever name Low Key. He was a shithook of Babylonian proportions and key figure in the gang rapes that put the Angels in headlines some years back. Forget all the pomp from that hack journalist who rode with them and sold us only a sliver of the true story. The periphery may be outlaws, cowboys, and idiots, but the Inner Ring, as Edgar called them, were servants of a dark god who consumed lost souls. These fucks dosed a black man, stuck a gun in his hand, then threw him into the crowd with eyes as wide as a berserker full of woad. Edgar, for all his faults, saw the Inner Ring as a threat. And he knew that their actions through the sixties had been a series of escalating spectacles of violence that would send thousands into a panic of blood and violence, enough to resurrect a dead god . . .

I'd stopped them once before, at Golden Gate Park. And I'd seen Low Key, now chapter boss in San Francisco, eyes like burning magnesium. He had a reputation as a killer and an aura tasting of electric malice. While the Grateful Dead played "Ripple" for a donkey's age, Low Key targeted another black man. He never saw me until the beer I'd bought drenched his greasy black locks and made me the target of his wrath. The beating he unleashed on me left my body so raw and broken I was pissing blood for a week. He moved like a mongoose, untouchable, graced with a body built and honed for violence, but when I abandoned offensive for defensive be became wild and infuriated as I blocked, dodged, parried . . . a circle grew around us and we may as well have been covered in the crimson sand of Rome as the plebes and Vestal Virgins cheered for their gladiators to stomp a mud hole in each other. Mano a mano, we went in circles, him landing only a third of his shots, me smiling, annoying him, and waiting for a big opening . . . until some internal clock in Low Key clanged midnight and he grimaced at me, saying with a ridiculously high voice, "Soon," then running into the crowd.

I have seen stranger shit than Low Key, from the depths of the cosmos to celestial plains only wizards gaze upon before death, but the coldness of his word actually scared me.

When I heard the Angels were doing security for the Stones . . . and the crowd was even bigger . . . turned out to be Altamont.

I didn't catch him until it was too late.

The kid was sigiled and armed. But Low Key was too busy gloating to see me come up on his hand, slip his ring off, and break the sigil's spell. Meredith Hunter was free of the ring's influence. But he was sapped, and when the crowd took the stage, he followed their collective movement, hoping rock and roll would save him . . . and Angel Alan Passaro took out his knife and stabbed twice. He was dead before he hit the ground, and before the ritual could be completed.

The crowd came between me and Low Key, denying me a chance at dropping a receipt on his face. He vanished that night, his ring hidden somewhere within Edgar's archives, but I was willing to bet he'd left a few disciples of the Inner Ring in the wings to hold court until he returned to lead the flock.

I shook the memory, and pressed open the door to the Magic 8-Ball with my shoulder, fists still coiled: it took an act of will to unlock my fingers so I could play it cool. The last digit released itself as the Sonics played "Strychnine."

The air was blue with fresh cigarette and cigar smoke, but the stink was of a career dive haunted by a million dead butts, spilled PBR, and rusty old blood. Locals hunched at the bar on the right, barely noticing my existence. Three Angels were on the right next to a curtained window and an old Seeburg with all four speakers shaking so conversation was a scream, racking up balls on the pool table. I walked to the jukebox as the Sonics dirged on about rat poison, and tried not to judge the poor souls here drowning in weak beers. From my periphery, the Angels considered me with sneers. Each was patched. The two on opposite sides of the pool table were waiting for the one with his back to me to make a shot. They stank, but not of magic. Just human grease and machine oil. The two waiting were the classic combo of Spaghetti and Meatball: thin and wiry blond with a dirty bandage around his left forearm, large and chunky brunette with gauze around bloody knuckles. Thin beards and weak mustaches dusted their countenance like a hastily dashed painting called "Trash by Afternoon Light." Over the table a weak lamp in a tired covering hovered like a stray flying saucer that escaped from *Plan 9 from Outer Space*.

The shooter was 180 pounds of well-backed muscle, but not the kind you see in Venice Beach—not cultivated, considered, scientific meat, but muscle from hauling, shoving, pushing, and throwing people around, the muscle of the street that gets a layer of padding from bruises and cuts. His skin was scabbed and his knuckles filthy. His back featured the flying school and MC insignia, and his chapter: Oakland.

I just prayed to Zeus and company that this wasn't some public school buddy of mine. They were a long way from home. Which meant going to a rally or muling horse or weed. But below that were a stab of words in Latin. *Mors tua, vita mea:* your death, my life.

The Sonics drifted off the airwaves. "Say, boys," I said, "spare a quarter? I'd really like to hear 'Dream Baby.'"

The shooter turned. Under his right eye was a burn mark the size of a silver dollar where someone had stubbed out a cigar. "Does it look like I care about your shit, faggot?" Spaghetti and Meatball stepped closer, flanking me on my left, the leader on my right.

"Funny you should use that word, though I'm not gay, since faggot is an old Anglo-Saxon word for kindling, and they used to burn gays like witches for their eerie powers. But seriously, if any of you had a quarter, I'd be grateful."

The leader's burned face was close enough for me to taste the day's ride he'd taken from Northern Cali. "You will be grateful if you leave now before I crack every rib in your body and leave you in a dumpster to feed the rats."

I smiled bigger. "Tell you what. If you beat me in a game of 8-Ball, which I assume is this establishment's claim to fame, you

can do just as you say, and brag to all your buddies how the Oakland Angels need to fight three to one to beat a single faggot." His
pupils pinned and he was a breath away from violence. "Or, you
can give me a chance to win a song on the jukebox. Unless you
think you can't win, mano a mano."

"Don't fight in here, Fife," said the bartender, an old Mexican man with a wide face and tired eyes. "I just redid the floors."
Through the haze, I hadn't noticed. But indeed, new hardwood
floors sat beneath our heels. "If you kill him, do it outside?"

"Seems fair," I said. "You game?" Fife was itching to drive his
skull against my nose. Then it happened—

The balls were racked. Spaghetti gave me his cue. Fife and I
stood like dueling fiends as Meatball lifted the rack. "Would you
care to break?" I asked.

He took a step back. "Ladies first."

I tsk-tsked as I set up my cue. "You sure have a lot of hate for
people who hurt no one."

"Less talk, more shots," Fife said.

I stood up. "You know, junior, you're really starting to bug
me."

The hot, quick sounds of blades snapping from their handles
made a chorus as Fife brought his up to my nose. "You're stalling,
dead man. Make this shot, or I'll bring you down here."

I smirked. "Tell you what. If I can win in one shot, you
boys hand over your knives and wallets, and let me go enjoy
Bobby Darin somewhere where hate doesn't drip off the nico-
tine-stained curtains. If I lose, well, you're going to break me into
a dozen pieces anyway, right?"

I played my smile just a little bit more loopy than usual.

"Let him fail, Fife," Spaghetti said, sitting on his stool. "You
got this."

"I want to see this magic trick," Meatball said, leaning against
the Seeburg.

I sprinkled a little Irish on my cue, pulled back, and adjusted my stance: I gave the ball a "one inch punch" I'd learned from Dr. Fuji. The white ball came alive, and I played the billiard surface like a pinball machine with one stroke, the solids racing to their resting homes until all that was left were stripes and the eight ball, on the edge of the side pocket, reminding me of Edgar's funeral. The white tapped it like a whisper and it dropped.

"Magic trick," Fife muttered, then his eyes narrowed. Fife swung his cue so fast it nearly caught me off guard, but my instincts snapped into survival mode and I moved with the speed of a prisoner down a rope.

I ducked the blow. The cue swung above the pool table, and Fife's vest flapped. There, tucked under his arm, was a holster. It was the last thing I saw before the cue crashed into the light above the table. Sparks, a hiss of action from the patrons behind me, my night eyes flashed on, and I was off to the races.

I tackled Fife and hugged him close, pinning his arm across his chest before we crashed into the Seeburg with a cacophony of broken glass. Fancy footwork and Jane Tarzan's wrestling tutorials allowed me to pop with my hips as I lifted Fife in the air, twisted, and drilled him to the ground hard enough to make him gasp.

The cavalry showed up in the form of a forearm around my neck, though I tucked my chin to my chest to avoid hearing the words *good night, sweet prince*. Meatball dragged me off Fife, just like I hoped he would. I resisted enough for show, Fife's left arm madly pinned against his chest, then let go, my arm sliding by Fife's side as Meatball pulled me back like a sardine tin.

On my feet, the darkness was sweet. Fife moved jaunty, covered in a dozen small cuts. Then Spaghetti was before me, hunting knife up.

Fife scrambled for his holster. "Where's my—"

But his Smith & Wesson M10 revolver was in Spaghetti's face, glinting in the dim and distant bar lights. "Let him go, Tripp," Spaghetti said. "He's got Fife's leverage."

The pressure left my chin and I told all three to get up and stand by the jukebox. They did, Fife's eyes so filled with hate they'd be dead ringers for a demon's.

"Well, boys," I said, massaging my neck. "It looks like you welched on your own deal. So you know what to do. Cash and keys on the table. And before you put up a fight, I don't want your fine vehicles." The top rail filled with scrunched up tens and twenties, loose quarters, and two keys as Fife held his ground.

"Don't be stupid," Meatball said. "We lost. Why the hell did you take a swing?"

"Because he's . . ." Fife said, then he shook his head. "I'm damned." Every vein in his body flexed. "I can't lose my ride to a goddamn—"

I pulled back the hammer. It shut him up.

"First of all, you're being rude. I'm not gay, but that doesn't mean I'm going to sit around until my last nerve is quashed by some queer-plastering idiot who clearly needs to reconsider his life choices of an all-male motorcycle club if he wants to avoid that which he hates." Fife seethed, but remained still. "Second of all, you're not paying attention. You'll get your wheels when I leave. Third, and this is the part I hope you chew on the most because one day it might save your life." I shoved the money into my pants pocket. "Tell Low Key that one day, he won't have a crowd to protect himself from me."

Fife growled, surged forward, and my finger itched.

Spaghetti and Meatball hooked his arms and held him in place while he screamed at me "I knew it! I knew you were one of those goddamn tricksters!"

While they danced on broken glass, restraining Fife, I pocketed the gun, picked up the cue, and smiled. "It's no trick." I hammered the white ball with a little Irish on it, and a metric ton of isometric pressure, the same kind that Bruce Lee used for the one-inch punch, plus a pinch of what Edgar called "the geometry of flash." The white ball slapped into a stripped ball . . .

. . . and all the round soldiers found their dugout.

"Just magic."

CHAPTER 10

LILITH GURGLED UP THE 10, BELLY FULL OF DINOSAUR BONES. I had a near-full bag of Sausage King jerky stuffed in my exposed mouth and chewed hard with my head out the window, the broken glass of the windshield the only thing sullying this oh-so-bright moment of victory: food, fuel, freedom . . . and a bull's eye on my car's face if LAPD or CHP wanted to give me the business.

Behind, hunting for keys in a sewer, were three sad Angels, one clearly a disciple of Low Key. Ahead was a day of demon hunting. At least there was a cool one hundred and change in my pocket, and my hunger was dissolving as the juice and jerky slid down my throat. The cash would be enough to replace my current nemesis: the busted windshield. With spidery cracks, it looked like someone had given someone with glasses four black eyes. Alicia was as powerful as she was petty, and was probably cackling into her afternoon sherry knowing I'd be driving with my head out the window like a mutt.

I stayed in one lane at sixty so everyone knew to get out of my way if they wanted to go home fast. With almost nothing but blind spots, I didn't much feel like passing. The El Monte Busway approached, a halfway mark to the Lincoln Heights Branch, and good God I hoped Moira was working her usual shift. Otherwise I'd have to fast talk my way to their special collections. Because that would be quicker, easier, and cleaner than double backing to the Thump & Grind and trying to get back into my office, and then rolling back due northwest to Nero Studios in the Valley. No. I had to make this stop count. Always go forward. That's what they said in basic, and in Korea. We weren't retreating when the Chinese came like a wall of death at Chosin—we were "advancing in the other direction."

Honks blared as my daydreaming reduced me to swerving. I pulled back in my lane. God, the past can kill you if you let it ride in front of you. Behind me was a blue Chevy four-door station wagon, riding my tail like I'd just eloped with its daughter. My left arm signaled to go around.

Honks responded.

They wanted Lilith to go faster.

My neck ached from being jammed out the window, so I didn't take another gander back. I hit the right-turn signal and pulled on to the tiny shoulder to let the disgruntled malcontent room to pass.

Skids from hard breaks ripped as the Chevy slowed to stay behind me. The exit towards Main approached. Juan's empty .38 and Fife's pistol were in my glove box. I wasn't keen on dragging trouble to the library. So I slowed, then hit the brake. Bang! The crash of taillights made me even happier, knowing I had cash to fix them, too.

Light flashed behind me.

"Damn it." I turned.

A cop's mobile light sat on the dashboard. The driver's side door opened and I slid back into my seat and put my hands at ten-and-two. The cop came up beside the car, plain clothes. This was no traffic stop. I relaxed my grip.

"License and registration."

No wisecrack about the glass? No posturing? This was strange. And so was she.

The Plain Jane cop was in jeans, a white blouse and black vest, shield clipped to her belt. Hair wild and mirror shades giving me a nice glimpse of how awful I looked. The sweat stains on my blue suit were turning the outfit into a strange, groovy pattern of dark and light. She had a hard face with zero humor. But her body was slight, like Nico's, with the ruffles of the blouse trying to cover what was clearly not there: hard packed muscle from a career in sports or being a tomboy.

My smile was already in place.

"What seems to be the problem, officer?"

"You want that alphabetical?" she said, without so much as a dusting of fun. "You're driving with a broken windshield on a highway, head out the window, and failed to pull over—"

"Officer, you didn't ID yourself as a member of L.A.'s law enforcement community," I said. "You honked."

"My light was on, and you busted my headlights."

"There were no sirens. And you busted my taillight. And you're not dressed for the highway patrol or the beat. So, let me ask you another question before I do anything so stupid as hand over my personal information to a stranger. How much is he paying you?"

"What?" Nerves serrated her voice, and I was very, very glad she had no sidearm and mine was safe in a glove box. "Give me your license and registration." Cars zoomed hard behind her and I was scared she'd get smashed if she made any sudden moves.

I sighed. "You're one of Aaron Piper's new lackeys."

Her eyebrows arched and dropped. "If you don't hand over your paperwork right now—"

I shook the bag of jerky, then stuck out the bag. "Hungry?"

She was an actress. She was always hungry.

"I promise, they are not poisoned." I pointed to the Sausage King's ugly mug on the bag. "Would he lie to you? Have one piece."

"Last chance," she said, taking a step back and assuming a stance that you only saw on gun ranges.

I dropped the bag and raised my hands. "By law you have to show me your identification."

"Right here," she pointed at her badge with her left hand, right one low, so she could grab what I suspected was a pistol tucked in her jeans.

My fingers closed into tiny tiger paws. "Kid, I'm late for a date with a librarian, so let me make this quick. That badge is fake. LAPD badges say "Police Officer" on top. Not "Police." And your badge number has a letter X to denote it's not real. These are from a movie set. As are you."

She bared her teeth, then tore something from a back holster: a .357 hand cannon. And I got a chill. "Get out of the car."

Shock retreated. "Nope."

"Then . . . tell me what I want to know."

"You mean what Aaron wants to know. You know, it's pretty lousy for a P.I. to send out actresses to do his dirty work. Lousy and lazy." The long barrel was still two inches from my nose and traffic rolled by like a parade. I pushed the barrel to one side. Yup, fake. "And I'm late."

She yanked back the gun, pointing it at heaven as if it was loaded. "Just tell me who hired you."

"That's privileged information. No dice. Aaron should have told you that. You know he's the absolute worst P.I. in the city? Like, I'm better, and I started today." I blinked. "How long have you been following me?"

She smirked. "I know about the girl in the motel, if that's what you mean."

"It is. What's your name?"

Her mirror gaze held me for a wild second. "Dorothy."

"Well, Dorothy, before you tell me another lie, allow me to reveal what Aaron didn't. You're messing with another P.I.'s case. That gives me cause to take him to court. And I bet you haven't signed anything; he only paid you some cold dollaro to do the work. You 'forgot' to return some gear from the last TV pilot you auditioned for, perhaps with other costumes that you use for meetings with directors and such, stuff nobody misses, but you didn't do the real homework for your role, hence the gimmick badge and pretend pistol."

Her smile dropped.

"And now you're trying to take a client away from me, one who has signed a contract and been notarized."

"You didn't notarize anything," Dorothy said.

"To anyone but an experienced tradesperson, it will appear so. And if this does go to court and we take the stand and do a round of he-said, she-said, well, I'll be the one in the black. Why? Glad you asked. You're impersonating a cop. In L.A. that's a felony." Her hand covered the fake badge and she reholstered her fake gun. "So, just so everything's jake, here are the facts. You know I know that you know that I know that you're not law enforcement. So I can have you arrested today and in prison for life. All it takes is a phone call, and, unlike your boss, cops love me." That lie hit her as hard the truth. I was on a roll! "So, tell me why Aaron sent you out to make my shit itch? And don't say 'needed the money,' honey, because you aren't a member of the ugly set. You get tired of being in commercials?" It sounded like tough, commanding language, but my guts were churning with jerky and fear. I'd been tailed by some rank amateur and now Nico's whereabouts were known to at least one other person. I didn't have time to move her again. I had to make this work.

Dorothy put her hand on the top of the car. "I was doing research for a role, and Aaron said he'd cut his normal rate if I did some legwork for him."

"So the badge and siren were your idea?"

She smiled. "My dad's a cop."

I laughed. "Then forget what I said about jail time." And per-haps not just a cop, but a detective. Time to tread lightly. Sweat beaded around my neck like a noose. I did not need L.A.'s finest anywhere near me, ever. They made the Goon Squad look like the Three Stooges. My math for law enforcement was thus: For every good cop who wanted to do right, there were two dozen thugs who liked power and authority, and were answerable to no one other than the brotherhood of blue. "Wendy, how much is he asking to have you do his dirty work for him?"

"Twenty an hour," she said. Behind her, traffic thickened and slowed.

The double-shot of sprained glass looked back at me. I sighed, dug in my wallet, and slipped out forty bucks, leaving me with about forty and change. "Here's my counter offer for three hours' work. I want you to take the night off. Go see a movie. Tell Aaron all I did was go to the library because I don't have a client."

"But you do."

I nodded. She was playing hardball. "Think you can get her to follow you? Be my guest, Wendy. I mean, she's had a rough day. Beaten, mauled, abused. But, yes, please, go make her a pawn in Aaron's stupid libertarian war with me. Steal my client with the disfigured face. Make her day worse. Be *that* part of the women's movement. You'll make Phyllis Schlafly proud."

Wendy sneered. I snapped out another twenty. "Go. Buy a copy of Simone de Beauvoir's *The Second Sex* and get on the win-ning team. But knock off the light and the badge routine. Felony is a felony, no matter who your dad is."

She pouted, then strode off back to her car.

I pulled away, head out the window like a dog.

CHAPTER 11

I GUNNED IT TOWARD THE EXIT, CONFIDENT THAT DOROTHY WASN'T a threat. Actresses are pretty easy to read when they don't have a script. Career liars, criminals, and politicians? I just assume they're full of bunk. But when an actress has to go off script, most of them reveal their weaknesses: being what the shrinks in this town call "authentic" and what I call "honest." And like a lot of children of cops, she's couldn't hide the terror of a felony charge that would make papa mad.

The highway cloistered. I leaned heavy on the horn and rallied through spaces not meant for a Dodge Dart. A chorus of angry honks attacked me like hornets. Peeling down the off ramp, I escaped the gridlock that would make the 5 a tailgate cemetery. Two greens later and I'd made it to Lincoln Heights Library.

Andrew Carnegie's guilty steel baron conscience over owning a chunk of the world's wealth had led him to believe that if you buy poor people things that make them feel rich, you might sneak into heaven—with the help of a healthy bribe for St. Peter to look the other way when reviewing how many workers coughed themselves to death, burned alive in accidents, or lost their kin in fights with the boss's goon squad.

That said, Lincoln Heights Library was spectacular. Creamy white walls extended in a weak and curvy V made an inviting sight in a city that worshipped images, not words. I parked outside, neck sore from craning, and shuffled as sure as my wingtips would allow up the steps to warm brown doors that were closing as a patron passed me by. The 6 p.m. sun was darkening.

I jammed my foot in and the heavy door was given a stern tug and vice-gripped my shoe hard enough that I grunted. "Damn, I thought I had at least five minutes."

The door pushed open. Before me was a humorless face, etched with hard lifelines, similar to Ares, but the disposition was pure Boston Irish.

"Brimstone."

Some accents are thick enough to stop a charging rhino. This one had twice the depth because it had been forged in the Depression, then the war. High canine teeth grimaced, and a clockwork buzzcut was sharp as a straight razor.

"Buzz," I said, then gave him a weak salute. "Just need to see Moira and I'll be out of what hair you have left."

"We're closed, Brimstone."

"No," I looked at my cuffs as if I had a watch. "I have five minutes. Please."

"We're closed to library cheats, Brimstone." He jutted his chin. "You want to make this personal?"

My hands raised in surrender. "I am very sorry to have borrowed a book for—"

Buzz gripped his belt. "Two years, one month, three days, not including holidays." He didn't pack a sidearm. Just a black baton, the kind cops the world over use to "brain" folks into walking straight on a crooked line.

"That's why I need to see Moira!" I said. "I'm here to pay off the fine."

"Let's see the cash."

"I'm using a check."

He unhooked the baton from his belt, and started doing small circles with his wrist. "We don't take checks from . . . why the hell are you dressed like that?"

My expression dropped. "I was at a funeral."

His braining-arm held still, Buzz squinted. "You Korean shits are all freaky bastards, you know that?" He tapped his head. "Those Chinks get into your head, Brimstone? You just sleeping until some commie rat turns you on us and you go all Kamikaze on the street?"

I smiled hard. "No, Buzz. I'm no commie agent. Were you ever a POW?"

"Never fool enough to get caught."

I snickered and cocked my head to the side, looking him over like a virgin in the front row of a floorshow. "Figured you'd never been tested that way. Never a day passed without the whole US army behind good old Buzz. Protecting him." I leaned in a hair. "Never faced the war alone." His pupils narrowed. "But I did. And I escaped. Saw the kind of hell you couldn't dream about, even if your buddies got shot to hamburger at Normandy." His veins flexed. "So if you think I'm scared of an old man with a stick who thinks his war is better than my war, then maybe you're not really a soldier at all. You're just a thug. A bully. Where I was raised, that makes you a shithook. You wanna go? Take a stab. But just remember, pushing people around doesn't make you American. It makes you a Nazi."

His hand arced back to brain me when thick heels clacked on tile, hard enough that Buzz winced and held still despite every ounce of him stuck in kill mode.

"Buzz, what are you doing with that thing off your belt?"

Her accent matched her outfit: pure Minnesota. God, except for the Indians and Mexicans, there was nobody really from California. She was new. Regulation two-inch school-marm heels, thick, near-orange hose lifted taut under the dark fabric of a regulation gray skirt and a floral blouse of purple, orange, and green. She was a dirty blond in her fifties, and working double-time with the pancake and eyeliner to make it seem she'd be thirty-nine forever. And since she wasn't a debonair black woman in her forties, she most certainly wasn't Moira. Moira also didn't smell of Oil of Olay and lilacs. "Park that stick, Buzz. And you?" she said with the conviction of a high school principal who'd found a JD smoking in the girl's room. "We're closed, sorry."

She didn't sound sorry. That was pure Minnesota "Nice."

Damn. If Buzz had taken a swing, I'd have some kind of leverage. Now gears had to be shifted. "I was hoping to see Moira about my library debts. I'm here to pay them off."

The lady put her hands behind her back. "Moira is at a conference, but I can take your name so you can come back tomorrow without accruing more dues."

"Gracious of you, Mrs . . ."

"Ms. Lucinda Merrill." There was nothing catty in her response. She was correcting me. "Not at all. But we are closed—"

"—and I would hate for you to spend an ounce of time here more than usual. But I'm on tour today and I would love to pay off my debts now, and not take advantage of your good nature. Please, Lucinda?"

Buzz practically hummed with violence in his clenched jaws while Ms. Merrill placed her hands on her hips. "That is very kind of you, but you should have observed the hours of operation."

"Then may I use your washroom?" I pleaded. "I've been stuck on the Ten for an hour and that second cup of coffee I had at lunch is eating a hole through my kidney. Please, Lucinda, it's been one hell of a day and I couldn't even get here in time to do the one good thing before I hit the road. Please?" I was banking on her Midwest commitment to manners being firmly entrenched with general rules of decorum and hospitality. "I really don't want to ruin the bushes outside."

"Oh for the love of Pete," she said, hand waving me in. "Just go already."

"Bless, you, Lucinda,"

I ran into the library, weaving in and out of the stacks. "No running! And you're going the wrong way!" Lucinda yelled, but I didn't listen. Moira's office was in the opposite end of the library, and I needed to get there. Because Moira, bless her, was one of the rarest collectors of the arcane in the Western hemisphere. I'd hoped to chat with her about hybrid demons in a young girl's mouth, and just my luck she was on a librarian holiday.

"Come back, Brimstone!" barked Buzz as my hand dipped into my wallet and yanked out a thinly shaved American Express made out to Mike Hunt. The stacks were thick enough to make you vanish once you turned a corner hard. Buzz prowled with heavy steps, so I grabbed some of my precious change and tossed it three stacks over as I went the other direction, hugged the wall, and ran alongside it like a rat heading home.

Moira's office had no windows facing the library, and I thanked the pantheon of actors in the cosmic dance we call existence for such a tiny miracle. I exhaled silently, wedged in the card above the latch, and slid down.

A tender click.

Slow, silent, and soft, I pushed open the door while, in the opposite side of the library, Buzz was picking up my change.

Door closed, I smelled Moira's room as my eyes adjusted: fresh Jasmine and old Pall Malls.

Her desk was an immaculate disaster area. But I'd visited enough times that I knew where in this unholy collection of old books, ash trays and stray papers was the one volume that might help. On her desk was an assortment of papers that she'd carefully laid down, a map of her administrative duties and her own travels in the arcane.

Which is why the Polaroid camera on her chair stuck out.

"Quit hiding, Brimstone!"

I stepped, gently, through the towers of arcane text and special collections while Buzz hunted for me in "Classics." Moira's new film hobby vanished from my mind. What I needed would not be hiding in plain sight.

The A-Z sleeves on the filing cabinet were a ruse. Paperwork for Moira was out, about, and spread around. Inside the cabinets was greater bounty. Slow and steady, I pressed the metal release with my thumb, gripped the handle, and pulled—

Locked.

Buzz may not have worked in intelligence, but he knew that if I wasn't in the bathroom I'd go to Moira's office. I had fifteen seconds.

I yanked a paperclip from a collection of papers and carbons on the cabinet, and another from the round magnet on her desk she called the Black Hole of Calcutta, shaped one in a lazy L hook, the other one straight, then went to work on the lock with breath slipping through my nose in time with my heartbeat. The hook rested at the bottom while the straight arm went straight for the tumblers.

"Better not be in the ladies' bathroom," Buzz groaned, thankfully distant . . . but not for long.

I raked through the tumblers, pulled with the straight arm, and inhaled. The lock released.

Paperclips hit the ground as I pulled the top drawer open.

The taste of magic books was like a cloying older woman's perfume. It reminded me of Edgar and I gagged.

Moira's private treasure chest lay before me, spines out, and I flipped until I found my target. I yanked it out, and two dark slivers fell out from the pages. I caught them between my fingers, turned them face up and gasped as the door opened.

Lights snapped on. The baton in Buzz's hand pointed directly at me.

"Going to smarten you up, Brimstone."

I held up the photos with a smile. "I think not, hero."

Buzz shook but did not move. No jive, the old solder was scared.

"Ain't technology grand? Those folks at Polaroid are wizards. No dark room needed, even when the pictures deserve to be enjoyed in the dark."

"Give those back," he growled.

I tucked the tome under my arm, grabbed the camera by its straps and looped its straps around my neck. "Normally the *L.A. Free Press* isn't interested in the love lives of librarians and security guards, but given the kink nature of Moira's photography, I think they might change their mind."

"I'm going to kill you." The heavy thud of thick heels approached.

"No, Buzz. You won't. Because that would get Moira in trouble. Murdering an unarmed man in an office, and Lucinda the witness heading this way."

He seethed, fumes damn near steaming out of his ears.

I put two twenties on the desk and pocketed the pictures in my left pocket as Lucinda popped in. "What on earth are you doing in here?"

Fury ate Buzz's command of speech, while I adjusted my weight and held the tome so tight in the crook of my arm you could only tell I was holding it from the back. "Oh, Buzz was kind enough to open this up so I could actually pay my fine." I started moving toward the door and Lucinda backed away. "Plus, Moira had borrowed my camera for her last trip to Greece. She loves new technology and knew I'd done some photo work back when I worked for Uncle Sam in Korea."

I tried to follow Lucinda's lead and leave, but Buzz stood between us. "I just love the look on people's faces when they see themselves on film," I said. "I bet Moira took enough great pictures to make some people famous. Right, Buzz?"

The thermonuclear explosion in Buzz's eyes detonated, but his killing hand dropped. He stood to the side, letting me pass, which I did with a quick step.

At the door, I thanked Lucinda while Buzz slammed Moira's office door shut, checking the lock with hard tugs, and then striding to catch me before I left.

I walked out backwards to keep the book out-of-sight. "Thanks so much, Lucinda. Sorry for the inconvenience."

She smiled, makeup softening in the onslaught of the late afternoon haze. "Not at all. Thank you for clearing your fines. Oh, and where did you say you were going on tour?"

I smiled as kind as a Sunday school teacher. "Oh, just running away to join the circus, as always. Afternoon, Lucinda. And Buzz?"

Cold murder was in the veteran's eyes.

I turned, adjusting my arm so the book, tucked so tight, emerged from my crook as I showed him my backside. "Say Hi to Moira for me."

I drove Lilith a short distance, hung down the wrong way down a one-way street, and parked behind a giant dusty Cadillac so I could catch my breath, stay out of Buzz's blast range, and review the spoils.

But first, I stole another glance at the two pictures.

There was Buzz, mouth deep between Moira's dark thighs, digging into her naughty bits with mouth wide open. You could follow Moira's form like a slash, as she'd obviously held the camera up high at an angle and clicked it while they were going to work on each other. The other had her riding him, half clothed, between the stacks, her looking up at the camera as if she knew someone who'd see it, lipstick smeared, glasses crooked. The only thing he was wearing were silver bracelets.

I smiled back at Moira. "Miss ya, Moira." I pocketed the explicit photos, removed the camera from my neck, and turned over the book that had been soaking in my pits.

Demons of the Orient, by the Reverend Montague Summers.

CHAPTER 12

EDGAR HAD KNOWN "MONTY" SUMMERS. I NEVER HEARD SPECIFICS, except grudging respect for the "fat pastor who dug like a rat into the catacombs of every parish and bishopric from London to Luzon." I had read his translations of *Malleus Maleficarum* first, for what young and bored circus roustabout could resist the tales of witch hunters during the fifteenth century during long hauls across Texas? Especially since books were rare as true love on the circuit. About the only other thing Edgar noted was that "Summers wrote far more books than he published," and mentioned two by name: *The Witch Lords of Africa* and the volume in my hand, *Demons of the Orient*.

From the driver's seat, I scanned for anything out of the ordinary. On the library side, kids took bikes out of the rack and pumped pedals to get dinner and miss a beating. The other side of the street was a handful of homeless people, barefoot as hippies and beaten by a cruel sun and cruel life, huddled under a single palm tree bent worse than a politician's spine. No threats. Just early evening sadness. I drew my finger around the outline of the book, realizing how much they were gateways to other places real, imagined, or nightmarish.

Summers was a mix of all three, but best known for collecting the folkloric tales of the occult from Europe. Vampires, witches, werewolves, and their assorted "kith and kin" were rendered with the kind of relish you expect from a melodramatic English teacher who gave up the stage for teaching the rug rats because they could never turn down the volume of their own hyperbole. Summers loved theater and plays and every tome he cranked out was written with high emphasis on the macabre, the grotesque, the bizarre. And yet he was recording the facts as much as embellishing them, or, as Edgar said, the stories were "all documented, all true." They just grew a little in the telling.

The book was a solid thousand pages. Time for a Joyride.

I took a deep breath and closed my eyes, a mantra playing in my head: *Tyger, Tyger, burning bright . . .*

The opening refrain from William Blake's poem raced through my mind with the beat of a parade drummer running late (1, 2, 1-2-3), short-circuiting my active mind so that my subconscious could bubble out of the ooze from which it ran my life without me knowing it, and offer me a deeper and fuller awareness. Edgar called it Transcendental Consciousness. I called it Joyriding: a state where my mind and body twined as if struck at exactly the same moment . . . and time became elastic. I was more than the sum of my parts and I moved like greased lightning in the world (*Tyger, Tyger, burning bright*) . . . fought with the conviction of a career pit fighter, made love so intense and timeless that minutes of bliss were born (*Tyger, Tyger, burning bright*), my favorite aspect . . .

I cracked the spine of *Demons of the Orient* and plowed through the pages with my fingers moving slower than my eye, each orb sucking in the words by near osmosis while my mind carved out a new cave for the information that was comprehended at a near instant and lodged among the tunnels of my brain filled with stray and disorganized memories: opening credits to *Challenge of the Yukon*, featuring Sergeant Preston of the Royal Canadian Mounted Police, the dirty jokes Professor Fuji used to make while imitating Groucho Marx ("What a gala day, and if it was more than a gal a day I'd *never* get out of *bed*!"), and the dark shadows of Edgar's jobs, tasks, cruelties that I'd covered in the gossamer web of denial, all of which held together by force of will as the letters, words, sentences, meaning and voice of *Demons of the Orient* filled in a new cave.

My skull smacked the headrest. Copper filled my mouth. The Joyride skidded to a halt. Jolting in my seat, I looked around to see the sun had dropped. Late six o'clock shadows trailed kids passing a basketball to each other, all of them loud and hopeful future stars. I sniffed and felt the drop of a drip.

The last yellowing pages of *Demons of the Orient* were stained with three drops of blood. Terror bit down on my nerves until memory did its work, and, thankfully, there was no evidence that I'd just raised the dead or given myself a curse by bleeding on the work of Montague Summers. I sucked in a deep breath, then exhaled hard. Nose bleeds and Joyrides were synonymous, especially when you crammed a thousand-page tome in your head. It was worse if you did anything physical. Fighting while Joyriding was never, ever, ever recommended. Even if you won, even if you moved like Bruce Lee on the Green Hornet, you'd probably wake up and be hit with an aneurysm.

I wiped my nose, and the book in my lap expanded in my mind. Ballooning facts, connections, and even Summers' hyperbolic voice filled my skull. Pressure grew as pages raced and the back of my eyes wanted to jump out of their sockets—

—POP!—

Tears streamed down my eyes, but my mind's eye saw every page clear, every image evoked, every symbol catalogued, pushing to find connections, clawing through the soft tissue of fresh meanings to hold on to that which I was hunting . . . seeking . . . in the swarm of knowledge I'd ingested like a hog on a soggy donut. Three deep breaths later, I'd latched onto the one symbol and image that mattered, Summer's voice cartoonish with glee as it discussed salacious and sexual material . . .

All three volumes of the erotic woodcuts are worthy of study, but none carry the weight of sin and abomination like Dreams of the Fisherman's Wife. *Hokusai's depiction of an ancient myth has many imitators but none so categorically affected as the original, for it was based on the true story of a Japanese fisherman who drowned at sea and the deal his wife makes with a Squidling and its child to save him from the underworld. While later Shinto writers and other righteous blasphemers placed a fabled ending on to the story and associated the popular Princess Tamatori with the Fisherman's wife, the true tale is far more important. Hokusai's Shunga diary recalls the details of his witnessing a local fisherwoman summoning an Octopus from the deep fathoms offshore. Upon her back she had carved a hex, the Black Shinto symbol for power and seduction, what would appear to Christian eyes as a twisted cross. The blood that dropped from her hexed flesh splashed the waters and brought the leviathan to the shore, where it suckled upon her labia and engorged her with cunnilingus as she writhed in sinful ecstasies upon the lapping shore. But where the most popular version of the Shunga depicts a second Molusk kissing the woman deeply, the original is far more frightening and worthy of vigilance. For it was from her mouth that a serpent emerged, as if a malign tongue. The fisherman's wife birthed a demon, rooted within her, a creature born of lust and desire and the monstrous seeds of the inhuman octopi. The demon snake was thin, eyeless, and without teeth. The alleged lost Shunga showed the same woman pleasuring herself with this demon, and upon its back was etched in yellow the ancient Shinto symbol for oblivion.*

I gasped. The tears upon my cheek had dried and my lungs felt as if I'd smoked a pack of Lucky Strikes and tried to hold my breath. The data was close to Nico's story, which was good, but not perfect. I only had an itch of what it meant . . . and the itch grew more annoying as I listed the contradictions: the snake thing in Maxine wasn't thin, but big, and it sure as hell had teeth . . . it wasn't interested in sex, but tearing Nico's face apart. Malice, not ecstasy or oblivion.

Damn it.

I flipped to the front of the book out of habit, but I could see the translation page when I blinked. "Published in English by Arcane House, published in German by Thule Publishing."

Thule?

My testicles retracted and the world dropped fifty degrees with each heartbeat. Edgar would scare the soul with tales of the Thule Society, the Occult Arm of the Nazi party. Norse legends, ancient Sumerian, and bullshit racial theories all fucked each other over in an orgy of nonsense that, nonetheless, also tapped into the real and dark magic of this spinning orb, and wreaked tortured havoc on its victims.

German translation of Japanese sex tome of sorcery. Axis magic? Some kind of blending?

"Fuck," I muttered to no one in particular, because whoever was messing with these powers was either powerful, or a fool. Or both.

From the secret embers of my childhood, a voice called out for Edgar. He'd know what to do. He'd be able to stop it. He had knowledge and power that exceeded mine by several orders of magnitude. And he was dead, for all intents and purposes. No running home to big bad Edgar, who'd just laugh and tell me to figure it out before the world ended.

Summers riding shotgun, I started up Lilith and rolled down the street looking for a payphone, preparing for a call I didn't want to make. Two booths had their lines cut, so I had to turn to North Broadway. I breathed ammonia and sadness as I plunked down a dime from one of the Hell's Angels.

"Happy Knight! Where every room is your own Castle!"

"Morris? Put me through to my room."

"Just be glad I'm a nice guy, James," he said, tone downright frosted. "I don't run this place on charity."

"You're a real Mahatma Gandhi."

"Who?"

"Just put me through to Nico."

Around me the sounds of traffic and blaring guitar did nothing to sooth my nerves. Then a click. "Yes?" Nico's voice was pregnant with expectation.

"It's Brimstone."

"Have you found Maxine?"

"Not yet. About to head up to your place of business."

"Then what have you been doing?"

That tone again, as if ordering a dog to recite *West Side Story* as punishment for bad behavior. Can't say I found it groovy. I blinked as my mouth followed my instinct. "Had to get gas. Also had to pay off a library debt. Sorry it's taking so long."

"No, no . . . I'm sorry. I'm so tired, and scared, and I saw on the news that if cops don't find someone within twenty-four-hours—"

"Nah, that's just what cops on TV say." It was also true. But my gut said there was no reason to worry her about Japanese sex magic and demon woodblocks just yet.

The door rattled and pushed in. I jammed my foot down to shut it. Outside, a bearded longhair with a gimp face was rattling his angry fists. "You're in my shower!" Glad it wasn't his toilet. I flashed my five fingers and mouthed "minutes" and, amazingly, that had him mollified enough to just stand out there with his flannel arms crossed, chewing his lip.

I focused on Nico. "How are you holding up?"

"All right. Morris brought me something to eat."

Anger coiled. "That was nice of him." And I'd pay off the tab. Last thing I wanted was any sense of obligation between them. He might feel sorry for her face, even some kinship because they were both mauled by life, but he was still a man and Nico, however scarred, was beyond his reach as a lay. Hell, she was beyond mine. "But Nico? I want to be clear, you can't open that door again. Not for Morris. Not for the president. Unless it's me. Our codeword is Blueberry Pancakes. Say it."

"Blueberry Pancakes."

Her voice stirred a hard longing, but I wasn't done with work. "Good. Just watch *Here's Lucy* or *Laugh In*, something fun to take the edge off this day. You must be bushwhacked."

She yawned as she spoke. "I'm tired but I don't think I can sleep until I know Maxine is okay. Or have you back . . . Mr. Brimstone."

"James is fine." And it was. I hated my last name. It crackled in my ear like a cop on the PA in the precinct, calling me to the line up or the front desk. No matter how pretty or sweet, any voice saying Brimstone raised one hackle. "And I will help her." Though I had no clue how. I blinked, and the tumblers in my head fell into place . . . because I knew who could help.

"Shit."

"James?"

Fists banged on glass. "Better run, rent's due, I'll call you in an hour. Rest up, Nico."

When the handle rested in the cradle, I took a look at the hard case outside. A creeping amount of gray was etched into his thick brown mass, his face scabbed and worn, and his beard was ragged and riddled with dancing dandruff that was likely not dandruff . . . about my height, less weight and more gnarled muscle from toughing it out on the street.

If I had gone to high school, he could have been in my class. Maybe a track star. Maybe a class clown. But something had derailed him so hard he ended up here . . .

. . . here, on the street, where death stalks every choice, and the man-made demons of drink, dope, and delirium are your co-workers and roommates, taking up lodging inside your skull, and you'll do anything for warmth against the dark, in bottles and needles . . . maybe he was a vet like me, but what he saw he couldn't swallow . . . maybe he was a rotten bastard who got what was coming to him via a karmic exchange played out in real time instead of waiting for reincarnation . . . maybe he made one bad choice, the worst choice, the kind that can't be forgiven . . .

"Get out of my house!"

I nodded, put a dollar on top of the phone.

He backed away as I folded the door to the side and stepped out. "Sorry to mess up your abode. I put rent on top. Hope that's fine."

His eyes were near feral. He shuffled inside, snatched the dollar, and examined it. He held it above his eyes. "*Novus Ordo Seclorum.*"

I nodded. *A New Order for the Ages* had been on dollar bills for a long time. Someone knew Latin before their life crashed. But the eyes were still wild. "I've seen it! The dark spiders, the shadows, the grinning men and their mouthless women! Hell has frozen over and the party is about to begin."

"Thanks for the tip, friend," I said, and gamely walked back towards Lilith.

"*Novus Ordo Seclorum!*"

The derelict's mumbo jumbo dogged me as Lilith headed me where I did not want to go. But there was no choice. My knowledge of Shinto magic was not enough to explain the differences in a demon's dental hygiene. I needed an expert. And that meant two things that made me squirm.

I was going to Beverly Hills. To see my ex.

CHAPTER 13

NOT KEEN ON ANY MORE HIGHWAY SHENANIGANS, I GUNNED Lilith through the byways of Chinatown and Mid-City, shucking and jiving with one hand on the horn. A series of green lights through Mid-City almost made me believe in a merciful god until I headed into the evening funk of West Hollywood. Brown bags littered the gutters like the corpses of squashed rats. The air fluttered with the launching of a dozen different burger wrappers that danced in and out of traffic like kamikaze birds. Welcome to the Sunset Strip.

Haight-Ashbury may have been the Mecca for hippies, but their Medina was the Strip. As seven p.m. broke the day into a blazing pink evening, the streets were filled with bright orange, sweaty brown, and faded red shirts, Indian headbands, and beads. Burning joints tussled with tobacco and made the air so thick with resin and nicotine that breathing too long would turn you into a groovy casualty. But there was a change in the uniform of the peace-and-love brigade. T-shirts hung off figures so thin you wondered if being a junkie was the next big fad, like hula-hoops and Orphan Annie decoder rings.

Watching the dopey smiles of L.A.'s love children, sadness crept up inside. Something had changed since Altamont. Their shadows . . . were wan. Their spirits a little paler. Woodstock hadn't ended the Vietnam War. Kent State had shaken them. Split them. Some got militant and dropped out of the world and lived as if they were Henry David Thoreau's poorer cousins, trying to make a crappy Walden into Shangri La. Others abandoned their beads for a corporate Monticello. That had bled their shadows pale. Once there had been a critical mass that could have had a chain reaction . . . instead they were scattered into a dozen Plan Bs. Some tuned in, turned on, and dropped out . . . and ended up here. Others had gone AWOL in America, living on communes and exploring lifestyles ranging from Roman to Puritan. Others sold their soul to rock and roll, caravanning behind buses filled with idols, hoping artists could be their life. And there were those who picked up a needle, and became wraiths of their former selves, or drank their way into a berserker rage, or popped enough pills to fade into a coma.

"Zombies at worst, sheep at best," Edgar had said once. But I liked hippies. There was so little malice, even if their leather headbands held back anger at injustice. I'd bashed through too much violence in East Oakland, the Iron Triangle of Richmond, the circuit and Korea not to wish, perhaps, that I could be one of them, a free flower child of abandon who made a life about living, feeling, being . . . but Edgar knew, as well as I did, that some of us are born to walk alone.

The sidewalks were crammed. Fuzzy guitars and thick bass blared from storefronts while singers I didn't know screamed and crooned and stole every possible emotional lick from the catalog of bluesmen whose names were every ounce as dangerous and cool as *Black Sabbath*. Howling Wolf. Lightning Hopkins. Big Mama Thornton. Hell, those names sounded like mob bosses and escaped monsters from the Universal lot. I circled the block until a spot opened up in front of Pet Palace, one of the only clean storefronts on the east side of the Strip.

The pennies between my fingers were hot as I pushed them into the meter, cranked the knob, and bought myself two minutes, Montague Summers in my left hand.

"Hey, man," said a twenty-something in hip huggers and a checkered top, wind caressing her hair like a web across her face. "You late for a wedding?"

I smiled. "Yup, just need to pick up the bride to be!" I pointed at Pet Palace and swallowed a sob.

"You marrying a dog?"

"I won't have you speak about my bride like that!" I said, gesturing as if I was an uptight Connecticut Yankee complaining about the nuts in his Waldorf Salad.

She laughed, deep and throaty. "Well if doesn't turn out, I love doggy style. So long as I keep the ring."

I read every ounce of her: young, starved, sexy, practiced, dressed like a hippie but working the daylight hours. She was a little drunk, comfortable being rude in public. And everything about her beauty being turned into this vulgar one act made me want to buy her a bowl of Ares's lemon chicken soup, and a one way ticket back to wherever she was from, and not see the Strip suck the life out her . . . she'd be a crone on the street faster than Dalko, my favorite little league washout, pitched a fastball. "I'll keep that in mind." I tipped an imaginary hat, then pressed open the door to Pet Palace, abandoning a wife for thirty bucks a night to talk to the one who'd actually said no.

Screams from every corner of the earth filled my ears. Macaws screeched, dogs howled, and I swear somewhere in the back there was a gorilla making love to a vending machine. The stink of the place was a zoo crossed with bleach and the heady afterglow of incense, which likely pleased no one but Isabella, who was no doubt in the back working her own magic to heal the critters of the animal world.

The front office was a tiny square with a handful of wooden chairs pressed against the back wall. Each held an owner who held a critter: a young girl with a macaw, an old lady with a snotty bulldog on her lap, but I was damned if I could see the love ape. At the counter was a fifty-year-old lady in a sweat-stained polo tee and red slacks with a freshly permed helmet of hair.

"You're incompetent," said the snotty bulldog woman to the desk gal, a Thai girl named Franca. "I said I had to leave before seven. And it's seven. I want to see Dr. Caylao. Now."

"She's very busy," said Franca, then saw me and her face soured. "Too busy, perhaps."

"I am *not* rescheduling," said the bouffant in slacks, her voice betraying a real north London accent, dented by about fifteen years of living in the States: a quiet indignity rumbling with a sense of privilege you have to be born with. "You will get off that duff of yours, and summon your boss, or else I will give you a reason to be upset."

She wasn't waiting on a pet. She was here for Dr. Caylao's *other* efforts. Same here. And the kid and old lady in the seats were ahead of me. I'd lost too much time. "Excuse me?"

The fifty-year-old turned and showed me a face so thick with pancake makeup and sculpted smears of blush and eye shadow that she reminded me of my old clown pals, Tick and Tock, sitting before each other, putting on each other's make up because they were twins (it was against the Clown code to let anyone else do it or see it, but Electric Magic tents had a lot of holes in them). In comparison this woman looked like spilled dinner. "Am I talking to you? No? Then mind your own business."

I kept my face pure pedestrian. "It's just that . . . isn't that your Triumph outside? The dirty green one?"

"So what if it is?"

"It's being lifted by the good folks of Peter's Tow Jobs."

"What?"

"Your meter must have run out."

"It did not!"

"Well you better put a quarter in or else you'll have to go down to the Pike in Long Beach to get her out." I loved that bit. People in L.A. think going to Long Beach is the greatest inconvenience since the outhouse, and the Pike's boardwalk was always crowded with tattooed bikers, exiles, and other assorted color that was being pushed out by the growing mass of hippies.

Fury shook the woman's eye, then her finger, which she wagged at Franca. "Tell the doctor I will be right back." She yanked the door behind her, but it couldn't slam, and she screeched under her breath.

The tension in the room dropped like an anvil. I turned to the two women in their chairs. "Ladies, I apologize. She's going to come in here twice as mad." Lilacs filled the air before I heard her voice.

"No doubt because she saw you, James."

I shuddered at the velvet voice that had just slapped me.

In white coat, beige blouse, gray skirt and five-inch naked heels was all five-foot-five of Isabella, one arm on the door. Her black hair was styled and wavy and her face said forty going on twenty-five. The only tell of the hard life she'd known was in her hands: deep scars and grooves from a childhood of labor, violence, and war. She turned to the patients. "Mrs. Devon, Ms. Frausto, I apologize for his conduct." Neither one of them spoke a word, just nodded at the strangeness before them. Meaning me in my prom/funeral outfit. "I will be with you in a minute, but I must see this gentleman out the back so that Mrs. Wentworth won't have a fit when she returns. You?" she said at me. "Come."

And there wasn't an ounce of joy in her words or actions. And that's when I noticed. The animals' screams had been reduced to panting. Down the short dark hall were waiting rooms, surgery rooms, and a bathroom, but the far back left was her office. Lilacs dusted the aromas of animals so much you'd be hard-pressed to remember that it was also a place of mange, poop, and death.

I enjoyed her backside, all the more pleasant as she tapped down the hallway . . . though it was also a rerun of our last moment together: me in the dark, her walking away. The office was small. Two chairs sat in front of medium-sized desk, and surrounding every wall like a layers of balconies were trinkets, charms, and artifacts from around the world, lilacs making everything smell safe.

She took her seat, crossed her legs, and held them fierce and tight like a judo master about to break someone's neck, skin the color of crushed cinnamon. "Sit, James." I sat. "Your hair looks like it was kissed by a hurricane."

"I've been blow drying it on the Ten."

"And your outfit? Chaperoning a kid to prom? I swear, without a woman in your life and left to your own devices, I think you'd end up wearing garbage bags and a fedora. Do you know how bad you smell? You're about one day away from looking like a vagrant. Where were you?"

"A funeral."

Her wan smile ebbed. "I'm sorry." The sarcastic lilt of a woman rearing up to read me the riot act on my flaws (an experience for which I did not have the time) dropped.

"It was Edgar."

Her eyes narrowed. "Then I rescind my apology and offer condolences. You stayed too long under his influence, James. It wasn't good for you." She *tsk-tsk-tsk*ed as only Filipinas can do, with a note of indignation and a mild amount of sympathy, all while wiping an imaginary bad smell away from her. Edgar had that effect on a lot of people. Izzy caught herself about to list all the reasons Edgar was bad news, then tapped the edge of her pristine desk. "So what brings you here? Do you have fleas?"

"Probably, but I have more urgent problems." My smile relaxed, and I raised Montague Summers. "Octopi. Of the Japanese erotic variety." I lay *Demons of the Orient* upon her desk.

She swore in Tagalog so sharp and fast it would have cut me to the quick if I'd been a hair closer. Her long, strong index finger pointed at the book with a short, sharp trimmed nail a hue of smoky red. "Are you still reading this racist *anak ng isang asong babae?*"

"I'm currently without my usual resources."

"So where did you get this junk?"

"The public library."

Izzy laughed like a firecracker going off and she never looked more beautiful. Most guys want to date or marry a still-shot, a cover of a glossy mag or a pinup model who is etched forever in a single lusty pose. An immortal moment, frozen in time. One that begins to rot as soon as it's taken, unless you were related to Dorian Gray. But what made Izzy beautiful was how life crackled through her, gave her energy. Sure, if she stood stock still you'd say she was gorgeous, but it was her spirit that made her truly beautiful, a rare mix of brains, guts, and sense of humor that made you want to make her laugh. "Oh James, I shouldn't laugh, but the library? You used a public library? You had such a good collection of dark folios."

If Izzy went down memory lane, I'd be here for every one of her cats' lives. "I need help, Izzy. And that book led me to you."

And the humor was replaced with the determined look of a professor about to battle a war of words. "Summers never went to the Philippines. And if he had, he would have never found what he was looking for, and he would have ended up with his head on a stick in Mindanao."

"I know. But he did go to Japan."

She gripped her knee with both hands. Hard. "Then why are you here, talking to a Filipina? Shouldn't you be sniffing around a Shinto temple or the Japanese consulate?"

The next move would sink me if I played it too hard. "I'm helping someone."

"How old is she?"

"She's a client."

"That's what you call it now?" Izzy stood, pointed at the door with a hand that had killed more Japanese soldiers than most American GIs. "Out. Now." She grabbed the book and pulled back for a mighty toss. "And take your idiot boyfriend Summers with you!"

I covered my face and pulled up my knee. "She was attacked by a demon." My heart beat three times before I dropped my foot. "A serpent emerged from her friend's mouth and slashed her face with fangs sharper than a barber's straight razor." My guard dropped. Izzy was still ready to throw a killer fastball, anger taut and muscles hard and hungry for combat. "Summers talked about Japanese women being possessed by sea demons . . . sexually."

Izzy raised an immaculately smooth and curved eyebrow.

My hands lay at my sides. My voice was just loud enough to be heard and not one decibel more. "We both know you sell . . . sexual aides of the unique variety to these old starlets, and I don't care about it except you're an expert on the side of erotic that touches the fantastic." I swallowed dust. "And I know you've seen the dark side of Shinto magic." Izzy had no thousand-yard-stare. The war she'd seen as a child, fought as a child, killed in as a child, was part of her nervous system as much as carny instincts was part of mine. "What attacked my client, it wasn't . . . normal. Something was done to warp even an *oni*." I told her the details and she listened, holding back the tsunami of desire to smack my five o'clock shadow off with one swipe. "So, sexual demons. Plus, this book was published in Germany by the Thule Society." She dropped the book on her desk as if it had been on fire. "I need your help, Izzy. I'm facing something a little bit outside my pay grade."

"What kind of help?"

"During the occupation, was there anything like these creatures that . . . touched on both cultures? Axis magic? Shinto sex demons? Twisted love children of Reich and Emperor? Can you help me?"

She turned her back to me. Not as a sign of disrespect, but as a note that her mind needed privacy. My guts sank, asking her to go back in time to a world of brutality only the hardest of soldiers knew, and in many ways worse. A girl in a man's war, fighting across Luzon for scraps of good, terrified that every step the collaborators would turn you into the *Kempeitai*, and you would end up in the hell of Bilibid. But I knew Izzy. There was a girl in trouble, hounded by demons.

Arms crossed, she faced me. "Yes."

CHAPTER 14

IZZY FLEXED HER ARMS, SQUEEZED HER BICEPS, AND LOOKED directly at me: not my eyes, me, the essence hovering before the windows to the soul, the core of who I was, the unvarnished version of my ego that hid in my mind. She talked to *that* and I held still and tried not to blink.

"A brothel near Manila, outside the old walled city, was run by a Japanese major." She wetted her tongue. "He was known to us as Major Kasamaan. He was part of the secret police, working with the collaborators. He had a jeep they said never ran out of fuel. He could drive forever across the island, hunting for guerrillas, hurting those in the barrios who helped the guerrillas in every way. And he targeted women for his brothel. Anyone who helped the guerrillas would have their daughters, or mothers, or even grandmothers dragged to the Hotel Kasamaan, as his brothel was known. No one ever left it."

As bad as this was, I knew it would get worse. Even the animals were quiet.

"They came for my friend, Makisig. She was a runner with the bamboo telegraph between my guerrilla unit and her bar-rio. She was seven." Izzy exhaled hard. "Someone snitched. We went to break her out, until the guerrillas heard she was at the Hotel Kasamaan. Then our leader, an American engineer, said no. Ten guerrillas were more important than one girl."

She leaned forward. "I slipped in myself. James, this was no hotel. It was no brothel. It was a church, for dark gods. The basement was littered with trinkets and sigils and signs. Some were Shinto, yes, others were German. Others . . . were not made by human hands."

I nodded.

"Maki was tied to a pole, along with four dead woman in a row. Flies were wild and ravenous and ate at my eye as I crept in the shadows of the fire pit at the center of the room. Major Kasamaan had his fingers in her . . . privates. Abusing her. I wanted to throw my little bolo into his eye when I saw her back arch, and—"

"I demand to see the vet!"

The woman from the front desk was screaming.

"I don't care if her hair is on fire. I will speak with her."

Rage twisted in Izzy's eyes. She stood in her heels, walked with the precision of a dagger, then left the room. The next sound I heard was the righteous old lady screaming as a door opened and was slammed. Izzy came back, captured by that moment of rage. She sat, then focused.

"A serpent burst between her lips. No toothless Japanese mollusk. No octopus. It was fanged, vicious, and its colors bled black and red and—"

"White," I said.

She nodded. "Maki was dead by the time the creature emerged and ate the corpses in the room, fallen Filipinos who he had used in experiments. Major Kasamaan died," she said, and I must admit I wondered how painful she made that day on earth. "But the creature . . . it grew as it ate the dead people. Including . . ." Her fingers interlocked as if in prayer. "I dropped a grenade and ran. Never saw it again."

"You did the right thing."

She dismissed my comment with a glare. "Save your consolations, James. I'm not a weak American girl crying for her mother's breast. The power you are dealing with is vile. If what attacked that girl was of the same beast . . ."

"You said it ate? Did it have teeth?"

She shook her head.

"Are you sure?"

"Don't doubt my memory."

"Just confirming how different my case is from yours. Confirms someone is messing with this magic. This serpent had teeth like daggers. It wasn't meant to kiss, or swallow. It was meant to tear and destroy . . . Which sounds more like a wolf to me."

"Japanese wolves are extinct."

"I know. But there was another member of the Axis that had a love affair with wolves. And the Thule society—"

She gasped, covering her mouth. "Yes, yes, yes. The major . . . he had a German liaison in Manila. His hands were covered—"

"In runes. A Thule society clown. Did you see him that night?"

She shook her head. "I have no idea what happened to him."

"Whatever happened, someone is messing with Axis magic." Fears spread behind my eyelids as I pressed my palms into my eye sockets, a flood of thoughts springing from my brain: *I just wanted rent, I didn't want to face dark magic, I didn't ask for it, in fact, I made sure I'd be clear of the Big Guys of Dark Stuff, I wanted small potatoes cases, cheating husbands and crazy old ladies, that was manna from heaven, and now I'm throat deep in the darkness again and it's reaching for my lip on my first goddamn day.*

I pulled the palms from my eyes, and the mashed sandy orange gave way to the reality of Izzy's beauty. "Got any Dubonnet?"

"Something better." She opened the bottom drawer of her desk and with one hand pulled out a heavy cash box that was locked. "James, there has been . . . lots of interest in Shinto magic these days. Many of these hippie peoples are looking East of India for the next fix of enlightenment. Tourists, more like it." Izzy's spat the word tourist with enough force to remove a tooth. Her brown eyes blared a hundred watts. "But not just Japanese spiritualism. German, too."

Teeth locked. "You mean Nazi."

She nodded.

"Damn it."

Edgar and I agreed on one thing: there was nothing worse than the scum-sucking turds of the Third Reich's occult mystics. *Degenerate pretenders*, was what Edgar called the Thule Society. Monstrous shithooks was more accurate. Edgar never told me what he did during the war, but his hints and clues and a couple of nights with a little too much gin with his tonic made it clear he'd been overseas, part of the shield and sword that destroyed Hitler's fortress in Europe. And the monsters he saw . . . like most of his generation he kept them to himself. Only difference with other people's fathers and uncles who kept their mouths shut about Normandy, Ortona, or Midway? Edgar fought actual monsters. "Who are these customers?"

"New. Down the strip. Called Iron Surplus. Sell mostly war junk to idiots. Some of my customers who enjoy my . . . cocktails," which was Izzy speak for mildly enchanted potions, lotions, and more that she learned from her Grandmother before the Japanese cut her head off in front of her, which makes her continuation of the family tradition of Kulam, or folk magic, sweet, even if most of what everyone wants is a thousand variations of Spanish Fly. "They are big, James. Tough boys."

"Good thing I only want to talk to them."

She *tsk-tsk-tsk*ed me again, removed a key from her lab coat pocket, and opened the cash box. "You're a trouble magnet, and you know it. If you're going into the mouth of needles, you will need some armor." She lifted what appeared to be a necklace, but with an iron pendant swinging from the bottom. The pendant's face held a large eye. On one side was a sword. The other a shield. At the bottom it said *Roma*.

"An anting-anting," I said. "I thought these charms were for criminals and outlaws."

She nodded. "I wore it during the war."

"Izzy, I can't take that—"

"Take? You'll return it as soon as you are done! Hold out your hand." I hesitated, and she snarled. "You walked with Edgar through the shadows of the unknown, and you can't trust me with my own people's magic? How typically American. I'm trying to help you and you think the little Filipina's magic charm is bunk."

"I am unworthy of it."

Her glare softened.

"Izzy, the last time I saw you was the night before . . ." I choked on emotions so warm and gooey they melted my insides like napalm. "When we were to be wed. And I always figured you didn't show up because . . . I wasn't worthy. And I get it. You wanted out of Electric Magic. You hated Edgar. And I chose you but—"

"Enough." She wiped away the word with her hand and took a long, deep breath. "You were a child, James. Even now. Part of you is a child. And I missed that because my childhood was slain by war. Your proposal was sweet. And I was too cowardly to break your heart when you asked. So I say yes, and then I know it's a no. But that doesn't mean I don't love you. Or find you worthy. Now take it."

I did.

"Put it on. Under your shirt."

I did.

"How do you feel?"

For a very warm second, there was only Izzy, strong, determined and beautiful, the tomgirl from Manila who hid on a US warship and came to the US with red hands . . . the girl who knew a thousand animal languages and could turn a wild dog into her best friend with a stern glance, who had lazy tomcats jumping through fire hoops, and could ride a bear with a hug until she stood on his shoulders like Mowgli . . . who tired of the circuit and left me there, a chump in a borrowed tux from Sir Reginald Barker (our tattooed geek who claimed to be British royalty), me sitting outside her tent with a cubic zirconia ring in my trembling fingers . . . the girl who ran away from our three-ring circus and became a vet, a healer of animals, and a quiet practitioner of her people's magic.

"James?"

"I feel," I took the damn thing off, "like a man wearing a bullet proof vest in a church."

"That amulet is no joke."

"I know, Izzy." I sighed. "That's why I took it off." Because the damn thing made me feel safe in the sadness of the past, an after-burn of wearing something that was designed to bend bad magic, ill fortune, and shit luck should it come your way. "It has a hell of a kick. And I'd rather not feel invulnerable unless I have to." I delicately wrapped the hemp rope and placed the anting-anting in my pocket. "I better go before those Nazis close up shop to go burn a synagogue. Mind if I use your phone real quick?"

She nodded, stood, and walked past me to go pick up business at the front. "Don't die, Brimstone," she said, hard and secure. "If you do, I'll have to bring you back to life and kill you myself." She laughed. I did, too. Then I dialed Happy Knight.

"Happy Knight, where the rest is our guarantee." The owner of the childish voice snorted, then giggled. It wasn't Morris. Some kid. High, stupid, or both.

"I need room 1A."

"Yeah, man, okay for Juan A!"

"I'm glad you crack yourself up, kid."

"Oh man, are you really talking to me right now?"

I smiled. "I am. What's your name, son?"

"Marco."

"Ah, Marco. You're an employee of Mr. Morris, correct?"

"Yeah, he's cleaning the pool. I didn't want to get the raccoon that was in the pump. Death is too heavy, man."

"Tragic. Marco, my name is Frank Stanley. I am the owner of the motel."

Silence.

"If you don't do as I instruct, I will have you arrested for being drugged on the job."

"No, I'm no head! I'm responsible! I timed it perfectly to end when I got to work."

Ah, the future. What wonders we will see with Marco, the world's greatest unintentional comedian. "Then prove it. Patch me into Room 1A."

"Okay, yeah, I got this one."

CLICK.

It rang. And rang. And rang.

I called back. "Marco—"

"I'm so sorry! I did what you said!"

"That's fine. The phone appears to be off the hook. I need you to knock on that door. I need you to see if my wife is still sleeping. She's very ill."

"Okay, I'll be right back, just hold on okay, boss?"

Tijuana brass crackled through my ear with so much treble it was like a trumpet giving birth and screaming all the way to the drop. Apparently this annoying music was one of Morris's splurges for customer service. I missed the silent darkness of the last call.

CLICK.

"Okay, I checked!"

"And? Where is she?"

"How should I know?"

"You just checked the room!"

"Oh, yeah. She's not there, man . . . whoever she is, she's gone."

Shattered glass thundered from my exposed ear. Women and animals screamed from the front. The receiver hit the floor as something at Pet Palace roared.

CHAPTER 15

WITH THE SPEED OF CHUCK YEAGER LATE FOR A DATE, ALL THE WORLD silent behind me, I chased the screams down the hall. Broken glass stained the ground of the office foyer. A large shadow filled the mouth of the hall. It turned and screamed at me with frothy intent and my night eyes took the details.

Six foot two, two hundred thick pounds. Jeans, white under-shirt, and red flannel shaking off his frame. Rock jaw, hair down to his shoulders and a five o'clock shadow that had been up all night and turned into a beard from nose to neck. Fists at his side like a gunslinger and around his neck hung his own amulet: a director's viewfinder, bouncing off his heaving chest. Worst, though, were his eyes: dilated, beady, and flashing red.

Fulton—the director of Nico's film.

I ran, he charged, but momentum was on my side. Shoulder hit chest. Hoisting his legs up, I drove them down to the ground. We slid into the foyer, and I hoped the shift to daylight would aid me in blinding him, if only for a second.

The slippery son-of-a-gun was faster than a greased pig on Easter morning. My right cheek ate an elbow in the fray, making Alicia's caning of my chin wake with fresh agony, thoughts going fuzzy for a cold second. He shook and shimmied and I tried to grab one of his arms to break. He'd had enough training to counter my grip, and enough strength to toss me a ways away.

And the taste of magic around this shithook was like burning sand.

I scrambled, and he was up, staring fire. Broken glass churned under my wingtips and his engineer boots. Fists flew, blocks and parries followed, and I dodged another elbow-kiss while Izzy grabbed the two patrons in the foyer and hustled them and their pets down the hall and, hopefully, out the back. All the while Fulton's fists charged while he frothed out grunts and groans from his mush. Broken glass crackled as I landed a couple of rib shots that bought me some distance, but didn't stop him from coming. Thank God I had Sausage King jerky in my blood instead of just exhaustion and floor biscuits.

I suckered him into shoving me back, and he kept coming as if cruising at his regular speed: breakneck for breaking necks, while the side of my face flared up like a balloon full of raw meat. Fulton ran through the patterns the Army had taught him, far more than most soldiers got, and as I breathed hard I realized he was probably a Ranger or Green Beret far from the sky . . . which meant I couldn't just get him to submit. Sleep or death was my only option. A left cross came and wiped the thinking from my brain, so I sidestepped, dove for a clothesline, and slipped in for my second "sleeper" of the day—

—until Fulton tossed me around like a drunk riding a bronco. The office bounced around me, desk to coffee pot to chair to wall, while I gripped tighter around Fulton's bull neck, but the fury that bled into his eyes was deeper than a bad stare and the taste of burning sand meant he wasn't going down, even without oxygen.

Fulton roared with the bellows of a minotaur.

"Ah, crap," I spat, and braced for impact.

BAM! I hit the desk at such an angle that my kidneys were almost evicted.

BAM-BAM! Twice his head rocked back into my swollen cheek. Rivets of agony pocked up my skull.

BAM-BAM-BAM! Three elbows in my ribs and I had to break the stranglehold or my lungs would be punctured.

I fell back into a waiting room chair, huffing.

"So, Fulton," I said, huffing while he massaged his neck. "Ready to give up and tell me where Maxine is?"

The woman's name triggered a scream and veins of rage emerged from his skin thicker than tent rope. With meaty hands, Fulton tore the top of the front desk off like Frankenstein's monster going ape on his own slab.

He swung for the bleachers as I dove across glass and dodged decapitation. Turning, he stood by my feet and raised the slab of desk to crush me. Thus, a gift presented itself. I drilled his balls with my wingtips and gave him the world's most atomic "gas pedal."

The embers of his red eyes smoldered, then shook, then dimmed. The slab of desk in his hands shook before dropping with the grace of a guillotine. I rolled to the right and the slab crashed to the ground, edge first. Fulton was on bended knees, a statue of power that had started to crumble. His flannel shirt was torn and, upon the bare skin of his shoulder blade, there was a mark that I thought was a tattoo until it flared black and red . . . a sigil.

He'd been magicked in some goddamn way.

Which meant he might be a victim. Not a perp. Not a predator.

I sat on my butt, ass cheeks a little tender from the pokes of broken glass. "Fulton, listen. Someone did this to you." His eyes clenched. Sweat dripped down his fat nose as if from an open wound and tapped the floor every second. The viewfinder swung like a pendulum from his thick, vein-pulsing neck. "I can help you. I can. But you need to listen closely."

He dropped to his knees, wheezing, eyes as shut as the dead.

"There's a Ancient Sumerian mantra that might help you."

His hands lay on the floor atop broken glass.

"But you have to say it just right."

He gripped shards with both hands.

"And you're clearly not listening to me."

His eyes opened.

"You're planning on jamming that glass into my eyes, aren't you?"

He snarled.

"Well, I tried."

He leapt at me as if a comic book werewolf drawn by Jack Kirby, a creature of rage and primal instinct that would not stop slashing until I was a stain of viscera on the wall, each paw clenching a glass dagger. But primal rage left his jaw wide open.

I hate fistfights.

I hate boxing.

I hate punches.

I hate ever having to turn my moneymakers into weapons of destruction.

And as that jacked up vet with a berserker brain lunged at me with ravenous intent, I was actually scared.

Scared I was going to kill him.

"Treat every fight like your last," Dr. Fuji said, all the while my hands were chopping at a malformed hat-rack with a dozen arms, "because one day you will be right." I ran through the sequences until they were blurs, and his steady diet of egg yokes and hemp oil felt like they were a joke that was eventually going to puke its way past my teeth, but Dr. Fuji was in charge of security for the show, and I'd been beat up so bad by a gang of hoods in Duluth for helping a black patron fix his tire that I'd endure any foul treatment that Dr. Fuji had in play. His American-Occupation English was flawless and word around the tents was he'd been a spy and

assassin throughout all of Asia, from Osaka to Samoa and all islands in between, but on the circuit he was our policeman, silently taking out rubes who had too much hooch and energy, breaking up fights on tour, his movie-star good looks being a great deflector of the usual bigotry we'd see with our foreign talent, but when it came, he endured, played the ignorant coolie and walked away, knowing he was the toughest SOB within a blast radius of a thousand miles. And Edgar got it in his mind to make me a protégé to "smarten me up" so I wouldn't wake up pissing blood from kicks to my kidney, and so I became the only ten-year-old apprentice to Fuji's teachings . . . judo, wrestling, wushu, karate, taji, aikido, words that felt weird in my mouth and were agony on my body. Fuji was a fan of all things violent, except boxing, which he called "idiot gladiatorial contests," but he knew the need of a good punch and how best to drop a man twice your size with a tiny fist at the right place—

Fulton pounced, and before you could yell *lights out*, a left cross snaked out of me with the full power of my spinning form, aura, chi, and chakras. When knuckles met chin, my ears popped. Shivers ran through my arm as Fulton's rock-jaw shook as if I'd punched a pineapple Jell-O mold.

Two slices from the broken glass came for my head, and I ducked and turned to avoid being headless. Twisting on my heel, I watched as a closed-eyed Fulton crashed into the wall, bounced to the floor, and then rolled onto all fours. His jaw hung down like a busted ventriloquist dummy.

He was down, but not out.

I gulped.

That punch was meant to destroy him, not annoy him.

A cut bled from his cheek, where my little green pinky ring had branded him as deep as the sigil on his back . . . which flared red and black.

He shook his jaw, and it snapped back into place as blood pooled around his fists, both still clutching shards. He craned his neck, eyes red, and growled.

"Put on the damn anting-anting, you idiot!" Izzy yelled from down her hallway.

Fulton looked back at her, so I ax-kicked his neck. His head bounced on the floor, but he pushed himself up, careened his neck.

His face was a mass of broken glass, streams of bright blood, and red eyes, a horror show thrown into a wrestling match.

I needed more than Fuji's teachings to work this guy over. I dipped one hand in my pocket when sirens roared. Their blaring wail stole Fulton's attention.

He rampaged through the hole he'd made in the glass door and people parted like the red sea.

Izzy stood in her doorway. "See how it works?"

I waded through the glass toward her, tried to say something clever, then gripped my sore jaw. "Yes, ma'am," I muttered.

"Go after him, James. Make him pay. Insurance doesn't cover you bringing monsters to my work place!" Izzy was cross-armed and all business.

I pantomimed tipping my hat as I hit the street.

"Don't play cowboy with me, James! Make this right!"

I pressed my cheek so I couldn't hear Izzy's voice rebound in my skull and hustled toward Lilith, wanting to hit the street before the fuzz landed. But the sirens were screaming and the light smacking me in the face. Now I had to deal with L.A.'s finest.

"Stop right there!"

I knew the voice. Hackles went apeshit.

The slow walk of a power-drunk cop ground my gears as the smug, fit face I'd wanted to punch more times than any sigil-soaked veteran grinned at me. And the fucker still smelled like lemons.

"Well! Jimmie Brimstone!" said Officer Richard Dixon. "What a charming turn of events!"

CHAPTER 16

DIXON GRINNED WITH HIS WIDE IRISH MUG, THE KIND THE English had tried to kick into oblivion for four hundred years but without permanent success. His beat-blues were as crisp and sharp as his blond buzz haircut, and they hung off a very wiry frame that packed a lot of kilojoules into taut muscles. Dixon was a gym rat and health freak, teetotaler, and wouldn't smoke if the IRA ordered it. Behind him, throngs of hippies, heads, and rich ladies with strange cats watched us like a one-act play.

"Thought you'd moved back to Oakland, *Jimmie*."

I smiled. "Know what the man said, you can't go home again."

"What brings you to LA?"

"Oh fame, fortune, my name in lights."

"You thinking of trading in that circus for Hollywood?"

"Everything's a circus if you look at it right: rubes, shit, and clowns."

Dixon snorted. "Shakespeare, you ain't. Tell me what happened here, *Jimmie*?"

Swallowing my loathing for his voice, that nickname, and the false sense of familiarity that was a mask for contempt draped in power, I said. "Well, Officer Dicks—"

"That's Dixon, *Jimmie*."

"Of course. Well, I was just visiting an old friend when, well, one of today's youths had what I think you experts in law enforcement call a 'freak out.' It sure scared me. He crashed through the door like a Loony Toon . . . get it? Or am I going too fast? Shouldn't you be writing this down?"

He crossed his hard, thin arms. Cuts and scrapes and scars buried under white-blond hair. "Blood on the floor and a lot of witnesses. Better hurry and get to the point, *Jimmie*, before I lose count of how many charges to stick to your good name."

My smile hitched. "Officer, I hope you're not threatening to brand me with crimes I didn't commit. Think of the pristine reputation of the LAPD." He was close enough for me to smell his citrus breath, courtesy of that lemon tea he always drank. Dixon was far more annoying than the crooked shits who did "night shopping" of local businesses, worked over guys on the beach for shit and giggles, or harassed the legions of beauties of this town because of "busted" tail lights. Serve and Protect became Use and Abuse.

No, if Dixon was one of those shitbirds, I'd make his life a living hell by putting sugar in his gas tank once a month and making sure whoever served him free coffee in this town did so with a side order of spit. Instead, Dixon was far, far more annoying.

He was straight. Legit. A square with a badge.

But he was also an asshole. Had been since Oakland, when I left my best "mate" behind when the circus came to town. Now? His best mate was the law. "Try my patience, *Jimmie*," Dixon said. "I've got all night."

But I didn't. "What can I say? Some Joe walked in here, broke through the glass of Isabella's shop, started tearing it down, I tried to help," I pointed at my swollen cheek, "got an elbow in the mush for my trouble, and when I kicked him in the balls he left."

"Why was he after you?"

"Never said he was. Motive is your job, officer. Not mine."

Dixon grimaced. "What did he look like?"

"Hard to tell. It happened so fast. But he was a white male. That I know for sure."

"You're making my shit itch, *Jimmie*." Every time he said my name like I was still a shithead kid at the docks, I wanted to break his jaw. There's nothing so vile as power fisted deep into a righteous asshole. "Guess I'll have to take you downtown for a round of mug shots of white males."

Fuck you, Dixon. If he got me in the hole . . . I'd never find Nico, I'd never find Maxine. Whatever trail was hot tonight would go colder than a nun's teat when I popped out. But Dixon wouldn't give me a break. He wouldn't take a bribe. And if I ran he'd follow, and tar me with the thousands of parking tickets Lilith had, then impound my girl for her two black eyes. Blood rushed through my veins so damn fast I felt sick, fearing the blue web of the LAPD.

"Officer Dixon!"

Izzy walked like a queen through the shattered glass. "How dare you accost this man, who did everything he could to save my office while you and your people were nowhere around! Useless. This man needs medical attention, not the third degree. And the criminal who did it ran out of here. Down that way!" She pointed down the Strip, then gave a near-perfect description of Fulton. "Tell me you are going after him, now, Officer! Tell me you are not letting a criminal get away!"

God bless you, Izzy.

Dixon nodded at her, grimaced at me. "We're not done, *Jimmie*."

"That way, Officers!" Izzy yelled, and Dixon was off like a bullet through the throng of long hairs and afros who'd stayed through all of Act One. One grease-faced teen applauded twice. Or was trying to catch an imaginary fairy.

"Thanks, Izzy," I said. "I owe you—"

I could not have stopped the slap even if I'd been Joyriding, and it hit my good cheek like a triple dose of thunder. "Idiot! Bringing your bad *kapalaran* to my office. Stop the monster, James. And fast. Go!"

I did, both cheeks smarting, anting-anting in my pocket.

Fishing for a dime, I made a call in a stained phone booth, cramped and stinking of ammonia and hash. Words pressed past my lips and shook my sore cheeks.

"Wild Card Casino, please."

CHAPTER 17

THE WEB OF CRACKS BEFORE ME CHEWED ON THE DARKENING sunset. Pain flexed in my face from Fulton's elbow, but I sat in Lilith and counted the stars around my vision as luck, because he could have probably torn my head off if he wanted to.

Nico was gone.

Maybe Fulton had found her, tore her apart . . . but unlikely. He'd have torn the doors off of her room. I didn't know where she was, who took her, if anyone. Would she have left a note if she knew where Maxine was?

The damsel-in-distress film I'd been in was now split into two. And if I didn't find both, my payment went up in smoke. There were only two leads in what was quickly becoming a gonzo goose chase. I revved Lilith's engine. It was Nazis before pornography. That had to be an aphorism somewhere in the underverse.

Worry doesn't make me drive fast, but closing times do. Most legit shops close at eight. Lilith roared into the evening traffic thickened with hash smoke from the open windows of Dodges and low riding Chevys. Guitars lathered in static and distortion trailed after the puffs of thick smoke. On the street, some kind of tortured animal man screamed and wailed with a posturing of blues musicians who'd seen far more of the evil in this world than these skinny wraiths of rock and roll could comprehend.

I revved up, shoved in an eight track that only worked when Lilith was in the mood, and rolled the pieces of danger I'd collected in my head. John Lee Hooker's growling voice hit me in the solar plexus as I drove like a dog with my head out the window, singing "Boom, Boom."

Wind drove its fingers through my hair like an invisible comb and I hadn't realized how sweaty I had been until being air dried while I shucked and jived through the rat race traffic of the Strip, neon signs brighter than the fading sun, ocean breeze as intoxicating as hope for the damned.

Hope and two leads was all I had to play with.

"Boom, boom."

The Wild Card Casino was a neon bunker built for giants and home to many gamblers on the Strip, and it soaked the night with blazing art deco sign with symbols of joy zipping on and off: a joker face, a cowboy, and the bottom half of a woman in go-go boots. It reminded me of a copy of *Zap*, a smart and dirty comic book I read in a port-o-san at Altamont, drawn by some head named Crumb, about a bug-eyed man chasing a woman that was only ass and legs and breasts but no head. I shook the image away, but the neon kept it resurrected. I double-parked a block away.

The red and yellow marquee proudly presented such talents as Steve and Eddie and that no-account putz and career has-been Frankie Mutts as the opener, with special guest "Lou Masters, the God of Magic." But underneath the display stood a man in three-piece burgundy suit who seemed to suck in all the light around him, and whose presence cut a swath of personal space, as if his double-breasted coat was punching the air in front of him. His hair was short, his sideburns trimmed, face dark and without an ounce of joy, brush mustache as trimmed and flawless as Robert Goulet's.

Just what you'd want in a Casino security agent.

I left Lilith and jogged to the front of the Casino as the six-foot-six enforcer came close and, hell, I almost backed away when he approached. "Cactus. You're looking well."

Cactus tilted his head to look at Lilith. "You should kick out those windows. Less hassles from the cops." I appreciated that he didn't mention buying new ones, considering his suit cost more than most of my organs on the black market. Cactus picked a glass shard from my shoulder, looked at Lilith, then back at me, trying to map my day. "You need to keep your guard up more. You're swelling up like bad fruit."

"Thanks, coach."

"You're dressed for a shotgun wedding," he said, flicking the glass without scratching his callused fingers. "Why?"

"Long story," I said. "And not why I called."

"Then talk," Cactus said. "I lose my men's respect if I seem an elitist bastard who can take smoke breaks whenever he wants." Just another reason Cactus was the best NCO we had. His sense of duty was far deeper than us white kids trying to be tougher than our fathers who beat the Emperor and the Fuhrer. Cactus could trace his family's warrior culture back to when the Apache warred with the Spanish. Wasting his time was an insult.

"I'm crashing into a mess of trouble."

He shook his head so gently it was hard to register his disdain. "That's why you called me? Muscle?"

"No. I just need a deck of cards."

Cactus considered me with the kind of hard stare you only see from former soldiers who end up in Westerns, glaring a thousand yards into the camera and trying to murder the audience as if they were a legion of SS soldiers. "Cards?"

"Yes. Standard-issue Bicycles will do."

"What kind of trouble requires a deck of cards?"

I laughed. "The kind I can handle, Cactus, but I'm currently locked out of my office, so if you could help me out, I'd be—"

"You're not answering my questions." Cactus had been a lieutenant in the Counter Intelligence Corps during the Second World War's last year, and rumor was he was an excellent investigator and interrogator himself, but by the time he was with me? Kicked down to Sergeant in a Marine platoon, freezing his sack off at Chosin, but no one knew why. But the command voice had stayed. He reached into his breast pocket "Name your trouble."

"Oh, nothing much. Just some young fans of the Third Reich, probably worshiping Hitler as a god, selling Nazi trinkets and whatnot to the next generation of junior fascist. Now, about those cards. I can pay now—"

Cactus tossed something blue and white. I snatched it from the air, old blue and white packaging. "Nice. God, no matter how bad my day gets, a new deck always makes me feel like things are going my way."

Cactus still glared death. "You're messing with Nazis. Why?"

"Private client business, Cactus."

"Client."

"I got my P. I. license."

His left eyebrow rose. "You're an investigator?"

"Licensed and bonded."

It was unclear who he was more furious with: me, for screwing around in his old profession, or the State of California, for making such a grievous mistake. "Ask me to help you."

"That's not why— "

He stepped forward, his voice low, cold, and deadly. "You knew I'd react to Nazis being in my backyard. You knew I'd view you having some dime store Pinkerton badge with rage. You want me to come with you. That bullshit carney psychology may fool the rubes you ran with as a kid, but they are horseshit to me.

You want the help of a friend, you ask. You want to get in the long line of white men feeding me bullshit, be my guest, but you will be the first one I break in half today." His breath was hotter than Mojave sand.

"Cactus?"

"Yes?"

"Will you help me beat up some Nazis?"

"Yes."

"Hey! You!" From just outside the Casino's mouth spewed a man in flared jeans and a sweat-stained silk shirt. "You're the asshole who had me thrown out! Hey, speak English?"

I held my breath for two reasons. First, if I didn't practice I'd lose my ability to hold it for five minutes: roughly twice the time it takes to get out of the Chinese Water Torture Cell, which Edgar thought was the "safest" way to teach. Also, it would help keep my mouth shut as Cactus dealt with this bozo. I massaged the deck and smiled: this would be fun.

The guy was twenty, drunk and high and angry, mustache like two blond feathers rubbing asses upon his lip. Cactus turned to face him. "I was on a roll in there, Chief!" The moron was stabbing the air in front of Cactus's face with his finger. "How dare you toss me out like I'm trash. You know how much money I throw in your direction?"

Cactus's voice was low, but clear, and without a trace of anger. "Mr. Coleman, you can't touch the waitresses. You were given a warning. We only give one warning."

"She lied!"

"She had no reason to lie."

"She's a lying dyke!"

"Her personal life is none of our business."

"I can't believe you're taking that whore's word over mine." Then he tapped Cactus's chest with each word: "I'm a fucking customer."

"Mr. Coleman, I'm warning you. Do not touch me again."

The feather lip laughed. "What are you going to do, Tonto? Get your silent Lone Ranger buddy to beat me up? Or are you guys wearing the wrong costumes for the eight o'clock magic show? Come on, Cowboys! Say hi-ho—"

"Silver" died on his lips, because when his finger touched Cactus at the end of "hi-ho," several things happened quick as lights out: Cactus gripped his hands, broke his wrist, spun himself around Coleman's back, and cupped Coleman's mouth shut like a drawbridge to imprison the scream.

"Mr. Coleman," he said, voice as level as before. "You were warned. We only give one warning. If you come back here, I will break your other wrist. If you come back a third time, I will break your ankle. You can do the math. Should you come back with a gang of friends, we will retaliate in kind. Or you can go home, try your luck at any of the Strip's fine gambling establishments."

Cactus shoved Feather-lip toward the parking lot, then strode off toward the VIP parking section without me.

"We can take my car," I said.

"Your windshield is busted and the LAPD has you on a 'suspicious character list.'"

I ran to keep up with Cactus' gait, tearing the plastic wrapping off the cards. "How the hell did you know . . . you have a police scanner."

Cactus smiled as we strode through the chained off section, guarded by a young Latino kid in short-sleeved dress shirt. "I didn't say that. Jesus? Tell Edward I am on a supply run. And nothing else."

The youth nodded, unchained the ritzy section. The streetlights crackled on as the evening darkened. But you'd spot this car in a black hole:

A 1950 Rolls-Royce Silver Dawn, waxed and shining as if it had run off the assembly in London and landed here. Edgar was a fan of British cars, and had a Silver Wraith. I'll say this for the British, they sure know how to name their cars. Cactus opened the driver's side door. "Get in the back." He sat inside. "And keep your head down."

"So the cops won't see me?"

He slammed the door and rolled down the window. "No. So nobody sees you."

"Don't want to be seen with your old army buddy?"

"No. Didn't buy this car to be viewed as some chauffeur."

I hid my sore mug, knowing he was right.

CHAPTER 18

"YOU BETTER HAVE A PLAN."

Laying across the back seat, I flicked off glass that was still stuck to the fabric of my slacks. It pinged off the window and landed on my thigh. "Of course I do."

"Improvising is not a plan." Well, that was a matter of opinion, but I did my best to make it sound as if I'd spent more hours than Ike on D-Day getting this sucker ready. Cactus finally said, "Fine, but if we die, I am hunting and killing you for eternity."

"Deal." But the lineup for inflicting my eternal misery started in Oakland. I placed the anting-anting in the car. For this plan to work, I needed bad luck.

Cactus drove to Iron Surplus in a car that probably weighed three times as much as Lilith and smelled like well-tended leather. The density was cozy, but it didn't make my day easier. My cheeks smarted as I rubbed away some of the worst pain from psycho-Fulton's smashfest. Whatever strength I'd gotten from the bag of jerky faded, but now didn't seem the right time to ask Cactus for drive-thru on the Strip. Food whenever you wanted it was, for me, a kind of dark magic. Like the rest of the country,

I'd felt the sharp edge of hunger gnaw my belly like rusty teeth in the thirties, and had been desperate enough to steal from those whom I thought had more.

But while Golden Arches sprang up across this country, as Kings of Burgers gobbled up more real estate and flooded the streets with mass-produced meat pabulum, I knew in my heart of hearts that this was some kind of Fat Faustian bargain. For twenty years I'd watched as the starved waistbands I'd known as a kid, held up with rope above skeletal ankles, had given way to wider and wider frames from those who'd never tasted real hunger, the taste of dust and bleeding gums, of sucking on bark, chewing on shoe leather. So I learned to cultivate my hunger away from the promises of two thousand calories in two minutes for two dollars.

Except In-N-Out. That stuff's sublime.

Night thickened. I took out the cards Cactus had thrown at me and began a mindless ritual I'd had since I turned ten on the road. I fanned the deck, took half, hit them on my knee, took half in each hand and cut them, slapped the pieces together and did a 360, then a Faro shuffle, a Hindu shuffle, then presented them over the seat. "Pick a card, Cactus. Any card."

He didn't look back. "You auditioning for a croupier?"

I folded the deck back into my hand. "I may need the work if I don't solve this case."

He snorted. "Don't get me wrong. I'm glad you found a job. Where did you get your gumshoe license?"

"Frank Gurney's Private Investigator's Full-Measure Certificate Class."

"I don't know Gurney."

"He lives in Sacramento. I did it via correspondence."

Cactus's eyes flared in the rear-view mirror. "A matchbook degree?"

"It's legit, Cactus. I studied, I passed, and I was certified by the State of California."

"I feel safer already."

Cactus sped up, hit the break, then reversed so fast that I bounced around the back seat like a Mexican jumping bean. When he stopped screeching the tires, I picked up the deck that had splattered like the Queen of Heart's army. "Easy, Cactus! What was that for?"

He opened the door quick. "Get out."

I shoved all the cards in my right pocket, the left currently holding the anting-anting, and pushed open the door. When I got out, I could see the hullabaloo. Cactus had wedged his car between a Volvo and a Voklswagen Beetle at the speed of *SHIT!*, tighter than a nun's naughty bits. Two blocks ahead, on the opposite side of the street, stood the three-story monster called Iron Surplus.

"They know we're coming?" Cactus said, flexing his knuckles until they cracked.

"Doubtful. And we need them in shape to chat. Which means, follow my lead." He looked back at me as if I'd said his ass was on fire. "I know, I know, I'm breaking with protocol, and you outrank me when it comes to raising Cain. But they're going to toss racist darts at you like Olympic champs, Cactus, and I can't have you going Karate Master all over them until I know what they know. Information is what we want, not body bags."

Cactus spat with a precision reserved for snipers and hit a stray cockroach on the street. "I won't leave here without breaking Nazi skulls." Rumor in my platoon was that Cactus had interrogated the worst of the worst: SS, Hitler Youth, the diehard fanatics who wet themselves thinking of the Third Reich as Xanadu, who cherished the destruction of the peoples of Europe, who cheered when the *Kristallnacht* sounded the klaxon for the first steps of the Holocaust. Cactus went into those minds to find out details about the absolute bottom dregs of humanity, to see what other horrors bled there in the pits of their nightmares.

For him, they were the supreme evil that walked the earth, and that we'd only barely stopped. "That's what you said we were here for. If this is a bait and switch, James, you can take those cards and—"

I strode across the street to a chorus of honks. "After we get the intel, Cactus. After we get the intel they are all yours. Just let me do the talking."

Three stories of poorly drawn M16s, Dog Soldier helmets, and combat boots made the face of Iron Surplus a garish eyesore even within the brightly colored dreamscape of the Strip as the sun kissed the horizon. There were two mannequins guarding the entrance like Roman centurions. One was decked out in the battle fatigues of a modern GI currently sweating bullets in the Mekong Delta. The other was a Prussian officer in a blue and gray greatcoat, complete with silly German helmet with a spike on top. A sign was taped to the wooden door. "No Dogs. No Home-less. No Hippies, Cowards, or Canadians."

My anger bristled. Back in the day, it said "No Black, No Dog, No Irish." Or "No Jews, No Blacks, No Trouble." Despite what politicians will feed you with your TV dinner, there are no good old days. Rome was filled with slavery. Colonial America, too, for all the good sense of the Declaration of Independence, which also shat on the savage "Indian." If a performer had the wrong skin drink at the wrong water fountain off the Chitlin Circuit, there'd be another dead black kid being cut from a tree, and touring Alabama and Mississippi I'd seen men and women hung from pine and oak.

The past? Goddamn did I want a future that looked nothing like it. I was glad to live in a world when Martin Luther King walked, and ashamed to be in the one that had him murdered. If there was any hope in humanity, it was in taking the best from the past and running like Jesse Owens away from the rest.

I shuffled the cards. "You ready?"

Cactus nodded. "I'll cover the door, and your back." He rolled his shoulders and I heard gunmetal beneath a double-breasted jacket.

"No guns unless there is no other option."

"That's up to them."

Arguing with Cactus was like moving a mountain: impossible and annoying. Guns were a trouble multiplier. And I could not afford a shootout and Dixon on my ass. The porn palaces of San Fernando awaited my arrival, and Maxine and Nico needed me alive if I was to find them.

I pulled the stupid big door.

Iron Surplus stank of old rubber, older sweat, and memories. It was a warehouse room with ranks and ranks of uniforms, dress and service. Gas masks hung on walls: gruesome clothes with filters and bug eyes which had tasted mustard gas in the Great War, modern diving masks with filters used by riot squads when they needed to poison a peaceful protest. Tables filled with boots. All used. Including pairs of russet leather combats from Korea, dusty gray dirt still in the treads. One still had a leg, the top end below the knee sawed off in red and white. I walked further. Blood dripped out of the cuffs of a Marine dress uniform as a bloody red stump of meat hung out of the hole. There was a ping-pong table full of severed heads and more flies than Alaska in spring, the buzzing worse than the track lighting high above my sweating head. Pieces. Everybody was in pieces.

Brimstone . . .

Hey, James!

Private!

Gotta light?

Gotta smoke?

Gotta spare blanket?

Gotta spare hand?

The hissing ghosts of my own mind awoke with the smell of distant battlefields and freshly made graveyards, of frozen blood and burning moonlight, waves of Red Chinese soldiers chasing us like a plague across the blue hellscape of Chosin.

Cactus shoved me. "Forward."

The ghosts receded as fresh sweat poured out of me and I was pretty sure this suit was blending into my skin like some super hero costume.

Four pairs of eyes sharpened me to the knifepoint of my current predicament.

Paler than spilled milk, each guy wore a green wife-beater and hair buzzed into box cuts. One was tall, one was short, and one was ugly as freshly made turd. The only customer in the store was a twelve-year-old kid with buck teeth buying a Marine t-shirt from a massive desk and display case at the back, next to the zig-zag stairs that went to the next floor. The kid put on his shirt as he left, as if making some statement to the generation he was growing into: I am not one of you. I am your enemy. I am going to read Steinbeck's war bullshit, forget *Grapes of Wrath*, lie about my age, and kill some gooks for Tricky Dick.

"Cold wash it," said the man at the desk as the kid passed by me and into the world. Behind the desk was a twisted mirror. My age. Similar build, but hitting the barbells ten times a day and showing off the goods by wearing nothing but a utility vest. Hints of gray in his dyed blond hair, right at the razor edge of his sideburns. Eyes baby blue. Stank of cigars and hate. "What do you want?"

"Fine store you have."

He crossed his arms, flexing his guns. "If you don't buy something, we don't want your kind in here."

"Kind?" The three other thugs did a lazy pincer movement around the tables of belts from long-dead men. "You don't serve the Irish?"

He looked me up and down. "We don't serve faggots. Or their mutt boyfriends."

I shuffled the cards to bring everyone's attention back to me and away from Cactus: the giant mirror in the store's left corner showed him standing silent as a sentry at the Tomb of the Unknown Soldier.

"Ah. Right. It must be the tux. See, I was at a funeral."

"Don't care if you were at the funeral of Robert E. Lee. Buy something, or leave. Now."

The glass case between us was full of buttons, bullets, and mementos. "Then I'll need your help to find it. I need an Iron Cross. An early one."

The cashier raised an eyebrow and the three thugs froze. "It's illegal to sell works of the Third Reich without proper authentication papers and being vetted by US Customs."

"Of course," I said. "But we both know that the Iron Cross pre-dates the rise of Hitler. The Prussian officer's uniform outside clearly shows you have material from the First Reich. And yet, I don't see anything out here from the era of Bismarck or the Kaiser."

He caught the line I was throwing him. "You want a pre-war Iron Cross?"

"Pre–World War Two. Something that might have been worn in the Great War would be fine. Perhaps by a corporal. One who served in Belgium." I smiled.

The guy smiled back, knowing full well who I was talking about. "That would be expensive."

"Don't let the tux fool you," I said, shuffling the cards again in my hand. "I just made out big at Wild Card. And Mr. Hayes over there," I said, nodding back to Cactus, "is a representative who will back my buy. In short, he's collateral. Show them your card, Mr. Smith."

Come on, Cactus, I thought. *Play along.*

Cactus's tough, weathered hand reached into his breast pocket.

Spit died in my mouth.

The three thugs secured themselves around him. The faint ghosts from piles of ragged gear chewed on my nerves

Brimstone, you didn't realize your name was Bull's Eye, put out that cigarette!

James, I can't feel my hands . . .

You're a coward, Brimstone! COWARD.

Slowly, Cactus retracted his hand.

In it was a black card. He handed it to the thug on his right.

"Says he's from the casino," said the thug with the one-eyebrow, and I choked back my surprise that the gimp could read.

"If the merchandise is up to snuff," I said, reigniting the patter, "you'll make out like bandits, enough to open new stores across the US. Heading East, of course. A fertile operation like this needs . . . breathing room."

He snickered. I'd overplayed my hand with Nazi gibberish. "What you're asking for is rarer than courage in a kike."

I grinned to hold back a left hook. "And time is pressing, as I'll be leaving for Brazil this evening. So perhaps you might have something less prized, but no less compelling." In the mirror, the thugs closed in on Cactus. "A pendant of the Thule Society? One with the two snakes, shaped like lightning, a precursor to the symbol of the SS."

The Nazi before me squinted his eyes. "Who are you?"

"James Brimstone." I shuffled my cards. "Perhaps you remember me from my teenage act: 'Brimstone, Master of Cards?'"

"Brimstone? That don't sound Irish."

I shuffled loud. "Can't all be born a Hitler."

"Well, Brimstone, you got ten seconds before I scalp you and your Injun buddy and throw your carcasses out the back of my store."

I cut the deck and folded the halves in each hand. And all the junior members of the Third Reich Club were eying the flash.

"See, that's the problem with you Nazis. Act first, think second, and I was about to offer you the chance to help me out with a problem because we likely have a mutual enemy, and instead you harass my friend here. And if you don't lay off, I'm afraid I'll have to raise you on scalping, and promise that should they move one more inch towards my friend they'll be staining that carpet crimson."

The Nazi snickered and pressed a button.

"You are one stupid cunt."

Thundering jackboots came from the upstairs, as if in waiting, and five guys ran down, each in matching hate-wear from 1939. The Nazi in front of me yelled "Grab the—"

Tyger, Tyger, Burning Bright!

You can always bank on an idiot picking violence whenever options are available: I spun on my heels and snapped three cards from my right and two from my left with the precision and accuracy of David's sling shot and watched in near slow-motion as my body Joyrode the Zen-like experience of a perpetual "now" while ten missiles shot across the room and at the thugs on the stairs:

Two kings and three eights lodged themselves into each thug's head about an eighth of an inch deep and with a satisfying "shluck." Not a bad Full House.

A pair of sevens sliced the hands of two reaching for weapons on their belts. The Rules for Stud Poker sliced the cheek of the one with the holster, while the joker cut his index finger right to the bone.

I glanced in the mirror to see, amazingly, Cactus had already dropped his thugs to quivering masses and was adjusting his cufflink. This was going too damn well!

Until I noticed the audience in the mirror.

Skulls in helmets, gas masks, skulls with grenades in their mouths, skulls eating other skulls, tables piled high with bones and dog tags, helmets teeming with maggots, and the snows of

145

Chosin raining down like a burial mound being built one flake at a time, growing ice around my feet.

Stay with us, James! Stay a while! Stay forever!

"*Tyger, Tyger!*"

I snapped back so hard my mind had whiplash and the Nazi in front of me started to become Technicolor triplets.

I never saw the three haymakers coming.

CHAPTER 19

ICE HIT MY FACE. IT TURNED TO MERCURY. GASPING, I WAS PULLED away from a deeper darkness. A single star swung in the sky, a pendulum of yellow that cast large shadows against my face.

"Wake him up."

"Yes, Christian."

Another splash of ice water, and mist preceded my sputtered breaths. Everything was taut, sore, and bleakly lit within my mind and throughout my body. Pain stretched across every inch of my midsection, as if they'd worked me over like a palooka training on a Porterhouse slab, right before being sent to the slaughter against the new champ. I blinked away burning tears and realized they'd largely left my face intact.

Then someone slapped me so hard my molars groaned.

"Rise and shine, Mr. Brimstone."

I lifted my chin. They stood in formation like a platoon of idiots. They were all heaving, holding bandages to their heads, or nursing gauzed hands that immobilized their trigger fingers. In front was the lead Nazi. "Christian," I said wetly, "I presume?"

He wiped his wet hand on his desert combat khakis. "Who are you, Brimstone?"

"Where's my friend?"

"The savage? Tied up. Just like you. But he's pulling the Silent Injun routine. Might have him sell cigars when I'm done. Or just drop his subhuman carcass into the Pacific. That depends on you."

Gently, I flexed my hands. They were both tied behind my back in a handcuff knot, a nasty variant of the clove hitch. This might take a second. And I had to play it smart. There were now three lives in danger besides my own, and all on my dime. That wasn't fair or right. Time to change the math. "Depends on me . . . what?"

"When you wanted Hitler's Iron Cross," Christian said as he kneeled into a sliver of yellow light, "I thought you might be some eccentric Jew collector. Those people are pretty self-hating. And rich. But you're no kike."

There was nothing I wanted more in that moment than to kick his grill of little Chiclet-white teeth down his throat. But I smiled. "No. I don't have that honor."

Christian snorted. "And that bullshit with the cards?"

"Actually learned that from a Jewish magician. Used them for circumcisions. Anyone in need of a bris?"

The slap dunked me into the darkness, then more water crashed, soaking me to shivers. Couldn't joke my way out, but, damn, they make it so easy. "What did you want with a Thule *Anhänger*?" He leaned in close enough for me to bite his nose. "Bullshit me, Brimstone, and I'll bury you on top of that half-breed and set you on fire."

Staring into the visage of this asshole, with his righteous and vile smirk, his absolute confidence in his command over life and death, every fiber of my soul wanted to beat him until he was toothless and broke. Yet, as my hands made the rope burn on my

wrist and silently and mindlessly worked the knot like I was crack-
ing a safe, I realized what I needed was to make friends with this
monster. For me, and for Cactus. Because something told me he
might not talk unless I became as vile as him. The words sprayed
from my mouth in pink mist. "We have a common enemy."

"Do we?"

"We both know the Thule Society is alive. And well."

"Rumors."

"But . . . someone is perverting their magic."

The laughter from six or so henchmen hammered my thin
skull.

"And who might that be?"

"Someone . . . versed in Shinto magic." The cackles continued. But they were diluted. Christian wasn't smiling. He stood
and glared down, arms of knotted muscle at his side. I gulped air,
the bonds loosening from my safe-cracking fingers pulling here,
and there, untangling the knot's clench. "Someone is using Axis
magic to create a bastard demon. And it ain't you, and it ain't me."

Christian raised his fist to his head, like he was a robot, and
everyone silenced. "What you speak of is an abomination."

"On that, we are agreed."

"Who is doing this?"

"That's what I'm trying to find out. I'm a private detective."

"You don't carry a license."

"I just got it. It's in my office, which is locked, which is a long
story. The point, Christian, is something about this rubs you raw
beyond the affront to Uncle Adolf. Something I said clicked in a
way you don't like. Help me, and I promise I'll put a stop to it."
There was a particular strand of anger in his face that was a loud
tell . . . Something had happened here that linked this to Nico's
case. He just needed to tell me.

"No," Christian said. "You will tell us everything you know,
Brimstone. And then we will take care of it."

I shook my head. "Can't work that way. And Rome is burning. Tell me what happened here that has your sack in a twist."

His face hardened to cover up some level of embarrassment ... Whatever had happened, it happened on his watch. "You have no leverage to threaten me," Christian said.

I sighed, leaned back in my chair, the bonds loose and wrists sore. "You really want to play hardball? You really want to give me no choice?"

"You have no choice."

"I knew you'd say that. Cactus?"

"Yes," came a voice from the dark, startling everyone. "*Semper Fi.*"

Cactus was a thousand times faster than me in a fight unless I was Joyriding. In the real dark, not the fog of my brain, I watched him cut down eight men like a freight train, punctuated by the crippling sounds of slaughter: wrists snapped, knees dislocated, and the guy who probably tied his hands likely needed a new collar bone. Christian spun, and above his waistband was the tell-tale handle of a Luger. His right hand slid behind him just as my ropes dropped.

I gripped his wrist with my right hand while my left arm snaked around his neck. Fuji called it the Manchurian Chicken Wing: I yanked his right hand up in a hammerlock, twisting his forearm and elbow out of joint. My left arm curled under his neck. Off balance, Christian struggled *into* my choke until he realized it was too late and his body sagged with blood being squeezed out of him. I pulled back, placed my knee against his twisted forearm to allow me my right hand back, then grabbed the Luger.

Another mighty squirm from Christian, but he was weak as a one-armed baby. I dropped him in my chair, kept the pistol at Christian's temple. One full water bucket sat next to two empty ones, dropped on their sides. "Cactus, are you—"

Cactus strutted toward me, fixing his cufflink and walking over the pile of thugs. "Did you get what you needed? My break is almost over."

"Not yet." I gave him the gun. "Keep an eye on the Nazi sleepover party you just created." Christian gasped, eyes fluttering, when I grabbed a third bucked of water and doused him like a carnival game of dunk the clown. "Morning, sunshine!"

Christian shook the water like a dog, tried to get up, and I shoved him back in the seat. "Unless you want my associate to turn this into a Nazi graveyard, sit tight and let us have a conversation."

"You won't make me talk!" Christian growled.

"I'm not interrogating you," I said, calm as June winds. "And I wasn't lying when I said we had a common enemy. Now, you know something about Shinto magic and Thule sorcery being mingled. Whoever's doing it, I want it to stop. You do, too. Help me stop them, and we'll all enjoy *schadenfreude* this Fall." Christian puckered, a prelude to spitting in my face.

My right hand cut the air like a knife and smacked him hard enough to shake his molars, rocking him back in his seat. He smiled, but didn't spit.

"Cute," I said. "But I won't tolerate disrespect. Do that again, I'll beat up someone who *doesn't* like it. Now tell me who's been harassing you for other Thule items."

"I'll never betray—"

"Oh lord, I'm not asking you to betray the Fuhrer. I'm not looking for a list of your customers across the city, state, country or world. Has anyone come in here looking for anything from the Thule society that set off your own radar? Something that did *not* feel right, even by your standards?"

His nostrils flared and contempt oozed out. I'd touched a sore spot.

"Help me get him, Christian," I said. Edgar always said you built connection with rubes by making a three decker sandwich of common goal, lots of eye contact, and repeating people's names. My hand stung and hung at my side, waiting for the next injury to preempt his insult. "Christian, what happened?"

His eyes were thin as dimes. "I fired someone."

"Who?"

"A no-account pretender." He looked at my hand. "Kurt Snow. Claimed he'd done work for the cause in Vietnam." I didn't want to know what kind of horror that meant. "Was a junior member here. But one day, we found part of our merch was stolen. Something rare."

"Something nautical," I ventured.

Christian's pale face dropped a sicker shade of white. "Yes."

"What?"

His breath was shorter. "Our supplier said it was the eye of a Kraken."

Beast of the North Sea. Scourge of Vikings. Symbol of the nightmare below the waves . . . Edgar had taken me to northern Norway once. Aboard our vessel, a Lapp deer hunter and guide named Cnutt told us the tales of his great grandfather, who'd been a whaler in the arctic and saw a creature the size of an island, a tentacled abomination that tore his ship to scrap and filled the water with screaming men that lashed about in a sea of blood as the serrated arms of the beast cut them to ribbons like an Imperial blender. Legend said that its root went into the dark heart of the earth, and it retracted itself to the core for slumber. During the war, the Thule Society had scoured occupied Scandinavia for anyone who had come close. The man's great grandfather was tortured, interrogated, and his survivor story had furnished him a later grave. "The Nazis never found the eye," I said. "If they had—"

"We would have won." Christian smiled.

I could hear Cactus' breath harden behind me. "But you didn't. Which means you don't have the eye." I leaned forward. "Not all of it. Since it would have gone to a higher bidder. You got something else." Which was as polite a way as I could say "You got conned, you Nazi shithook."

Christian grunted.

"And Kurt stole whatever it was. Where is Kurt Snow?"

Christian glared into the dark.

"Ah. You went to collect. And he was gone."

Christian swung his face at me. "He wasn't even German! He was an actor! One of those Jew method fucks who pretends to be like their character! We tore his apartment to shreds and found nothing!"

"What did it look like? The eye?"

Christian clamped his mouth until Cactus' breath was over my right shoulder. In his hand was a Hitler Youth hunting knife. "I'll skin his balls."

"A black pearl," Christian said, quick. "On a chain. Our seller said it was a fragment. That it was part of the Kraken's eye, which was made up of a million tiny eyes. It casts no reflection. And if you stare too long into it . . ." He shook his head. "That's all I know."

Now he was lying. But I didn't care. "Thank you," I said to the Nazi shithook. "Cactus, let's go." We walked away from the pile of little Supermen.

Cactus' fury was so loud his aura was punching my backside. As we descended the stairs into the main room, a pall came over me. At first, I thought it was the post-adrenaline gut-check. But as we approached the main floor, ghost murmurs become whispers.

You're walking between two worlds, Brimstone. And soon you'll fall through the crack.

I landed on the main floor and Cactus said, "I forgot something."

His words were a distant echo as I strode through the tables covered in mounds of material touched by the dead.

See you soon, Brimstone.

"Not if I see you fuckers first," I said.

Cactus strode by me. "You move too slow." I followed him out into the now-dark street.

Neon and screaming guitars embraced me through the night air as we got back to Cactus's car. And, as if on a timer, I slammed the door of his car as screams filled the building. Smoke coughed out of the cracks. Flames followed. We sat and watched as Nazis ran out of Iron Surplus like rats from a sinking steamer.

"Well," I said. "That was subtle."

Cactus glared at me in the rearview mirror. "You didn't say anything about destruction of property."

I smiled, looking at the roasting hoard of Third Reich bull-shit. "No. I didn't."

Cactus smiled back.

I enjoyed the moment, because it wouldn't last. Someone had an aspect of a Kraken, some Shinto mojo, and that spelled a nightmare waiting for me on the set of a dirty movie.

CACTUS SPED THROUGH THE STRIP UNTIL THE BRIGHT LIGHTS OF WILD Card covered us, then slowed down to a professionally cool 10 mph before dropping me off by double-parked Lilith, complete with a ticket.

"Thanks for the help, Cactus," I said, opening the door. "Sorry we couldn't go in guns blazing."

"We left guns blazing."

I caressed the anting-anting in my pocket. "You don't fear the fire marshal will retrace our steps?"

"Their world was illegal. Those shits won't tell anyone any-thing." He turned, one arm over the seat. "Now beat it, Brim-stone."

I stepped out. "You mad? I gave you what you wanted. A chance to trash more Hitler Youth."

"You made nice with shadows."

Rubbing my ribs, I sighed. "There was no way Christian was giving up anything unless we broke his world a little, Cactus. He had to see us as losers. He had to think he was winning for me to tear down his confidence. It's psychological warfare. And we won."

Cactus snorted. "It's not just winning that matters, Brimstone. How you win defines what you win. Now go." As I walked away, he rolled down the window. "Be careful how you win, Private. You can only cheat death so many times." He tossed something as he peeled away, mighty engine roaring.

A fresh pack of Bicycle cards landed at my feet.

"Thanks, Cactus," I said to his exhaust.

My skin itched. My clothes stuck like tattoos. If I could smell myself I'm sure it wouldn't be springtime fresh. Now I was to go make good with the beautiful people of Nero Studios. Where there was likely some demon of the Axis living in the body of a porn actress, maybe protected by a feral Vietnam vet who destroyed Izzy's store like Godzilla in a China shop.

All I wanted was a Dubonnet on the rocks and to peel these pants and shirt off, hit the YMCA for a shower, and avoid the unspeakable truth that swirled around me in the neon night.

I was a terrible P.I.

Leaning against Lilith, I counted up my injuries. My face was raw and sore. Thankfully, nothing was swollen too bad. That wasn't magic, but my family's DNA. Years of suffering toiling under the grey skies of Ireland, stretching back to the Gaelic invasion of the emerald Isle, had helped forge a people built to suffer. Lots of Brimstones were boxers, thugs, wrestlers, as well as soldiers and laborers for other people's wishes and wars. And that gift was no small change when I looked at the utter mess I was in.

I tore the parking ticket and tossed it to the wind, then walked to the payphone outside the casino. It worked and didn't smell like an outhouse. I fished for change until I realized I wouldn't need it.

I tapped "o" and brought the receiver to my ear. A dull click was followed by a muddy voice.

"Operator, how may I direct your call?"

"Police, non-emergency line."

"Are you in any danger now, sir?"

The pieces of the day flew through me like saucers from an Ed Wood movie, messy and shaky. "No, well, maybe." Maybe I should hand this off before anyone else gets hurt.

"Sir, are you still there? Do you need assistance?

Don't waste your time with the Marks, James. Their lives and deaths are playthings for the Awakened. Think of all the rubes who handed over money to see a "Man Eating Chicken," or try to outfight Hercules, or pick on Fuji, or, indeed, try to outfox our tricks. They are a resource to be strip-mined, cast aside, so that we may do great things, things they will never do. They're like the wild Irish garbage you emerged from by chance. They are the evolutionary background noise for our greatness. Don't mourn them. Don't pity them. Feel no obligation to those that are inferior. If they vanish, no one will notice their absence.

"I would."

"Sir? I'm sorry, I didn't understand."

"It's all right. I think I got this one under control."

"Sir, I'm sending a car to your location."

I hung up, walked back to Lilith, rolled down the window, and revved her up.

Edgar was wrong. We mattered. The great unwashed. We weren't just history's sad statistics without shape, form, or flavor. I was one of them. So was Maxine. So was Nico.

And I was going to find them, or die trying.

CHAPTER 20

RIDING THE 101 WITH MY HEAD OUT THE WINDOW TO "THE OTHER Hollywood," the sun a murky stain on the lip of the dark horizon, I considered the facts. Someone screwed around with a Kraken's eye and old Shinto water demons on the set of Nero Studio's latest porn picture, which had a Greek overtone. Maxine was targeted for possession, but Nico was the target for abuse.

But why?

Leverage? Looks were currency in the Valley and everywhere else. People will do anything for fame. For beauty. Power. L.A. is built on humanity's desperate need for illusions. A dime-store sorcerer, not anyone of consequence, might be dipping into the valley for an even more desperate kind of victim, or tool.

Yet serpents in the mouths of women involved in carnal sex spoke to passion as much as power, the need for the sensual and sexual. Most Nazi magic was about domination, violence, control. In short, Fulton: a berserker rage. If I'd cut off his arm and beat him with it, he'd probably yank off his leg for a proper duel. But his rage and Nico's scars seemed separate.

Traffic slowed and denied me the whoosh of racing through air. The oppressive heat of the Valley sunk into me. Behind, an engine revved, the telltale sound of an annoyed citizen who will cut close to death to shoot an inch further than his sidesaddle companions, causing everyone else to stab their brakes. And he was coming up behind me. There was a gap on my right as someone pulled left. I looked back.

A dirty white Chevy Nova revved up, aiming for my out-stuck head.

I ducked inside Lilith to avoid getting lynched by their right-side mirror. "Where's the fire, hero?" I said.

Traffic dipped to a crawl.

The Nova was packed with girls, hair big and wild, thick makeup sliding down their faces. The one on the right had a frizzy perm and freckles, mascara bleeding down the side of her face as if auditioning for the Grand Guignol. They were clapping in unison and saying what I assumed was the title of the song, which sounded like "All Right Now" and made me wish for the subtle tones of Charlie Parker or the mad genius of Coltrane.

"Hey, boy," she said, "You got a date for the prom?" The entire car cackled.

"Thanks," I said. "But I ride alone."

"Ooooh! So tall, dark, and mysterious. Then who beat up that face of yours?"

"Nazis. Can you believe it?"

"Damn!" she said, playing the hellcat, even if she didn't look old enough to buy Cools without being carded. "We got a war hero here! Where you going, war hero?"

"Nero Studios."

One of the giggling group in the back shouted. "That's the porno place!" The car screamed as it moved slower than piss up hill.

"You a porno actor, war hero?" said the beautiful nightmare.

I shook my head. I'd seen enough action on the circuit that nudie cuties, stag films, or dirty booths and films held no attraction, though like everyone else I wanted to see Jane Russell in *The Outlaw*. "Going to visit a friend. You guys know the main hub for those people? My friend forgot to give me the address."

"You have friends who work there?"

"Laura, don't talk to the creep!" someone in the back said. But Laura was enjoying her command of the moment.

"I do," I said.

"We're all actresses."

Of course they were. "Really?"

We edged across pavement as she laughed. "Don't laugh." I hadn't. "Did a Coke commercial last year. My agent is getting me McDonald's."

"Terrific, Laura. Stick with soda pop and burgers. My friend's having a bad time in these pictures. I'm there to bring her home."

"Oh, fuck off!" she said, the flick-switch of her anger so loud and proud. "You're some bible-thumping do-gooder telling a woman what she can and can't do, right? Maybe your friend chose to be there."

"Oh, not this discussion," said someone in the back.

"Didn't you read 'A Bunny's Tale'?" I said, curious where all this anger was coming from.

"Gloria Steinem can kiss my ass!" Laura said. "She got paid to be a Bunny at the Playboy Club, didn't she? Now she's telling me what I can and can't do with my own body? If I make money doing what I want with it, who cares?"

"Laura!"

"Shut up, Mandy!" Laura said, then she jabbed her finger at me. "And you, don't even think about dragging your friend from what she wants to do. Men always think they know better, so long as they're the ones driving."

Just then the traffic picked up and the Nova peeled away while Laura gave me two barrels of her middle finger. "Fuck off, War Hero! Go kill some babies in Cambodia instead!"

Honks blared behind me and I hit the gas with my toe as the girls of tomorrow peeled off into the future, leaving this stunned road kid from the Depression in their dust.

The heat thickened as you rode in the valley, an invisible oppressor. Even if L.A. was the basin, San Fernando had a drag, as if civilization had forced itself on slumbering lands that did not want to awake. Cars zipped by without their headlights on, stray bullets of the 101 en route to becoming 90 mph caskets. So much life shooting forward as we removed ourselves from the cluster of shared misery in the traffic jam, the chances of meeting again far worse than those for dying alone. Drivers tapped on their yellow headlights in the wake of the stray bullets, as if they'd been a warning about the future accidents in our way. Accidents. Chance. Luck. These ruled the world far more than well-oiled blueprints. We searched for patterns in the wreckage. Reverse engineer from the point of destruction or disaster the construction of a life. There were two lives I was trying to reconstruct from a supernatural disaster. And I prayed they weren't already destroyed.

I'd just wanted a P.I. license to pick up small change for a small life. I did not want to have one foot in the door of occult. If I had, I would have taken Edgar's offer and run off into strange adventures of the mind-bending kind.

Now I was stuck between.

Between worlds.

Like the ghosts said.

When traffic cleared, I ducked inside Lilith, opened the glove compartment and tore out an eight track. Once it was shoved in the stereo's maw, I craned my neck again with my head outside the car, and drove hard as Count Basie and Nelson Riddle fought each other for supremacy and a part of my backside stiffened as I pulled off at Studio City, denizen of Hollywood powerhouses in tall buildings. You could tell because the cars in the Mobil and 76 gas station there were hot rods, limos, and Cadillacs being serviced by Latino youths whom the drivers barked at as if giving orders to a fresh batch of shave-tail recruits. Hating the rich was my natural pastime.

I pulled into a 76 with a store attached and parked next to a burgundy Thunderbird, which denoted someone of much lower status than a director, producer, actor, or attorney. Writer or stuntman was the spread. Near the diesel pump was a cherry red cabin for a long-haul truck, which always reminded me of a chicken's head, freshly plucked, courtesy of the old geek trick I'd seen a hundred times from Zed the Pinhead, biting a chicken's head off as a finale. It made chicken fights seem downright humane.

In the rearview mirror, my hair was somewhere between Conway Twitty and Frankenstein's bride. Vitalis and Pomade together couldn't tag-team my mane into submission, so I patted it down as best I could and left Lilith to cool down in the dark.

The track lighting sizzled like a diner's griddle and Mr. Clean had clearly wiped the walls with all the grime of foot traffic, so everything was covered in the lemony haze of chemical cleaner. Refreshing. At the desk, standing before the rows of candy bars and packs of gum, must be the owner of the Thunderbird, as the man in the AC hat in front of the skin mags was, I deduced, the trucker. Behind the desk, a tired Latino in his fifties with steel-gray hair and an inch of fat on his body listened to the ranting from a youth who was barely old enough to shave and yet had hair down to his shoulders. He held a binder full of scripts, maybe three, as if he'd written *Ben Hur II*. "Come on, man," he said to the Latino. "Just tell me if she was in here."

"Sir," said the manager. "I don't keep track of my customers' whereabouts."

"But she said she'd meet me here."

"I can't help you with that. You'll have to buy something. This is not a recreation center."

The youth snorted. "I'll fucking buy something. Give me two more weeks and I'll buy this gas station with my royalties, turn this place into a bookstore, and fire your lazy ass."

The man chomped down his jaw at the insult and pointed at the door. "Go."

"No, I'm buying something now." He grabbed a fistful of candy bars and smushed them on the table. "I want these ones."

"Fifty-five cents." I tried not to whistle about the rise in prices.

"Actually," the kid said. "I've changed my mind." He turned away and walked straight toward me. "What are you looking at, grandpa?"

"A thief. You broke it, you bought it."

He got close enough to smell the coffee and cigs on his breath. "You can't break a candy bar."

"You can, you did, and you'll pay the man."

"Or what, grandpa?"

I lifted my chin. "Easy, hero. You and I both know you don't get to ruin someone else's property and walk away as if your shit don't stink. You're not one of the Warner Brothers yet. Though I suspect you're writing for them."

"Who told you?"

"You did. You'd turn a gas station into a bookstore, which only a writer would think is clever. You mentioned royalties, which means you're selling something," and I pointed at the binder, "probably scripts. And your girl didn't show up. Which means you're not an actor. Now pay the man before I tell Mr. Warner and company about how some inky hands Underwood treats the staff at his favorite petrol station."

The writer shook for a second, then found his balls. "And who the fuck are you?"

"Stunt man," I said. "Hence the outfit. And I've got far more stroke with Jack Warner's film world than you do. So, if you want to get out of here with a sliver of your career intact, apologize to the good man who did nothing wrong, and I'll do what I can to help you."

There used to be days when all I would do, day in and day out, was lie about who I was, where I was from, and what I could do, whatever Edgar asked of me, in the Circus and out on his . . . projects, like Altamont. Lying was comfortable and fun when you vanished from people's memory the next day. "Or you can start something you won't be able to finish."

The writer scoffed. "Like a low rent stunt double can change my fate."

"Never said I'd do that. Said I'd help. Also, you're about sixty seconds from seeing just how badly a low-rent stunt man can act." I leaned with my left shoulder and he got flummoxed, so he didn't see my right hand dart in and grab his binder.

"Hey! That's mine!"

I slapped away his hands, shifted my weight, and jabbed his solar plexus like a staff-strike to the chest. He crashed on his ass, slapping down a rain of candy bars.

"Stay down," I said. "Or I'll toss this epic into the wind." The rage of the artist was palpable, but not threatening, as I leafed through the pages. "*Cyborgia*? This a green-eyed monster flick?"

"You wouldn't understand it."

"Ah. It's one of them art-films down at Nero Studios."

The kid's face went white. "That fucking place? No way! I'm a writer, not some hack making pornos at that perv palace!"

"Where is that, exactly?"

"How the hell should I know? You some kind of stunt man for pornos?"

"Something like that." I shook the binder at him. "Now say you're sorry to the nice man, buy what you broke, and get lost before I get unhappy."

After a short fume, cash hit the desk and a "sorry" rolled out of his lips, so I tossed him his script. The hack fucked off into the great unknown.

I was collecting the Paydays and Juicy Fruits from the floor when a voice above said, "Thank you, sir." I stood, and the cashier relaxed his crossed arms.

"Just sorry you have to put up with that nonsense."

"It's part of the job. You asked about Nero Studios?"

I laid down a pack of Juicy Fruit, the best part of my C-Rations in Korea. "I did." I let the statement hang. Because anyone looking for Nero Studios would be damn humble and quiet about it, whether they were looking to be in a skin flick or to meet those who are already on dirty celluloid. But when the silence dragged I dropped a reason. "Supposed to pick up a friend of mine."

He nodded. "They moved to Van Nuys. Corner of Stagg and Orion."

"Lots of people ask for directions?" I said.

"Yeah. *Bellezas perdidas.* Young and old. Where else do beauties go when the studio is done with them?"

I nodded. "Hell of a good point, friend." I took out some change, laid it on the table. "For making a mess."

"But you cleaned it up! At least take some gum."

So I did.

Chewing two sticks of sweet plastic, I drove Lilith over the L.A. River on Tujunga Ave, heading for the 170.

That's when headlights bit my ass.

CHAPTER 21

THE FRONT FENDER SURGED LIKE THE JAWS OF A ROTTWEILER.

I ducked inside Lilith. The cracked window stared back like the sockets of a skull filled with cobwebs. Flying blind, I reached in my pocket for the anting-anting before—

CRASH!!!

I bounced forward, Juicy Fruit spat out, and the amulet dropping into the passenger side. Damn it.

Lilith jutted forward into the unknown and jostled the madman behind me. Forward was now a one-way ticket to an early grave. And I'd had enough fun at cemeteries today.

Left hand gripping the steering wheel, I pulled Lilith into reverse, then swung my right arm over the seat so I could see through the back window.

It wasn't the hack writer's T-bird, but a red and black Lincoln Continental Sedan. Preferred ride of Alicia Price's goon squad, and the pain in my chest from her hammer shot awoke from its slumber. Apparently, crashing a funeral, crippling my windshield, and attempting to break my neck wasn't enough for the Pacific's jilted Queen of Magic. Death was racing at 90 mph.

So I hit reverse and stabbed the gas.

Kar-RANG!

Fresh bruises blossomed in my guts as tires burned asphalt and generated enough smoke to choke a dragon. My body turned to iron. I refused to let Lilith give any quarter. The exhaust and burning tire smoke blurred any chance of seeing the driver. Cars whipped by in the passing lanes as we fought each other for the title of Champ of Going Nowhere Fast, until Lilith, in her glory, lurched forward, and the ground beneath the car started to give more and more. There was no way out with me putting my head out the window. Horns blared in my ear as dozens of two-ton bullets shot past this insane duel I was losing, the anting-anting laying in the foot space of the passenger side like a candy bar out of reach. Another lurch forward and Lilith screamed at being shoved. She was being pushed around, and I didn't like it. I reached for the glove box.

BANG!

Broken glass filled the back seat. I coughed, acrid smoke filling the car, popped the glove box, and grabbed. The back window was a jagged maw of shards and teeth. I gripped the handle of a revolver, hoping to hell it was Fife's pistol and not Juan's bulletless .38.

I dropped into first, shot off into the passenger lane blind. The cracked window before me was a map of cut glass with all roads leading to death. Honks and screeches followed as I'd hoped. I caused a minor traffic jam while pushing Lilith to 100, cars filling in the space between me and the Continental. I gunned it forward, gazing into the rear view. The Continental was wedged behind two cars. Horns blared and then shots fired. But it gave me enough time and distance to execute my only possible move.

I gunned it forward, head out the window, fishtailing Lilith until she was leading with her rear, and the Continental was facing me, grill to grill. I stabbed the accelerator and drilled it forward and fired one shot. Glass shattered, and the air was nothing but shivs and shards. I kept the pistol trained and focused and fired at the windshield of the Continental. In the heartbeat before I squeezed off another round and filled my nose with the pungent cobalt flavor of gunshots, I saw my assailant.

Bald, wearing a tux with a bowtie, and wearing shades while driving in the dark, one hand on the wheel, the other holding a Beretta 70. That smile was pure rictus from ear to ear. Skin the color of milk with a hint of piss. Bow tie around his neck. A neck with a speaker embedded in its folds.

Shanks. Shanks smiled with the visage of a skull. Shanks nodded, as if to acknowledge that I'd killed him before, and he'd remembered. Shanks was Alicia Price's favorite heavy. Because she kept Shanks' brain in a jar and bought him new corpses to animate. Yet with that smile, you always knew it was Shanks.

"Hello, Brimstone!" he said without moving his lips, voice cackling and crackling as if he was shouting through a drive-in speaker, the sound emanating from his bow tie. His head tilted. "Lady Alicia Price sends her regards!"

Four more shots rang out as I ducked. Foam from the seats flew in the air. Lilith was being gutted from the inside.

"If you would ever be so kind as to tell her the spell for opening Edgar's casket, I will stop turning you into human shrapnel!" Then Shanks laughed with the cadence of a man gurgling barbed wire and napalm.

Our engines gunned it at each other. I counted to three, then snapped off another slug. Shanks ducked, awkwardly, and my headshot went into his shoulder before he popped up again like a whack-a-mole. "Nice to see you, Shanks!" I yelled, then fired again, blowing off more of his shoulder. "But I'd rather eat a bullet than give her Edgar's brain!" He popped up again and I ducked. He fired once and my rearview mirror landed in my lap. Shanks was able to control bodies from vast distance. But good

God, he was rather mechanical when it came to surprises. Fast as hell, but mechanical.

"Oh, I know, Brimstone!" Shanks said.

I twisted my wrist so that the pistol stuck out at 80 degrees.

"The request is on her behalf."

I grabbed the mirror and lifted it until Shank's rictus was in sight and I'd calculated just where I had to lift to squeeze off a bull's eye.

"Your death is on mine!"

I snapped off a round. My wrist flared with pain from the awkward kickback.

But we were lurching forward! Lilith was driving that Continental back. I dropped the mirror, grabbed the wheel, and dared to pull myself up and hit the brake.

Shanks head ended with his bottom jaw. The rest was splashed across the back seat. And yet, that bow tie screeched at me. "Not again! Not again! You will pay for this, Brimstone! I will make it a slow death! I will eat your eyes while you watch! I will defecate into your toothless mouth! I will—"

I fired a fourth bullet into his throat. Static squealed out, voice getting higher and more distant, each threat more volatile and vile than the last, but whatever Shank had left to share was lost to all but dogs and cats who were tuned to his frequency.

Night, glass, and tiny itches covered every inch of my skin, suit, and nerves. Distant sirens howled like coyotes. I reversed, spun Lilith into the right of way, and carried on toward Nero Studios. The lack of windshield was refreshing and the whole valley roared in my ears. The rush of wind pulled stray glass from my hair and shards caressed my skin before leaving. Sweat and small streams of blood mingled around my ears, and I could taste the gunfire. The foam from Lilith's seat swirled in the roar of the outside world ramming through her as we shot forward to find answers, and I hoped the trail of blasted heads and broken glass didn't come back to me. I mean, how many cops would think to look for a man who murdered a twice-dead corpse in the heart of the dirty pictures industry?

I exited the freeway and found myself quickly surrounded by suburban majesty. Van Nuys' main drag was eerily quiet. Unlike the Strip, there were only street lamps to throw nets of light from their high reaches. The darkness was thick, but not oppressive, as kids in flares exited The Royal Times theater, laughing. The marquee said *M*A*S*H*. With no windshield, and Lilith purring at a low murmur, I strained but heard their laughter.

"Hawkeye is the best! I've seen this five times and he's still the man, man!"

"Five times? Shit, you know this is about Vietnam, right?"

"Mitchell, it's just a movie. Don't turn it political."

"Everything's political."

"To you, everything is about Vietnam."

"Yeah, was *Airport* about Vietnam, Mitchell?"

"*Airport* was a gas."

"*Airport* was shit."

"Everyone's a critic."

"*M*A*S*H* was just dumb fun."

I hit the brakes before I knew it and the tires skidded louder than a chandelier crashing on a ballroom floor. I was out the door before I could blink.

The gang of teens in flares and flannel and feathered hair of assorted lengths looked at me like the Frankenstein monster just ran off the Universal lot.

"*M*A*S*H* isn't a comedy," I said. "It isn't about Vietnam. And it ain't the kissing cousin of *Airport*. It's about Korea. You know? The Korean War? Of course you don't. You don't have enough pubic hair among you to make a third-rate beard. But before any of you were a gleam in your daddy's eye, your older brothers and even your fathers were fighting off an invasion of

North Koreans and Red Chinese from a country that had just been born. Sound familiar? Well, that's where the similarities stop. Those battles were frozen affairs, the kind of cold that would give an Eskimo pneumonia. This movie you saw? That's about Vietnam. But the novel? Wait, did you know it was a book first? Did you read it? It's a horror show and not a tepid warning. Did they excise the crucifixion scene? Did you see how they beat a man's depression with attempted murder? Did you know that the crux of these theories and ideas were taken from a Holocaust survivor? Did you know that everything that made that book sage was pissed out to make a film that was easy to swallow since you're all either indifferent or think everything is about you?"

There was red spit flying from my words thanks to a small cut on my lip.

I gazed into the wide eyes of these kids. Just kids. And I knew I was in shock. My adrenaline raged and soon would become empty. Fury shook me to keep me steady. I'd lost track of how many times death had come for me, but when they send a dead man to kill you, you tend to remember you're alive not by dint of a divine plan so much as a cosmic accident, a celestial joke, a bad pun from an indifferent universe.

The teens of Van Nuys huddled together. Then, the girl with curled hair and razor thin frame tapped her cigarette. "Why the hell are you dressed like it's the prom?"

The night filled with the cackle of shrill laughter as I pulled the door open and sank back in. The malicious joy of teenagers stabbed me in the back as I headed for Stagg and Orion, sinking in deep long before the cross street comes into view. But I didn't need to verify the signs. I passed Jaguars and Mustangs, preferred rides of the newly rich and aging powerful. Houses here were bigger than motels. Even still, looming at the end of the street was a massive structure.

Roman columns dominated the front. In the headlights the royal color of purple was radiant. The windows were blacked out like skull sockets, but within them I knew there were living things. I parked, grabbed the anting-anting. The two guns I'd collected looked like an insurance policy I was leaving behind. I scrounged for the pack of cards.

The Bicycle pack had caught a bullet.

"Thanks, Shanks. I guess we're even." Now I was weaponless and needed trouble to find me.

I placed the anting-anting in one pocket, and figured I'd do what I had to if I needed another hand cannon. In the looming dark of the mansion, I felt naked without a gun or a deck of cards. But I closed Lilith's door gently, shook off the worse of the broken glass like a shaggy dog coming out of the rain, and walked toward the mansion.

Embedded within the columns was a loot bag of Ancient Greek and Roman words, prayers, and poems, none of it connected, none of it linked.

Praise Bacchus!

Behold your secret name when speaking to the Goddess of love!

I came, I saw, I conquered!

But the one on the center was essentially a long *tabella defixionis.*

Those who enter the domain of Lady Octavia surrender their will to the demons of lust and enlightenment, and upon reading this are bound to serve the limits of ecstasy in the hopes of finding the bliss of the one true mind and experiencing resplendent pleasures and horrors within the prison of their hearts.

"Sure," I said to no one. "Sounds groovy."

I approached the black front door, an obelisk of opal, and rang the doorbell. Inside, there was thick silence. A hungry quiet. The kind that would likely swallow screams of pain or pleasure.

The door opened without so much as a squeak. No one was there, until I realized I needed to look down.

A tanned midget with a cigar who smelled like burning sand and had the thickest coke-bottle specs I'd ever seen glared up at me with yellow teeth. "Yeah? What do youz want?"

CHAPTER 22

"I'M RICHARD GRAHAM," I SAID. THE AC BLASTED ME LIKE AN arctic wind tinged with the scent of sex.

"And I'm Muhammad Ali," he said, the Brooklyn accent thicker than the Century Sam cigar smoke he was puffing with every word. "Scram, head, we're making a movie."

"I'm Maxine's brother."

The words died in his mouth before he had time to crack wise, meaning he wasn't stupid. "Maxine?"

"She's an actress. Her roommate said she'd be here."

He sniffed something in the air, then gave my clothes the once over. "You living in dat suit full time?"

My voice rose, face squinting with fatigue that was 70-percent dead-honest. "I left our cousin's wedding on a red-eye Greyhound. I haven't had food or a hot shower in two days and none of this matters—just tell me, where is Maxine?"

"Shh!" said the midget. "We're making movies here, kid. I don't know where ya think your sister is but it's—"

I stepped closer, so my foot was at the lip of the door frame. "You're TV Smite." If you've ever seen a fear-frozen midget, you know how hard it is not to laugh. My face was numb, my guts hurt, and tiny cuts across my body were too fresh and raw to allow me the chance to let loose and snort at the fear-locked munchkin. "You're the writer. You wrote the script that's going to make Maxine a star. She told me about you. And Octavia. Please, TV, it's been a heck of a day."

TV grimaced.

"Please?"

The door closed upon my face.

Rats.

The thick thud of TV's orthotic shoes rattled off.

Playing family was a stretch, but the fact that I showed up meant I would bring cops if they didn't accommodate, even if only for appearances and to finally get me out.

I was about to bang and scream, but I heard the faint *tip* and *tap* of heels on a polished floor. I stood back. The door opened.

She was a vision in black and purple. Alabaster skin, raven hair minus a streak of white, eyeliner and shadow dark and sharp, lashes like Venus flytraps colored midnight. Lilacs and nightshade preceded her presence, and she tasted as good as that first cigarette in the morning. The purple sash over her shoulder crossed an ample bosom that pressed hard against a black dress. A slit ran from her inner thigh, revealing frighteningly thin legs ending in five-inch gold heels and exposed purple toenails. "Mr. Graham? I'm Octavia Bliss. I'm your sister's producer."

She offered me a hand older than her face or legs: the wrinkles around the knuckles meant she was roughly forty-five, but that didn't diminish her flame by one watt. Across her index finger was draped a ring with the face of a woman and hair of snakes wrapping around her fingers in a silver band. A gorgon, one of three ancient sisters, most famous being Medusa, but something told me my Octavia Bliss preferred the immortal firstborn, Stheno. Easier on the eyes.

I took the hand, half-expecting it to bite. When it didn't I clasped hers with mine. "It's great to finally meet the lady who will make my sister a star."

"Too kind," she said, accent pure Georgia peach and ramped up for effect. I half-expected a black manservant to be at her beck and call. She had the bearing of a queen. Lipstick tarred to her face for a well-practiced smile, the kind worn by all women who grew up pretty and used it to maximum advantage in an unfair world run by men. "And we're all very excited about her debut. But we're shooting—"

"Oh," I said, interrupting with nervous excitement. "And I won't get in the way. I'm just so late to the party I rented a car once I got into Los Angeles and drove up here to see her. We can have it be a surprise

"That's wonderful!" She mimicked my idiotic excitement. "What I meant to say is that we're shooting on assignment. Maxine isn't here just now, but will be back soon. And, sadly, we can't have you go to the shoot because of liability issues. Only cast and crew. You know, city hall!"

I laughed. "Oh, don't get me started on municipal politics! The fat cats in Madison are my public enemy number one."

She laughed. "Then you know my pain! We're still shooting another part of the film, so —"

"Of course, I'll just wait here until they return! Just stick me in the wing of the mansion where I won't get in the way."

She gripped my hand and pulled me inside. "I wouldn't have it any other way! TV?"

The clunk-clunk of his feet announced his arrival before he puffed smoke so hard he might as well have been the Little Engine That Stank Like Diesel. "Yeah?"

"Why don't you escort Mr. Graham to the apartments?" She turned to me. "We call them that because we have so many night shoots, people just have a nightcap and stay put rather than drive into the city."

"Wow, bed and breakfast as well as a movie studio. You're an impressive woman, Ms. Bliss."

"Oh, you have no idea," she said with a cattish note. "Forgive me, Mr. Graham."

"Richard."

She smiled, in total control. "I can't recall what line of business you were in."

"I sell used office furniture in downtown Madison."

I savored the look of horror and boredom in her smile. "Fascinating. Now, I must get back to our shoot here."

"You shoot movies *in* this mansion?"

"That's why I had it constructed. But I promise, Mr. Graham, we won't abandon you to walk the halls. You will have every possible comfort. And when Maxine returns, you will be the first to know."

She lifted her hand. I kissed it with the full bow of a Confederate gentleman, since that was clearly what she wanted. "TV, take him to the west wing." Then she turned on her heels and I enjoyed the show of her taut ass leaving down a dark corridor to the right.

"So," I said, looking down at TV, who was chewing his cigar in his yellow teeth. "You must get this a lot, but—"

"I ain't a goddamn munchkin," he said, thick finger pointing daggers at me. "Now follow me. I got a script to rewrite."

Octavia's mansion was a white-walled warren of epic proportions. TV led me down the same corridor she took, but hung a left. I could smell spices. Old BBQ and fresh stew. The walls were lined with pictures of doves, drawings of doves, mosaics of doves. The bird of Aphrodite, or Venus, to use her Roman name. Fitting for her house. Not for the Nazi magic I came here to suss out. If Maxine or Nico were still alive, the clues to their existence were here.

"TV? You're a writer?"

"Meh," he said, grunting along as if handling the jobs of a man-servant were beneath him. Perhaps he had a point. A scriptwriter handling the door meant this house was not in order. They'd have a bodyguard or something. That meant the grounds were weaker. The "shoot" she mentioned was probably her sending all resources out to find Fulton, Maxine, and Nico. Because if the stars and director were gone, who were they filming?

"Would I have seen your work?"

He snorted. "Howz do I know what you've seen, Mack?"

"It's Richard, not Mack."

"Says youz."

"Do you just write scripts?"

He craned his neck to see me. "Who wants to know?"

"Me. Richard."

"You ask a lot of question for a used desk guy."

"I'm a people person, TV. Talking to people helps me help them help themselves."

He snorted. "You're a salesman. You don't make anything."

"That matters to you?"

"In dis world, there are builders, facilitators, and sheep."

Builders . . . TV was either a libertarian, or a Freemason, or both. "That doesn't sound very nice."

"Nice has nuthin' ta do with it. If you made those chairs and desk, you'd be a builder. You make something for others. If you buy a thing, and don't build something on your own, you're a sheep. If you just move the work of others into the hands of sheep, you're a facilitator. You don't retain substance beyond da slick slap of cash in your hand, profiting off da guys who make this world."

We approached a patch of light from an open door, and the sweet smell of hickory and fried onions made me salivate like a demon tasting his first kill. "And what does that make you, TV?"

"Builder. Writers make things."

I enjoyed this bizarre game of libertarian chess, so I focused on the questions as we passed by the patch of light on the right. The kitchen. A black man in a red-splattered apron was cutting ribs on a stainless steel table with what appeared to be a culinary hacksaw. He took no notice of us, consumed with his work. "But everyone can write. Wouldn't that make us all builders?"

"Ha!" TV said. "You can write words. Scribble your name on a check. You ain't got the stones for *real* writing."

"What's real writing, TV?"

"Blood, sweat, and tears, Mack. Taking someth'n out of your skull and making it real. Dis . . . movie is out of my head. Sure, Octavia made it her own. She's a hell of a skirt. But I was da one who went to the library, read Ovid, read Marcus Aurelius, read enough dirty Roman theater to make a bathhouse fag blush." He chomped down on his cigar, realizing he was overplaying his hand by trying to win this baloney argument. As far as TV knew, I thought Maxine was in a real moving picture, not a dirty porno flick. I swallowed the juicy taste of BBQ from my mouth and carried on like the Midwest idiot that everyone in California believed existed between Nebraska and Ohio. "Well, I can assure you, TV, that I also give blood, sweat, and tears when selling my customers the best possible deals to set up their own businesses. These builders you mention need materials. Desks, chairs, lamps. And I spend most of my days on the road between St. Paul and Milwaukee hunting for the treasures to help their dreams come true. I help the builders build."

"Keep telling yourself dat, Mack." He stopped midway down the west wing of the Apartments at Nero Studios, took out a ring of keys, and found the one for the door. "Sit tight. I'll be back with some snacks. You a teetotaler?"

"Only when my clients are."

He grunted. "Facilitators. Each one of ya is a different slice of vanilla." He pushed open the door and waited for me to enter.

I did.

"Light's on the left."

I flicked the switch.

The single mattress and nightstand lay before me. The room's colors of smoky red carpet and amber walls made me think of a bloody honeycomb. "Sit tight, Mack," TV said. "Back soon." The last word was punctuated with enough velocity for me to get the point. He closed the door behind me. The lock's tumblers dropped with an ominous *click*. The anting-anting in my pocket was downright taunting me now. I was in a locked room at a dirty movie studio where bad magic had scarred a beautiful girl.

I waited until TV's footfalls were distant.

American Express in hand, I worked the lock with the plastic edge and prayed this wasn't the kind of sexhouse that had dungeons.

Bending for my life, the lock slid open. The darkness outside was pregnant with silence and my wingtips made sounds so soft they'd only wake a church mouse. Darkness is a vocabulary all its own, a feel . . . I can see fine in it, but reading what it's telling me has always been a chore. It's like staring into a well of clear water that the wind just rippled, distorting the message of what's inside even when you've taken the plunge.

But I tasted it. A hint of magic. Just like when I met Nico. It wasn't the house. Those hexes and curses outside were for show. New spiritualism was pretty much a shell game for gurus making a mint off distorted images of the East, selling them to rich white folks whose Catholic upbringings made being a capitalist success story a guilty pleasure they had to assuage with crystals, mantras, and the poorly understood workings of Zen . . . They didn't taste like anything, not even the greasy remains on hamburger wrapper. Magic, though, real, honest-to-goodness magic, was like a slap of bad candy in your mouth.

Here, it was thin. Still distant. An electric burn with sugary tones. I flicked my room's light switch and the flavor led me further into the dark. The apartment wing had a right turn down the hall. The walls were littered with framed oil paintings of doves, and then garish spectacles from Rome. They weren't original works from great masters, but a novice imitating their style. In each, the eyes of the central figures were too big. They smelled not of magic, but of limited talent.

One showed a Thracian tossing his net upon a tiger, trident poised for victory against the giant beast. Another depicted Julius Caesar charging into a mob of Gauls upon a white stallion. Another featured an orgy of the gods, with Jupiter in his many animal forms—swan, horse, bull—defiling goddesses and mortal women.

But the last pulled my short and curlies. It was the best rendered, sharpest, and most realistic of the bunch. Which made it terrifying.

Juno, wife of Jupiter, stood at the tip of a precipice. She held the head of her husband. Before her was a crowd of lion-clothed women, doing the same with the severed heads of their husbands.

My balls retracted as I passed it by, following the dirty, burnt aroma until it was interrupted by something . . . sweet.

Around another corner, the sweetness hung before a door on the right. I was at the heart of the apartments, like the dreaded final room in *Masque of the Red Death*, and I worried I would find a clock that tolled me into oblivion, or a key to the mystery of the two missing girls.

The knob was iced. The AC roaming the halls would make an Eskimo shiver. One hard turn and the door opened. Humidity and somber red light hit me, and the pungent aroma of sex stained every sense.

On black sheets a woman was being drilled by a guy. There was a pillow under her ass and he held her legs up so he could keep his rhythm tight and regular. Everything smelled of sweat and oil, lust and tangs of flavor gracing the humidity of their session.

"Golly," I said, announcing my arrival. "I guess this isn't the shitter!"

The guy jumped back, pulling out his willie, but good God it took awhile, given its length. He covered himself up. "Shit, Terra," he said. "Is this creep your husband?"

The redhead on the bed crossed her legs, hands over her bush. "Not any of the ones I remember." She was buxom, with far more curves than Nico. Older, my vintage, and in full command of her beauty. She touched herself and smiled. "You late for a wedding, friend?"

"No," I said, playing innocent and shocked but trying to be polite and pretending I couldn't taste the aroma of her clit with every word. "I'm Richard, Maxine's brother."

Her name was like a gunshot to the young guy with the horse dong. "I need to shower before the finale, Terra." Something tells me he was in the climax of the film and saw Maxine go serpent berserk on Nico.

"Thanks for the wake-up, Riley," she said. He pushed past me into the darkness with a handful of clothes. Terra pulled a black silk sheet over her form with such a careless air it only covered her bottom half, with one leg exposed like the slit of a skirt. "Such a good boy. Always makes me feel younger. He's going to be a big star. A big, big star." She winked to let me in on a joke so obvious even a moron could decode. "Maxine's big brother, huh?"

The taste of magic crept through the atmosphere of fresh sex on clean sheets. "Yes," I said, keeping up the gosh-wow Mid-Western naïveté. "Richard. Are you the star of the film?"

"Bless your heart," Terra said. "Your sister's the star, Dick. I'm what they call the antagonist. The big bad queen who wants her youth . . . or something." Something broke her patter. Probably the memory of the demon that emerged from Maxine's mouth. "How can I help you?"

"I've been looking all around for Maxine, but can't seem to find her."

Terra's cattish attitude received a new polish. "Well, I don't keep track of other people's schedules. But she might be—"

"What da hell is youz doing?" TV had moved silently in his big black shoes, high ball glass in his hand. "Told ya to stay in the room."

"Relax, munchkin," Terra said. "This is Maxine's brother."

"Don't call me dat!" TV said. "Unless you wants me to write you out of the flick."

"Then I'll ask Octavia, pretty please with a cherry on top, let me back in," Terra said, and the fume in her gaze was matched by TV. The hate between them was strong and mutual. "Now give the nice man his drink. He's visiting his sister, the star of our film, and we don't want to be rude. He and I were having a very nice chat."

"We're filming," TV said, thrusting a glass at me: the sides were studded with fake diamonds, making it a challenge to hold if you didn't have career calluses as thick as camel toes. "Can't have tourists making noise and walking around da place."

"Which is why Mr. Graham is staying right here until Octavia's done."

"Octavia said—"

"Octavia doesn't want us making a fuss with all the excitement today."

"I don't want to be any trouble," I said.

"You're not!" Terra said. "Now if we need you, TV, I'll be sure to ring the bell."

TV plucked his cigar from his mouth. "I'll be happy to ring your bell, Terra."

TV clunked down the hall in the darkness, turned the corner, then vanished.

"I apologize for the manners of our esteemed screenwriter," Terra said, throwing off her sheet. "But our producer thinks he's a genius, so we must suffer his poor taste and foul aroma while trying to make a beautiful film." She rose from the bed, her legs strong and graceful from years of dancing, with just enough flesh on them to reveal her age. She had not been an ingénue in a good long time, but her firm, sweet cheeks were hung like a ripe apple, a ride that was built for comfort, not speed. I tracked her whole body as she gave me her back and studied a coat rack from which hung robes, scarves, and slips.

Then I saw it.

Across her right shoulder blade, a tiny sigil had been carved faintly on her skin . . . so faint it was invisible to the naked eye. But if you'd spent as much time in the dark as I had, you could pick up a sigil like a faded radio signal on a radar screen.

But the sigil, goddamn it . . . it wasn't Roman, Greek, Egyptian, Jewish, Japanese, and it . . . moved, as if I had some kinda reading problem like dyslexia. Whatever it was, it was fighting me to stay hid, and the shape was a complete unknown.

CHAPTER 23

I BIT DOWN AND FORCED THE IMAGE THROUGH MY MIND AGAIN, threw it against my memories and hoping my joyride with Montague Summers might yield a tool, an insight, a goddamn nugget of wisdom . . . But all that came back was a taste, the one that I'd been tracking, the one that now had a hint of substance beyond the tremulous flavor of magic.

Blood and iron.

Terra took a black silk robe, casting it across her shoulders before threading her arms into the sleeves. Upon the backside was embroidered a golden Japanese Kraken. She pulled her hair from the inside and let it drape the creature, turned, and tightened her belt. "Please, Dick. Make yourself at home while I freshen up. Just don't run along the corridors making TV even more grumpy than usual."

"I'm grateful for the company," I said, raising the glass as she smiled, turned, and walked into her bathroom. The door closed.

I put the glass on her nightstand as Terra turned the taps. The water covered up the sounds of her peeing out whatever that young stud had done. The magic on my tongue split . . . half went to the washroom, the other half to the nightstand. I reached for the nightstand knob as Terra flushed.

She opened the door, the silk robe caressing her white body, lightly tied like a Christmas present that had almost been unwrapped. I was fanning out the top sheet. "Sorry, when I get nervous I like to make the bed."

God, that sounded better than I could have hoped.

Terra walked toward me. Freckles emerged. Wrinkles. And her beauty didn't drop one iota. And it was refreshing. She was playing a full-grown woman, and she owned it like a soldier owns his rifle. "Well, aren't you a domesticated gentleman." The sheet landed and she cut herself between me and the bed. I drew myself up as she placed a long-fingered hand upon my chest. The taste of magic on her back was stronger, but I couldn't make out the sigil. I'd have to touch it and, if I could, taste it myself. Then I'd need to see what was hidden in that nightstand.

"Dick," she said, playfully, right hand reaching for my neck, "would you like to lie down and wait for your sister here?"

"Oh, wow," I said, "I'm sure you have things to do."

Her red nails wove into my hair.

"Only one thing comes to mind."

She pressed me to her and our lips touched. Brandy and cigarettes stained my mouth as I wrapped my arms around her, but gentle, hands on the small of her back instead of grabbing her ass and lifting her to the nearest wall. She must lead. Few Midwest used-office-furniture salesmen were secretly Rudolph Valentino.

Tongues wrestling in hard moves, she messed with my hair as I drank a bit deeper, as any man would, but she set the tone. A little bite. A little lick. Ramping me up. Wanted me to make a big move. Every ounce of me wanted to assume command, but I teased back, gulping air. "Wait, weren't you just with that other guy?"

Her eyes were hungry. She wasn't used to men resisting. "He's a boy." She gripped both ass cheeks and ground herself into my crotch. "I need a man." She snaked her right leg around me and I was forced to grab two handfuls of her ass. Both legs tied in a bow around my back, I brought her up so she could look down and kiss me hard, long, gnashing. Then her breath was in my ear. "Fuck me."

A thousand erotic forms and flavors paraded through my mind, and I wanted to jam her against the wall, pinning her to the door, and thrash ourselves against any surface as I ground deeper and deeper into her mysteries . . . but that was me, not Richard.

My fingers kneaded into her firm ass as I turned toward the bed. I laid her down across the dirty sheets that I fanned out, but her legs were still tied around me. "Don't bother undressing," she said. "Drop your pants and fuck me. Now."

I dove into her mouth. Terra's hands tore at my belt buckle and zipper with a skill and acumen best reserved for jewelers and clockmakers, and soon she grabbed my throbbing piece.

Her eyes lit up with a hint of honest shock. "Oh, wow. You're really big. "

I smiled. "Thank you."

"No," she said, pulling me closer, "thank you." She used my piece to strike her pussy lips, each time saying, "thank you," in breathier and breathier whispers until I felt her open up to receive me. She guided me in until I filled her. Her mouth parted in a long "Oh, that's so good." And it was clear Terra was a talker.

Like Nico.

I surged forward, driving hard, and Terra seethed with pleasure until I controlled my shit and wiped Nico from my mind. Focus, I screamed at myself. You have a job to do, and blasting off right now will not get it done.

I regulated my breathing like a snake charmer and began again. Another stroke inside her and I was learning more from her mystery. She'd had a kid, once upon a time, and there was room to begin with, hence the need for boys with lion pricks. The difference with mine? I was what they call "full." Spend enough time with Tantric Shamans on the circuit, and you learn how to fill a woman, any woman, with what you have, thanks to a silent mantra in my brain that ran whenever I entered a woman. Circular breathing finished the spell. And Terra was releasing her legs, then tightening them, unsure of how much I'd brought to the dance, since what I have is substantial, and I'd found her erogenous zone.

Her eyes widened, then shut. "Oh fuck."

My pants peeled off my skin and dropped to my ankles as I pulled back, almost out, and then slowly, surely, pushed straight and hard into Terra until my balls tapped her ass. The black robe was splayed open, and she moved as if swimming in an oil slick, writhing as I moved. "How . . . how do you know how to . . ." I gripped her ass tighter. My churning rhythm cut off all capacity to make full sentences. She gripped the sheets, eyes rolling back as I sent wave after wave of full, slick pleasure. She tightened around my piece. Her legs shook. Her sweet spot was on the left, so I ground there, pulling her ass to and fro as she held her breath and everything seized. I quickened. Her elbows locked, head rolling back, and then I just pounded into her and everything clenched until she shook, rising and falling like an out of control Bride of Frankenstein who got hit with too much juice. Taut, she shook, eased her frozen spine, and then breathed out with a moan.

"Oh fuck," Terra said as I slowed things down. "I haven't come so fast since high school . . . Where the hell did you learn to move like that?"

Looking down, I smiled. "High school. I was pretty popular."

"I don't doubt it." She exhaled hard. "But . . . you haven't finished."

"It would be rude to finish first."

She laughed, hips starting to grind again, though in gentle circles instead of a bucking bronco. "A gentleman, with a giant cock? God, it's almost worth being on this picture."

"Is there a problem with the picture?"

Her mask dropped back, knowing she'd said too much in the heat of the moment. "Not right now. Here, let's try something different."

Terra gasped as she slowly pulled away from me, turned, and went on all fours. The robe was covering the sigil, but the taste was in the air, dirty and loud. She presented her ass in the air like a wild animal. "Take me."

I griped my piece and used it as a paint brush, teasing her sex with it. She moaned with wet shivers.

I rubbed it hard, forward and back. Her face lay upon a pillow, writhing with eyes shut. She licked the front of her teeth with a sweeping gait, breath hitching like a rabid dog until I plunged myself deep inside. Her mouth gaped and stretched as I pulled her ass to me and tapped that spot of her few men can reach.

Her eyes shot open. "Oh God." Terra threw her red mane back, gripped the bed, and banged towards me to bring her to a climax. She was all business. And so was I.

I caressed her back, pulled back the robe, and touched the indecipherable sigil.

A flare of pain rammed my mind's eye and for a second, my balls retracted.

"Something wrong?"

I grabbed her ass. "Just lightheaded."

She pushed back and forward. "You're working too hard. Let mama help."

And fuck if that didn't work. But that sigil was too strong to be fucked with . . . I needed a plan B.

Tantric Shamans are a weird breed. They call their pieces the Godhead, which is damn presumptuous, but they also fought demons at the behest of Matrikas, Hindu Goddesses. Part of their journey is using sexual congress to understand the divine nature of creation in the universe, of sex being a game of question and answer. So it was that some Shamans could cast a spell in which a woman whom they slept with could only tell the truth. The catch, of course, was that if the spell was cast on a woman who was forced against her will, the man's Godhead would shrivel up and become the nesting ground for fresh maggots. Hence, it was rarely used.

But Terra was about to climax again and my balls were packed, loaded, and itching for release. With my right hand gripping her ass, my right hand snaked under the black silk. The sigil was warm as my hand slid up her spine to her neck and she kept jamming into me.

My fingers kneaded the Tantric code into pressure points. Terra banged back at me with desperate thrusts. All ten of my fingers then clamped down at just the right angles as I stabbed one more time against her sweet spot.

Terra exhaled deep. Everything hummed. "Terra, can you hear me?"

She looked straight ahead. Couldn't see her face.

"Yes," she said, breathless, sweat glistening on her uncovered skin.

I switched to circular breathing to reduce the thrum of lust about to break. "Terra, you will tell me the truth, and I will finish our partnership."

"Yes."

"Where is Maxine?"

"She ran away, after what she did."

"What did she do?"

". . ."

My ten fingers squeezed harder and she moaned.

"She . . . hurt Nico."

"Where's Nico?"

She shook. "I don't know."

"When did you see her last?"

"This morning, before Maxine attacked her, her face . . . oh God, I don't care, I still love her."

"Who?"

"Nico."

Questions blistered in my mind and my concentration was fading while my fingers quaked and my member shook.

"What did Maxine do?"

"Attacked Nico. With a snake."

Terra shook harder, emotions for Nico running wild. Damn it, everything was starting to hurt, and while Edgar made sure I had a deep threshold for pain, this wasn't the arena I used it in. "Who gave you the sigil on your back? Octavia?"

"I don't understand."

Shit. She didn't know it was there. "Do you feel there's a phantom itch on your left shoulder?"

"Yes."

"When did it happen?"

"When we started shooting."

My piece was no longer listening. It began to drive Terra into ecstasy.

My hands shook. "Who . . . was in your bed . . . when you first noticed?"

That was it, I was going to come.

"Nico."

My hands released their pressure points and gripped two glorious handfuls of ass and I pounded away like it was prom night. Terra screamed as her sex gripped me, tried to stop the train of pleasure, but it was too late. We came at the exact same time and, for a brief, weightless moment, we were one.

We caught our breath. I began to pull myself out. Terra whined. "Do you have to? You feel good in me." So I shuffled out of my shoes and the pants around my ankles, and returned inside her sweet darkness, but lay to the side until we were spooning.

"That was unreal, Dick," she said. "What did you do to me?"

"Honest affection," I said.

She took my hand and braided our fingers, then cupped her large left breast. "That was too dirty to be so sweet. Downright cosmic."

I lay down with a woman who slept with Nico before all hell broke loose. A woman who had a sigil on her back, and didn't know it. The ethics of magic was a world I was still negotiating. Edgar believed magic made you above ethics. But I knew that wasn't the case. And I knew that what I'd done was crossing a line. "Terra?"

"Yes, Dick?"

"Please don't tell Maxine what we did." Terra turned to look at me as I applied the "Gosh, Wow" face of a Midwestern man caught in a guilt trip. "I mean, she might be mad if she found out her brother was romancing the star."

A funny smile and kind yet embarrassed look came upon her face. She cupped my face. "Oh, sweetie, I'm not the star. Your sister is. Her and another girl. Me? I'm a cheap piece of luster for a very Roman epic."

"What?" I said. "But you're gorgeous."

She smiled. "I am. And I'm old enough to be your little sister's mother." A dirty thought crept across her visage and she grinned like a cat. "Kiss me."

I did.

When she pulled back, she grabbed the highball glass from the nightstand that TV had brought, slugged it back, then exhaled hard. "Pardon me while I freshen up. Make yourself comfortable. I may have some spare clothes in the bottom drawer. Your outfit is . . . a little ripe."

She left me on the bed, drained but sated and confused. The bathroom door shut. I peeled off my shoes so that the gucky pants I was wearing could air out. But I wasn't going to hunt for clothes.

I slid across the bed and reached for the nightstand drawer, breathing deep so that the aroma of our lovemaking wasn't lost too fast. And here, I could taste the hint of magic that had led me here. When the shower's hiss awoke in the bathroom, I pulled open the drawer.

CHAPTER 25

CRUMPLED PACKS OF COOLS, A VARIETY OF LIGHTERS, AND TWO hashish pipes covered something that had the tang of dirty sorcery. I plunged my hand in and wiped away the fire hazards. A wooden block sat at the bottom of the nightstand with a wax cover. I tasted sparks and ash as I gripped the wax's corner and pulled slow and sure so that nothing would tear or crease.

The image glared back, an image inspired by the one I'd seen in Montague Summer's book during my Joyride.

A beautiful woman with black hair and alabaster skin, tied to the rocks on a storming shore. A snake birthed from her mouth, wide as a strongman's arm, fangs sharp and serrated, leaping at the viewer with malicious intent and red eyes, and within the pupils were dark inscriptions, twisted runes whose meaning was fathomless as the darkness in which they swam, just like the sigil on Terra's back. The style was Japanese, Edo period, but the raven-haired woman was buxom, like a German model. The entire visual tasted of old blood, and I chewed on it, searching for more clues within the catacombs of my memory, books I'd read, tales I'd heard, as if this flavor might link up. Otherwise, it was just another stack of information that someone here was playing with the dark fringe of the occult, warping it to their desires. Right now, money was on Octavia: she created a film company that catered to young people who would do as they were told and not ask questions because of daydreams of stardom. That was a bottomless trough from which to draw in victims for any kind of experiment. But why would she? And was Nico involved, seducing other women? Or was she a master's pet, like I'd been to Edgar?

I needed to talk to Octavia, and fast.

The shower died.

I pushed the nightstand drawer with enough pressure that it shut fast and quiet. I slid off the bed and dove for the bottom drawer of a dresser filled with beads, rings, bracelets and perfumes that made the air taste like vanilla.

The bathroom door opened. Terra was naked and glorious but for the towel in her hand that she used to wring out her hair. "Say, Dick, I was wondering . . ."

I pulled out a pair of striped plaid trousers so thin I could barely get my arm down one leg, let alone my thigh. "What's that, Terra?" Beneath them was a pair of terracotta slacks. God, what happened to gray, black, and blue as the colors of manhood? They went with everything. What went with Terracotta except . . . more terracotta?

"I could have sworn that Maxine . . . said you guys were . . . from Milwaukee —"

I sprang from the floor and caught her before she collapsed. Terra's eyes rolled back, mouth agape, as I gently brought her to the shaggy floor. I checked a pulse. Her breath. She was alive, and breathing hard, but something had knocked her out.

The highball glass sat upon the nightstand.

TV had drugged it.

I pulled her from the floor and lay her upon the bed, propping up her right side so that should she vomit it wouldn't be fatal.

The sigil on her shoulder . . . hissed, and for the briefest of seconds I tasted blood and iron. But it was still a goddamn jumble.

"Fuck," I muttered. There was no running to Edgar from now on in. No knocking at his chamber door and getting his wisdom and insight along with insults and punishments. "Never touch a foreign sigil, boy," Edgar had told me when I thought I saw one on the carcass of a deer in Montana. "Little scratches hold big power. And when they're thrust upon someone else, you know it's about one thing: obedience."

Charms. Control. Slavery.

Someone wanted to control Terra on the set where Maxine sprouted a demon and Nico got scarred. A love triangle? Maybe. But even if this was a Roman bathhouse with cameras, these were not crimes of passion. Time, effort, control, calculation.

I could almost hear Edgar laughing. *Listen to my adept playing detective. All he needs is a cocaine habit and a fat foil to ask stupid questions and he'd be bound to find Moriarty in the nick of time.*

I shook Edgar's voice away and focused on the sigil.

It was the only fresh clue I had. I took a breath, and did what Edgar wouldn't.

My lips touched the sigil.

Burning filled my corneas as my eyes fell out of their sockets like two bowling balls into the gutter of the universe, and time and space cut each other to ribbons and through the hack and the slash I plunged into a starless abyss where everything tasted of blood and iron and the screams of the damned were answered with the howls of the insane before my consciousness landed at the seat of a high throne made of the skulls of children, and in its lap sat a giant heart of black velvet that pulsed like a heartbeat, a clock, a countdown to oblivion, and behind me the hideous creak of a door opened and there within the crack of light the black heart mutated into a figure of lithe desire, a pulsing creature of maws and tentacles, a call to worship, to be enthralled . . . and this vision of seductive terror and the promise of brutal joys whispered but one word to me as its eyes opened to reveal the gaze of a demon snake . . .

"Brimstone."

I snapped back from Terra's body. Blood and iron fled from my lips as the aromas and tastes of this world crashed into my mouth.

The creature, whatever it was, that goddamn creature . . . knew me.

I turned to the door.

TV stared at me, a .44 in his mashed and thick fingers. "Ah hell," he said, as I stood with terracotta slacks in one hand and Terra on the bed. "Get those pants on."

I did. They were snug, and revealing, but they fit and were cleaner on my sweaty skin than my sticky blues. "I just want to see my sister."

"Yeah," TV said. "And it woulda been easier if you'd taken a powder, instead of Red. Maybe you'd have woken up and ya sis would be back."

"Why would you drug me instead of letting me wait here? Where is she?"

TV plucked out his cigar. "Yer voice is giving me gas, kid."

Mercy, it was hard to keep the witty comebacks from spewing past my teeth, but I was Richard, not James, and keeping up appearances increased my survival rate far more than pithy jokes shoved at an asshole dwarf. "Where is Maxine?"

"Here's what's going to happen," he said, walking forward in his clunky loafers. "Yer going to get in your miserable excuse for a car. Yer going to fuck off to parts unknown. And yer going to wait for your sister to contact youz. Don't like it, I'll drag your dead weight out of this room. We can't have people nailing our actresses like it's a whorehouse. We're a respected film company, Mack."

Murder. The little man was willing to murder me to protect whatever happened to Maxine. My opinion of TV was starting to change. Perhaps he wasn't a bitter slice of unfortunate DNA in a deformed body. Was he magic? If he was a familiar, as some little folks are, I would have tasted the stink of his link to a sorcerer. Unless he was covering up.

He puffed his Century Sam. "Hurry up with that zipper, clown. I got laundry ta do."

It was the same cigar. It wasn't ashed away. A charm, perhaps? Smoke could hide many things . . . maybe even the taste of magic.

That meant TV was no joke. And this was a showdown.

He had a gun. I had pants.

But at my feet was my suit coat and Izzy's gift. I'd found enough trouble. Time to make some.

"Okay," I said, hands in the air. "Can I take my clothes? Please? It's my only suit."

"Grab it, townie, and all your gear. And then scram."

I did, quicker than he could see.

On the floor I worked a little scarf routine, pulling the bulges of my clothes to hide my hands from TV's eyes as they tunneled through the stained fabric still dusted with Lilith's glass eyes. "Need my keys."

"Hurry up, I ain't getting younger."

The thick braid of the anting-anting was across my palm as I pulled myself up and attempted to put on my jacket while looking like a nervous wreck.

"Ya mudder still dress you? Get those sleeves in. I ain't got all night."

And as he let the collar fall down upon my naked shoulder, the face of the anting-anting dropped. The charm hung down with a weight of magic that tasted like overripe coco jam, sweet, strong, and sticky. Bandits wore anting-antings to escape from danger and hails of bullets. I hoped it would be enough to stop a menacing dwarf with a ten-cent stogie and secondhand Colt.

TV's eyes flared. "Sad world, guys starting to wear jewelry."

"We can't all be born with your good looks," I sneered.

He raised the gun so it would hit anywhere between my balls and neck if he got shoved. "You finally grew a pair . . . something tells me you ain't really nobody's brother."

"And something tells me you're going to tell me where Maxine is."

TV huffed a laugh that was so bitter and acrid it might as well have been the last breath of a dying ghoul. "You got a lotta guts for a dead man walking. But that necklace doesn't look bullet proof."

"Funny thing about this necklace, Tiny, is that it protects the wearer. But you never know how. Why, some of those bullets might turn into goose feathers, or just go 'pop' like kid's cereal when milk hits the sugar. Or maybe it will ricochet like a pinball shot, crack that stogie out of your maw, and leave you exposed."

That word scared him. Yup, whatever supernatural hijinks were infecting this place, TV was tied to them. Like Terra. Like Nico. Which meant I had to go to the top of the food chain. "What has Octavia done with Maxine?"

Dark fire forged in TV's eyes. "Don't you talk about the Boss like that, or I'll take my chance with your goddamn trinket and see if it can stop a full clip."

"Where is she?"

Thunder cracked from the front of the house, and TV's attention slipped from me for a sliver.

Springing forward, I gripped his wrist and pulled it back. A shot fired out as we tumbled into the hallway. I tore the gun out of his hand as he kicked my shin hard enough to wake the dead. I flipped the pistol, pointing straight down on the little murderous man, as another sound crackled from the front of the house. Electric and loud and clear.

"Vice! Open up or we will tear down this door!"

CHAPTER 26

VICE. THE WORD SHOT UP MY SPINE LIKE POISON. OF ALL THE departments of the LAPD, Vice's reputation was the most brutal. A law unto themselves, they were an All-American version of the SS. They answered to no one, had informants in the Valley, the Strip, and even the regular Hollywood: anywhere that might bloom a good time or bad trip. Dirty movies, it appeared, were their game, too.

TV chewed his stogie as I punctuated the air with the gun. "Where do you hide here?" I whispered.

He grimaced, clearly wanting me to die under his glare.

"Right now? We're helping each other. Later, try and kill me. But if you don't hide us, we're both spending the night downtown in handcuffs. What would Octavia think then?" The logic made his eyes shake, because being angry wasn't going to help us a lick. He turned on his heels and marched into the dark hallway.

"Move," he grunted.

In the distance I heard Octavia's voice. "TV! Get the door!" He growled, but marched forward.

A cop barked, "Open this door or we're breaking it down!"

We turned another corner as Octavia's heels clicked behind us. "I'm coming!" Stifling a chuckle at her choice of words, I increased my gait as TV's little legs scissored down a stretch of dark paneled halls that smelled of dust more than magic.

"Look, we have a warrant!" said a distant cop voice.

"Ah, shit," TV said, picking up his pace. "We need to scram."

"I'm not leaving this house without Maxine."

"Who said we was leaving da mansion?" One last turn and the center of the oubliette was a dead end with laundry chute. The little bastard had led me into a compromising position. "Me first," he said, but I pinched a nerve in his neck and he hissed like an asthmatic cobra.

"Not so fast. Something tells me you might run away if you get the chance."

He rubbed his shoulder. "Wanna go? Head first?"

"We go together."

"Revoltin'."

"Just get in the chute, handsome. The cavalry is coming."

TV muttered as he reset the cigar in his mouth, turned, and climbed into the chute. "Just sit at the top, like's it's a slide." He shook. "When this is ovah, I'm gonna piss in your skull."

I gripped his shoulder again, a little harder. "I've given worse eulogies." Cop shoes on tile and hardwood approached. I took a deep breath and then dove in, gun in TV's back so the little bastard would get no funny ideas, but then silently clicking the safety so I didn't have a corpse clogging the drain.

Riding down the chute, we slid into pure darkness, TV blotting whatever light there was at the end of the tunnel so all my night eyes could see was his crumpled backside. We banged on the sides, my fingers gripping TV's shoulder. Gaining speed, we cut our way hard and fast until the dull light of the drop mouth was before us and I realized what we were heading toward: the laundry bins of dirty movies.

"Gross." I got out before we tumbled out of the chute.

We bounced against the hard embrace of a concrete floor. At impact, TV rolled out of my grip like a greased bowling ball. I got to one knee as he took off with goblin-like speed. I clicked off the safety of the pistol. "Close," I said as he crested a corner. "But you can't outrun a bullet. Hands up." TV did so, but with one hand around the crested corner. "Where I can—"

"—see 'em?" he said with mischief, and then smacked on the lights. Searing wattages covered my night eyes in sparks and the tiny bastard vanished before it came back. A dirty laugh echoed as a door slammed. I ran, but he was gone, the laundry door locked. My wallet was upstairs. I'd need to improvise some kind of key. But TV would be long gone, a little man hiding himself and what I expected to be his magic in a big house where he knew the ins and outs.

Damn it. I tried to stifle the rising tide of doubt in my abilities by focusing on what could be done: survive, find Maxine, find Nico, get the hell out of here.

I took stock of myself and the room. My naked shoulder sported a fine abrasion from the serrated landing, but everything else seemed dandy. The terracotta trousers were a bit snug for my vintage, but looked good. The anting-anting lay across my chest, useless at stopping midgets from escaping, it would appear. Or polluted because of what I presumed was an anti-magic stogie.

The laundry room was cool, damp, and gray. Large washers and dryers were stacked against the far wall. Shelves held Dazzle, everyone's favorite laundry soap, the one with the beautiful lady with the doe eyes holding a baby: the magic brand that could take out the worst stains of all kinds, wine, nicotine . . . blood.

The washer's maw was open. The dryer was shut and full.

Seems TV had done me something of a favor. I tucked the .44 into my waistband, just above my ass crack, then opened the dryer.

Dirty magic fell out. Loincloths covered in faint blood splatter sat on my feet. And I tasted blood, iron, and something worse. I spat, but it stayed. The cloth was shredded, the kind of damage you'd get from wild fangs. The kind that marred Nico's face forever. The kind that takes you three rounds of Dazzle to get clean.

But this was only the second.

The cloth was cold. Washed and dried twice, but abandoned.

And something familiar. Not magic. But strong and rich. I licked my parched lips, then brought the loincloth to my mouth.

Nico. Her scent was still warm upon the cold sheets.

I pressed the faint slice of blood to my lips—

Lava filled my eyes and choked whatever scream had tried to emerge from my gaping mouth: the world bled away, paralytic stitches of terrible pain cut through me, a red tower rose from a sea of churning humanity that was tied to each other, eating each other, rutting the pieces, and from above this mote was a tower . . . that rose into a snake's neck, the tower head gazing at me. Its eyes flexed, and there was a twisted swastika etched on its iris. *"Brimstone!"*

"No!" I screamed as I yanked the cloth. It dropped as I clutched my mouth. Damn it, I was making enough noise to call in an artillery barrage on my head. I kicked myself, then leaned against the chute mouth. Senses flaring, I counted down from a ten in Sanskrit while the whispers from above plucked at the hair deep in my ears.

"You see, Detective Morse," said Octavia's luscious voice. "There was no need to beat down our door. My palace is always open for the LAPD."

"Much obliged, Octavia," said the detective. "As soon as we're done searching every nook and cranny, we'll let you get back to your art movies."

"You're a very modern man, Detective."

Cop shoes marched into the apartment wing for a post-raid sex party and that goddamn midget had locked me in the laundry room while he planned his next foul move. The only good news was that he couldn't do anything loudly. But then again, neither could I.

The room was musty, and outside of the bloody sheets there wasn't a hint of magic. No windows. Only sound was the groans of Vice and the women who had become their graft. The ant-ing-anting bounced on my chest, too thick to use for a lock pick. I searched the shelves by the washer for anything that might act as a wedge to get me out of here before something far worse than a bitter midget showed up. The box of Dazzle had a ragged maw. I tore off a strip from the side, not wanting to cut the beauti-ful visage of the Dazzle gal. Thirty seconds later, I worked the lock with a slice of cardboard, but the eyes of the soap box beauty queen followed me like a pervert. The cardboard was too soft. Even when I flexed it out it wouldn't hold itself taut enough to catch the lock.

Tearing it out of the door jam, I looked for a trashcan. But the little laundry room had none. Every laundry room has trash. For lint. Stray receipts.

TV had taken it with him. Which means there was some-thing in that trashcan. Something washed out of the sheets that might be tied to . . .

I closed my eyes.

I recalled the red tower and the snake.

I recalled the throne room with the tentacle heart.

The box of Dazzle softened as the woman's lips shook.

"Brimstone . . ." said the girl on the box. *"Help me."*

CHAPTER 27

"MAXINE," I WHISPERED.

"Help me, Brimstone," screamed the visage of a woman possessed, a voice tortured with the numbness of terror, the scream hitting me as if from the other end of twenty-foot pipe.

"Where are you?"

"Close . . . I saw you."

"How?"

Her visage wavered. *"The demon in me . . . said your name. It fears you."*

Great. Now if that could only help me unlock a door. "Are you still on the set?"

"It's coming . . . I can't speak too long."

"How can you see me?"

Her beautiful face and knowing smile spouted out a voice so distant. *"Its power . . . it's immense . . . it flows through . . . but it's killing me. Stop it . . . stop her . . ."*

"Octavia? Is Nico okay? Is she close? Maxine!"

Distant screams filled my ears as I muzzled the box of Dazzle. Then the visage went silent.

Maxine was alive. And the bastard demon inside her was powerful enough that she could speak through . . . images of herself. Images. Film. Sex. Power. In the darkness of a soiled laundry room, I felt everything come down on me. This wasn't just a case of idiot novices fucking around with bad mojo, or even second-generation Nazis playing with toys they don't understand. I'd seen perverse evil in glimpses. The throne with a heart. The snake tower. The magic that was in play was darker, harder, and deeper than I'd anticipated.

Though I didn't know it, I was gripping the anting-anting for all it was worth. But fear flickered in my mind. Folk magic might not be strong enough to stop whatever it was that held Maxine captive. And Nico, too.

I took it off and slipped it into the ass pocket of my groovy terracotta slacks. I'd never gotten anywhere in life by avoiding trouble. I was rewarded in a handful of heartbeats.

Through the maw of the chute, the grinding sound of sex and lies went from murmurs and thuds to words and gasps.

"That's it, copper. I've been bad. Make the cuffs tight, and use a lot of force."

"Oh, your nightstick is so hard, and big."

"Yes, officer, I'll do whatever you say."

These were countered with cop grunts.

"Going to have to fuck the slut out of you."

"You're going to take it all in and beg for more."

"You have the right to suck my dick."

My jaws clenched at the unbridled vocabulary of the small-dicked man who craves power to dominate, the curses of guys who never got invited to bliss, but stole it and fucked it with all the charm of a fascist interrogation.

Suddenly, something shot down from the chute with a hiss. I leapt from the wall to find a pile of rope at my feet. Black rope with red eyes.

I had seen snakes in India, Australia, Africa, and South and Central America, not to mention the garter snakes of my short youth in Oakland. This behemoth raised a head the size of a football. The taste of magic was oily and slick. It was some monster snake from Parts Unknown and its diamond eyes glared at me with starvation.

"Easy, pal," I whispered, taking two slow steps toward the laundry. Last thing I wanted was the members of Team Vice blaming me for interrupting their sick graft and closing this house down. One gunshot and everyone's party was over. "I'm pretty much ninety percent jerky at this point."

The forked tongue tasted air. The diamond eyes flexed and focused on me as the head rose. Clear and confident that it could eat the big mouse. And from the chute, the dirty talk rolled like a slinky from the top of the stairs.

"Yeah, like that. Ohhh, God. Don't stop."

"I can't take it! You're too big!"

"You taste like heaven."

My back hit the dryer as the beast before me rose. "Whoever raised you didn't skimp on meals," I said. "Why don't you take a snack break and a nap and leave this tough old skin and bones behind?"

"Yeah, you like it like this, you dirty whore."

"Your ass is mine, bitch."

"Did I say stop sucking?"

It reared back.

"God, I hate when snakes don't listen to reason."

I stepped on the bloody sheet, the box of Dazzle on my right.

The bastard snake hissed.

"Damn it."

The critter snapped its head out like a flying dagger. I twisted away as the snake's head punched through the washer's door as if it were butter. The thunder of the blow so loud it might even pull a cop out of free sex. Instead, the women moaned even louder.

"You're making me come! Fuck!"

"Harder, I need you harder . . . yes, yes, yes!"

"Mmmmmm."

The snake retracted like a boxer pulling back for his hay-maker, and in that sliver of time all I could think to do was yank up the sheet like a suburban matador.

The snake's head hovered, irises dilated and tongue snap-ping out. The natural monster no longer seemed sure of its tar-get. Tasting the blood from a demon snake's tooth will do that to you, I suppose. The frayed metal punched in and out of the dryer gave me an idea: I didn't want to die this way, so I hoped the idea turned out to be brilliant.

Above, the sound of hands slapping asses, of beer guts gig-gling, and of hair being pulled were trailed by the huff and guff of cops fucking film stars and believing they were gods.

I shook out the sheet. "Grrr."

The beast hissed, moving back. Arms wide, holding the sheet at neck level like a matador's cape, I slowly slid my bobbing head to the left as I held the rest of my body straight: if the snake was as dumb as most rubes, he'd think I was standing in front of the washer. The plan: have it dart into the face of the washer, wrap its head in this dirty magic sheet, and hope to God I could strangle it before it wrapped around a limb and crushed it like a fortune cookie.

The critter sized me up with another flash of its tongue, then opened its mouth.

Tiny razors ridged the mouth around the large striking fangs. It was trying to scare me. It was working. Those fangs looked strong. Maybe strong enough to jimmy a lock.

"Toro, toro, toro!"

A BRIMSTONE FILES NOVEL

The jaw unhinged and the void of doom in its gullet whispered death. It rattled its head once and tore through the air, aimed right at my face, not body.

Sacrilege spilled down through the chute:

"Fuck, God, fuck!"

"Fuck me, Jesus Christ!"

"Lord, I'm going to suck you dry!"

Serrated teeth and fangs cut the darkness, so I snapped my head back and it changed directions, head swimming through the air and never taking its wild eyes from me. I pulled the sheet up to my chin. It reared back with a hiss.

"Not a fan of dirty snake linen, are we?" Talking helped remind you that your lungs were still jake and needed air to make you move at your best. I lifted the sheet to my eyes. Through the stained fabric, I saw the snake slither back. I moved my whole body in front of the washer, its lid up and the closest thing I had to a guillotine.

"Round two, Seth," I said, dipping the sheet, nerves settling with the words. "Come and take a bite out of Brimstone!" Venomous intent drove the snake's head forward with the accuracy of a sharpshooter.

Just what I wanted.

I bent backwards, arching my back over the washer, and the snake's head cut a close shave, the bottom of the jaw nearly at eye level as it passed over my face. The bladed teeth almost hooked my protruding chin. I clapped my hands together, trapping the cloth around it. The snake shook, stronger than a college kid hitting the gridiron. I twisted across the top of the washer, sliding my hand up the snake's body until I felt the tensile strength of its neck flex. It knew what I was planning and didn't like it one iota. Tough cookies.

My hands flexed with the strength of a man who'd made a life hitting tent pegs into the ground to earn his keep before he was old enough to read, hands trained to hold cards a million different ways and use them as weapons, hands that could squeeze the life out of a man three times his size if he had to.

The snake fought my grip and lost as I shoved its head to the edge of the washer's lip.

Above came the gurgle of men about to climax, a sickening sound given their character.

"Gah . . . oh gawd!"

"Oh, oh . . ."

"Ugh!"

With my left, I slammed the lid down, then kept pressing. The machine shook while the savage beast fought against impending decapitation. But his number was punched. I ground the lid into its neck until the flexing went taut. And for one moment it became an expensive and erect snakeskin cane.

Above, the men grunted in breath and the ladies said smooth words.

Beneath my hand, the lid snapped closed.

Blood gurgled from the lip as I tore with my left hand, hard and fast, and separated head from body. I tossed the body into a darkened corner as blood seeped into the sheet thick, fast, and sticky. Then I heard a heavy thud and tumble as the lid closed.

I lifted the lid.

The wide-eyed head of my opponent glared out at me in death stare, jaws as wide as two hands, fangs like samurai swords pulled back for the last cut of the blade. A small prayer fell from my lips.

We met as enemies on a blood-soaked plain.

One of us fell, neither to blame.

Next time, my friend, I may fall.

And see you soon, one and all.

But not today.

I plucked the critter's head from the bottom of the articulator, then closed the lid and laid it down. Tearing a piece of the cloth, I planned to use it to yank out a tooth for a lock pick.

The doorknob rattled.

And I had a better idea.

CHAPTER 28

TV FOUND ME PRONE ON THE GROUND, SILENT AND STILL. THE SNAKE'S mouth was at my neck, head and body held together by my hands. In the dark, the snake's blood might as well have been mine, covering my neck and hands, as if we'd had a life-and-death struggle and the snake was reading a death poem instead of yours truly.

"Well done, Charlie." TV loomed above. One hand was behind his back. The other held a key. I manipulated the snake's slither with my hand. "Drain dat venom inta da bastard." He pulled out his hand and revealed a white mouse. "Then you get dessert."

I held "Charlie" still, and then launched his head at TV like a shot.

"Gah!" TV shrilled and dropped the mouse and keys, as the ghost head of his killer pet bounced off his head. I did a kip up, caught the head, then came down with it on TV, who had landed on his knees, hands up. I flexed out Charlie's teeth and held them at TV's eye.

"Shh!" I said, picking up the keys and shoving them into the tight pocket of my slacks. I flexed the snake's head. "Laundry's done."

Above, cop grunts became low murmurs and the fake laughter of women who endured the presence of rotten men. I drew the pistol with my left hand and indicated the door, then pulled back Charlie's head. But I didn't drop it.

The hallway was taupe, lit with weak lights. I closed the door behind me with an elbow. There was a tiny bathroom on the right, while the hall stretched deep and long. Chlorine and bleach mingled in the moist air. I tapped TV's massive head and pointed at the bathroom.

Inside, door closed, I laid my back on the bathroom door and took in the little man whose big snake had tried to kill me. "You can move fast for a fellow with tiny legs."

He crossed his arms, chewing that cigar . . . which had yet to ash and remained at the same size as when I'd come to the door. "And youz as ugly as you are tall. You may be a good fibber with the gals, but I don't buy you an ounce. You ain't no brother."

"And you're no ordinary midget."

He sneered.

"Why did you try and drug me?"

"Why'd ya pull a pistol?" He had stones for a little man, that was certain.

"You mean the pistol that you were going to use on me? So, once again from the top, why lace my drink with knockout drops?"

He grunted. "Ah, I waz just gonna drop ya off at the bus station with a beautiful creature and send you back to Wisconsin."

"Because you don't want me to find Maxine."

He smiled. "Whoz said she was lost?"

Then I lifted Charlie's head and TV's smile shook. "Hard to tell what kind of snake is in the room when it's darting for your eyes. But up close, I realized your dear Charlie was a rare breed of Australian Tiger Snake, the Red Dwarf, the small version of a much larger beast. Very poisonous. Some aboriginals believed their venom had magical properties."

TV puffed. "You going to scare me with fairy tales?"

"No, TV. I'm going to give you a choice. See, this venom in raw form kills anybody full sized. But, oddly enough, in children and those of . . . small stature, it's a powerful elixir for getting at the truth. Rare, but popular with parents. So, you're either going to tell me where Maxine is, or I'm going to press these fangs into you so hard you'll finally drop that cheap trick you've been chewing on. The one that covers up whatever stain of sorcery is on your skin."

He sneered. "So. You know a little magic. Think you can scare me?"

"Me? Nah. I'm wearing ridiculous slacks and don't much like blasting people into the great unknown. And, hell, I'm not even sure that if I did you wouldn't rebound back with a legion of Charlies in a chariot made of fire and pulled by a minotaur." I looked at Charlie. "But pretty sure that the venom in these teeth will make you sing like a tortured angel in the heart of Pandemonium. So, tell me where Maxine is. Tell me where Nico is. Tell me who is responsible, or it's fangs for the memories."

Slowly, the little bastard plucked his forever-burning cigar from his mouth, spit at the ground with enough disdain to make a nun faint, and jutted his chin up to meet my approaching hand. "Do your worst, dabbler. I ain't saying shit!"

Charlie's fangs bit into TV's arm and I pressed down as he growled and fought the painful scream coming from his guts. Seconds later, his eyes went white.

I dropped Charlie's head on the floor. "That's not good."

CHAPTER 29

TV LURCHED BACKWARDS, HEAD ABOUT TO PLANT ITSELF ON THE concrete floor, mouth agape and eyes like piss-stained milk. Lunging, I gripped his armpits before the rest of his body fell hard. The cigar's cherry smacked concrete and sparks flew with a hiss. The taste of magic was bitter and sharp, like coffee grounds soaked in vinegar.

His weight hooked my hands and dragged me down with him, as if he were an anchor of steel being dropped from a cloud. Pulling hard against the dense man's collapse, my back ached, shoulder blades yanked forward before being yanked back.

Pound for pound, TV may have been the densest creature I'd ever held. With a supreme effort I had him against the bathroom wall, the burning cigar at his feet, eyes still swimming in pus.

"TV?" I said, looming over him. "TV, can you hear me?"

His neck twitched, face contorting. "Yeah . . ." the word fell out of his mouth like a long-lost letter, distant and faded. "Yeah." The veins in his face turned blue, then flexed.

This was bad. Tiger snake venom didn't push people into a coma. It was a truth serum, and a very rough kind, but one's eyes were clear and focused. Not . . . whatever this was.

"TV, where is Maxine?"

His lips curled. "Can't say. She won't let me."

"Octavia?" His skin covered in hives, as if allergic to my words. "TV, is Nico here? Who is behind the attack on Maxine and Nico?"

"Can't say." He started shaking. And that's when I tasted it.

I turned him over, pulled down his collar.

Burned into his flesh with an arcane stylus was another sigil. Same blurry style as Terra Nova, but clearer, as if done in a hurry or against a stronger foe. I could make out the symbol: a pile of rope tied around what appeared to be a snake's mouth. A spell of silence, cut into his body. A hiss rose from the floor. Blood had fallen out of TV's nose and kissed the cigar's cherry.

Dying. The little bastard was dying on me. The sigil was going to kill him to keep the venom from working. I just signed this man's death warrant with my own blood.

In the back of mind, Edgar laughed.

I wiped my lips across my forearm. "Double damn."

I clamped my mouth onto the dwarf's wound and sucked as hard as I could while my mind raced for the only thing that might help. TV shook as the venom stopped in its tracks and retreated into the blood gathering in my mush. I dug into my back pocket and grabbed the anting-anting. The little man gasped as if something broke and I tore my mouth off the wound, spat blood and venom at the wall, and tied the anting-anting to his arm above two holes made by a dead snake's fangs.

TV convulsed as if in a seizure. I plucked the cigar from the ground and shoved into his mouth.

"Ow!" My hand snapped back. He damn near chewed off my knuckle. "Hey, a little gratitude would be nice."

TV's face huffed and puffed and chewed the cigar, and the rotten flavor of bad coffee and spilled vinegar began to fade. Whatever was in that stogie it was more powerful than a two-cent puff from Century Sam. Damn thing was strong enough to cover up the arcane. You don't grab such trinkets at Kress's five-and-dime on Hollywood. Someone had access to potent materials, beyond the Kraken's eye and dirty Japanese squid books.

TV's breathing eased as he took in smoke. The veins above the rope of the anting-anting began to lighten from the black and blue that crisscrossed his face. The more he puffed, the easier he breathed, and the more his natural, creepy color came back to his face and crept down his haggard neck. The amulet of the anting-anting swung like a pendulum above the floor.

I turned on the sink and grabbed a mouth full of water, spitting out the rest of the truth venom and TV's blood.

"Gah!" Part of my tongue was numb. No matter how much venom I spat out, some was in me. Truth serums . . . are not quite charms.

Terror gripped my balls like a vice. My cover as Maxine's brother was thin and now on fire, but I didn't fancy being trapped in this Roman nightmare of porn and vice cops and have my own secrets spilled.

And as if on cue, a voice pricked up from the ground. "So's, who are ya? Really?"

My fingers dug into the porcelain sink like a doll's neck I wanted to snap. "James Brimstone."

"Ha!" TV said. "Stupid name. Must be a Brit."

"Stupid name of the guy who just saved your life."

"After jamming a snake in my arm."

I turned. "You did it first."

TV's defiant and pudgy face puffed up. "Fine. Consider us jake. Now get da hell outa here before I getz mad."

I washed snake blood off my chest and arms. "I'm not going anywhere without Maxine and Nico. Tell me where they are, and I'll leave that charm on your arm so you can live."

TV grimaced while he puffed. A trickle of blood ran from his nose as he shook, spat, and sucked in air. "Youz don't get it. I can't help ya. No one here can. What's going down is going to happen, even with da accident."

I sluiced off the light-red water. "Accident? What happened on set, that wasn't supposed to happen? Maxine wasn't supposed to attack Nico?"

TV puffed in and out with the rhythm of his breath, a tiny human forge with a cigar that wouldn't die. "Lips are sealed, Brimstone."

"Thanks to that sigil on your back."

His eyes went wide. "Don't know nothin' about 'dat.'"

"TV, you may be an idiot, but you're not stupid. And someone is making you do these things. And I know who. She's covered her actual dabbling in the arcane with all this Greek and Roman nonsense. She has money, power, influence, and apparently a bottomless supply of actors no one will miss as she screws around with things she can't control."

His chest rose and fell as if whatever I said next would kill him.

"Tell me how I can save Maxine. Tell me where Nico is. And I promise, I'll not only let you go, I'll put you in touch with the only legit hands that can remove a sigil that is burned so deep. You'd be free."

That last word was like cold water splashed into his face, a slap of clarity in a hazy world, a wish dangled before him on a very sharp hook.

"Free?" TV said. "Ain't no such thing. Not here at da doll house, not nowhere. Look, yous'z saved my life, but if . . . if I'm asked, I'll cut you through with a rusty nail. Free?" He hissed in breath. "Wouldn't know what it felt like if it drilled me in the guts."

Sitting there on the floor, leaning against the wall with a stain of blood and venom, sucking in smoke and breathing out disdain, TV was a tragic sight. There were . . . places where people were controlled with dark magic stabbed into their skin. Forever. Whatever skills he had in the arcane, they weren't enough to save him. For the first time since coming into my line of sight, I actually felt pity for old TV.

Then I drilled him in the chin with a straight right so hard I bet Cactus would have been proud.

TV's head bounced off the wall. His cigar dropped to the floor and rolled under the sink. "Sorry, friend," I said, checking his pockets. "But I believe you. Can't have you stabbing me in the back after I saved your life. Too damn tragic, even for me."

TV's wallet was starved, but I had to look at the driver's license. "Tiberius Valentino?" I said, then let it rest on his tiny knee. "And you thought Brimstone was tacky." There was nothing of value stitched into TV's clothes. But the anting-anting hung off his arm like a warning bell: *Don't leave me behind! See how I saved him? Do you want to run around this place on your lonesome?*

But venom still dripped from TV's wound. Venom that had tainted my own blood. I was compromised in a major way in a house full of dark magic. Serums and poisons weren't charms, but Edgar fed me enough of them that they didn't last long. I needed time without the truth coming out of me . . . or an anting-anting to cut the poison's power.

And it was tied around the arm of a midget who had tried to kill me.

I got up, grabbed the keys from my pocket, then opened the bathroom door. TV was now being missed by Octavia. She'd send someone after him. Time to hustle.

I opened the door to the chorine-and-bleach haze of the hallway. Even with terracotta slacks and a pistol, I felt naked as a babe in a house that aimed to kill me. Time for the prey to become the predator.

CHAPTER 30

MOISTURE DRIPPED OFF THE TAUPE WALLS. WHICH MEANT ONE THING: Octavia was rich enough to have an underground pool in the valley, a pool where no one could see you, one hidden from the elements. Perhaps buried deep enough to stifle the screams of those who had become toys for blasphemous spells.

I passed a winding, dark staircase that led to the main floor, then halted. The moans and groans of the Vice squad's second round of sexual graft was in full swing, far slower and more grinding than the first but no less repugnant. I was as liberated a man for my age as I knew, and as far as I was concerned, a lady could use her body for whatever she wanted. But there was a story emerging from Nero Studios: one where you served the will of someone else. Cops paid in flesh. Sigils as slavery. Your life controlled by others.

Edgar's voice giggled in my head. *Yes, James. Just establish my death among my peers, buy me the gift of oblivion from this world, and you will be free and our partnership broken.* But it was no partnership. It was master and servant. I had no beef with dirty pictures, but I was going to burn this place to the ground, even if I died trying.

A thick wooden door waited at the end of the hallway, deep, sweaty groves on its skin like black scars from a thousand lashes. The aroma of chemicals thickened with each step. The brass lock on the door matched the brass key on TV's ring. I clocked the hammer on my pistol and turned the key. The tumblers dropped like gasps in a drowning man's throat. The door opened into darkness. My night eyes steadied. A sauna of dark tiles shimmered before me. Everything echoed. My breath, my steps, the closing of the door behind me. The air was rife with chemicals meant to burn and kill life. The taste of sanitized death.

An exposed doorway sat on the opposite side of sauna. The darkness was deeper, but the heavy drip of a faucet head made it clear it was the shower, probably before the entrance to the pool. I'd search this floor and, if there was nothing here, no Maxine or Nico or snakes the size of midgets, I'd wait until the last moan of Vice had turned into a snore and then sneak upstairs and get Octavia, who had to be the sorcerer TV was serving.

I stepped into the shower. It was twenty feet long and I hated to think of all the fluids that had washed down the drain's cross-hatched mouths. On the opposite side was another large wooden door.

My feet gripped the concrete of the shower floor, when giggles and laughter came at me from both sides: the pool door, and the entrance to the sauna.

"Damn it!" There was only one move to make.

I dropped my trousers, tossed the keys and gun into the pile on the floor outside the shower, and turned the nozzle at full blast. Iced water flowed until I could adjust the nozzle to a happy medium that hopefully reduced the shrinky-dink effect to my lonesome member.

Lights snapped on from the sauna, but the first voice I heard came from the pool door. "Come on, Rachel! Let's do another lap!"

"After what we did, boss, I need a shower."

Then, from the sauna end, two more voices. "You haven't lived until you've had a sauna party."

"Sure thing, baby."

On each side of me came a buxom twenty-something dragging a slimy member of Vice. To my right, from the shower, was a soft brown-haired gal with the body of a swimmer, hard muscles beneath her skin, small, pert breasts and a doe-eyed faced streaked with garish eyeliner thanks to swimming and sex. Her beau was hirsute with a thick mustache, wavy hair, and a bronze body from tanning; a career Angelino who made Vice his heaven. To my left approached a strawberry blond with a choker featuring a bull that resembled the mark of Augustus Caesar. She had many rich curves, tanned to a high gloss of bronze, and devilish eyes to counter a dimple-sharp smile. Her Vice was a milky-white novice, five o'clock shadow creeping on his face, still wearing his briefs and black socks.

All four pairs of eyes took me in as if I was a rat in the pantry.

"Who the hell is this guy?" Mustache said.

Baby Face also moved to the fore to protect his girl. "What's your name?"

"James Brimstone," I muttered, the snake venom in my blood still so damn strong that I couldn't keep my mouth shut from telling the truth. I thought of a dozen great lies . . . but before they pierced my lips a stabbing pain thundered in my heart. Damn it!

But maybe there was enough truth I could drop to get myself out of this jam.

Mustache mouthed. "What are you doing here?"

"I'm taking a shower." I rubbed my hair. "I just had sex with Terra Nova."

Whew! No stabbing needles of agony in my heart. I couldn't lie, but I could pick what truth to share so long as I didn't hear a question. I blasted each ear again.

The girls laughed, covering their mouths, then spoke to each man while the shower blasted my ears and I prayed that TV didn't wake up and ruin everything. I pulled out of the stream. "I'll leave once I finish my shower," I said, dopey and stupid as both men looked me over, then looked at my clothes. The gun's nose stuck out from one of the folds. In the dark, it didn't look like anything more than a patch of gray. With the lights on, it might as well be smoking.

"Hey!"

The water stopped.

Mustache's long, strong arm stretched out alongside me, hands clawing the faucet.

"We asked you a question."

"I can't hear well with water in my ear," I said, honestly.

The slap came fast and obvious but I had to take the hit: the left side of my head stung as the water dripped out of my right ear. "How about now?"

"Only my right ear," I said.

The next slap came, right on cue.

"You a Midnight Cowboy?" Mustache said.

"No," I said. "I'm a private dick."

Both Svelte and Choker loved that line, and so did the Baby Face. "Come on, Cirello. We're off duty."

"Fuck you, Heinz," Cirello said, then glared at me. "Creepy bastard." Cirello crossed his arms as I knocked the last warm drip of water from my ears. He gripped Svelte's wrist. "Stay out of our way."

"Planning on it."

"Hey, I wanted to shower," Svelte said, holding her ground. "Why don't you sit in the sauna for a—"

Cirello yanked. "I wasn't asking."

"Let her go."

All three words spilled out of me as the last drip dropped on the tiles.

Cirello's eyebrow arched. "What was that, Cowboy?"

"You're pretending not to hear me because you think I don't have the guts to threaten a cop," I said, oh-so-honestly, and realized my fate was being sealed tighter than a noose. "But I do."

The finger of authority jammed in my face. "You threatening me?"

"Your use of rhetorical questions is a real indicator of your stupidity."

"You calling me . . . don't call me stupid, faggot!"

"I'm not gay, but appreciate the compliment."

"It's not a compliment!"

"Only to idiots."

His fist reeled back so fast I almost didn't see it coming. Thankfully, the venom hadn't killed an iota of my reflexes. Cirello's punch came at me hard and fast and missed by a country mile as I ducked to the right and turned my body to one side. His fist crashed into the shower's concrete wall at full speed, and my now-dry ears enjoyed the wet crunch.

"Goddamnit!" Cirello said, pulling back a mangled fist while his adrenal glands flooded him with so much machismo his face was a blanket of white, hot rage with a hairy lip.

"Cirello! Don't!" Heinz said, reaching out, but too slow to stop it.

Cirello's left hand swung in a wide hook, straight for my jaw. I ducked, and he tried again, this time aiming for a body blow to crack my ribs. I slid on my heels and watched as his left hand banged into the faucet. Blood rained from fresh cuts and his face was white with pain. "I'm going to kill you!" he grunted in a whisper.

"No. You won't. Too many witnesses. You'd have to kill them all, and you look lazier than Charles Manson having other people do his dirty work." Heinz moved forward and I shook my head. It kept him in place. "Here's what you're going to do. You're going to take your partner and leave the party. Grab your clothes and just roll out. Tell everyone there was a car accident and his mangled hands were from stabbing the dashboard." I was relieved as hell that telling other people to lie wasn't in and of itself a lie, and pondered for the briefest of seconds on the philosophical quandaries of snake-venom truth serum before I remembered I was naked at a sex palace.

Cerillo staggered back, two limp wrists pointing at me. "Kill him, Heinz!"

Heinz looked at his partner, then me.

"Pretty sure killing me increases the bad news for you two. You'll have to murder these two ladies as witnesses. And then maybe some of your brothers in blue who think murdering women is bad mojo. Then you'll be forced to turn on each other when Internal Affairs goes ape. Or, and this is just a suggestion, given freely by a naked man dripping before you, you could go get that hand looked after, make up a great lie about beating a guy so bad your hands broke, and call it a night."

Heinz surveyed the whole situation like a far future computer tabulating probabilities on punch cards. He nodded at the door. "Let's go, Cirello." His partner fumed. "I'll make sure you see Nurse Lola."

The name made his eyes switch from rage to lust, then back again for one last dagger-stare at me. "Got your name, Brimstone. When we meet again, you'll be the one dragged to the ER."

"I doubt it," I said, honesty chugging wildly. "I hate violence. It's the lowest form of entertainment. But I've broken tougher critters than you. Including tonight." I smiled, because when you're that honest, anything else would be disrespectful.

The ladies' eyes went wide, mouths were covered by painted nails. And we all waited for Cirello's next move.

His eyes bunched. He huffed once in my general direction, and then he lifted his mangled hands. Tears pulsed out the sides of his lids. He grimaced with gooey spit on his teeth. No words came, but agony hissed within his breath as Heinz pulled him away, giving the illusion that our hero of the busted hands was one step away from beating me to death, regardless of the pain of fifteen broken bones, crushed knuckles, and ripped skin.

Cirello staggered out, Heinz pulling up the rear. They shuffled past my clothes.

The butt of the gun still hung out like a traffic light in the desert and Heinz kicked the pile, with a familiar clack on the ground.

Heinz looked back.

If I said anything, I'd reveal the pistol. If I said nothing, he'd look at the floor. So I did something that was not in the Gentleman's Guide to Proper Conduct. I grabbed Choker by the shoulders and mashed her mouth to mine.

She surprised me by biting mine, pulling it down, and then licking the damage. Svelte's taut breasts then stabbed my backside as her hands weaved across my chest and down my thigh.

"You're a real bastard, Brimstone," Heinz said as he dragged his partner out the far door.

If there hadn't been a tongue in my mouth, and a soft hand around my cock, I would have said, "Indeed."

CHAPTER 31

CHOKER AND SVELTE WORKED ME OVER LIKE A VETERAN TAG TEAM, and I didn't stop them. I had to work out the venom in me or the next time someone asked me a question I wouldn't just shove my foot in my mouth, but probably a gun. Which meant sweating out the venom, and keeping their mouths occupied, as well as mine. Wordless and primal sex. Not my forte, but my only route to finding Maxine and Nico.

I cupped each woman's ass, sliding my hand down the cracks and hearing the gasp in different tones. Choker had a quiet burr, making her breath sound like moans, and her mouth had the taste of Chesterfields and Spearmint with the flavor sucked dry. I was surprised at how much I loved the combination. Svelte was dirty and innocent with a sweet and high pitch, her tongue thick and strong, curling at the tip like a cresting tide.

I massaged each woman's ass. Each got two fingers making hard circles around their rear doors. "Let's do it with steam," I said, looking hard at Svelte, tapping her asshole so her breath hitched. "Get it going." I slid my hand away and she hissed, and then I pulled Choker to me. I grabbed both ass cheeks, and lifted her up. Then I shot Svelte the look of a coach who is tired of her shit. "Now."

She did as she was told, and I felt like a shitbird. But I couldn't handle questions. They would screw with the truth serum in my blood. I promised myself I'd attend a feminist rally with Svelte when this was all said and done, but right now I had to fuck my way out of the hole I'd dug.

I grabbed both of Choker's cheeks and lifted. She dutifully wrapped her arms around my neck and hitched her legs onto my hips. My cock was mashed against her sex, standing straight up as the hunger for each other thrummed. I walked backwards until my knees hit the sauna's bench and I sat with Choker, her smile electric, hands cupping my face. I licked my lip and she pulled me closer. We hovered an angel's hair apart, and desire was telling me to dive deep inside, pull her hair until those hard nipples arched skyward, and drive her steady and sure to a climax. But there were two to satiate. And I needed to be wordless.

I grabbed a fistful of Choker's hair, pushing her kiss deeper as she panted like an animal in heat, then pulled her head back. She gasped. "Oh fuck, I want you now."

She was good. I would have thought she was lying, given her day job. But the wetness clinging to my cock from her snatch was dewy, thick and honest.

I nodded, then lifted her until her ass was on the long bench. "Get on all fours."

She licked her smile. "Groovy."

Something hissed. A whiff of steam filled the air. Svelte had poured water on the red rocks. She saw us and bit her top lip and pulled it down with a gentle nibble.

I nodded from the end of the large bench where Choker sat, sweet cheeks in the air. "Back against the wall. Legs spread." She walked with the precision of a Russian ballerina, sat as instructed, legs spread wide, right on the bench, left on the floor. Choker's face and Svelte's sweet sex were only a tumbler apart when I caressed Choker's pussy lips from behind. Steam covered us with watery ghosts who stuck to our skin.

"God," Svelte said. "Watching this is so . . ."

I had no time for conversation, or else I was doomed. Quicker than I wanted, I dove into Choker. Her ass flexed as she moaned, but before a word was dropped from her lips her face was pushed onto Svelte's glistening clit.

Svelte hissed, then "ooh'd" as the daisy-chain I'd made worked into thrumming fashion while the sauna turned us into ghosts.

We found our rhythm. I ground an iteration from the Lost Kama Sutra known as the Bliss Hounds into Choker, a chugging position that made my thrusts go through one lover and into the next, Choker into Svelte, a ravenous cradling of passions and guttural desires that made our breathing sync with grunts and moans. We rocked like a runaway train, and Choker's whole body shook as I dug into both cheeks then did long, hard, slow strokes while she rocked back, each thrust complimented by driving her ass cheeks together until . . . I released, and passion ran its own speed and thundered from me. I gasped, then jammed her to a climax that rippled wet and fast into Svelte. Our chain sizzled with screams . . . then gasps . . . then there was only electric steam . . . I centered myself with thoughts of pillars, columns, and rods of iron as both women came at the same time: Choker's gushing voice filled Svelte, who sang one hallowed note of ecstasy.

I pressed Choker's cheeks together hard as I pulled out slow.

"That was mystic," she said with wet lips, looking up at Svelte.

Svelte was catching her breath, muscled stomach rippling with defined abs and above their outline her dark, hard nipples hung from sweet breasts. "Never felt that. Even on set. Even with Fulton."

If there was an erection-killer in my world, it was the psycho director Fulton who had destroyed Izzy's office. I wanted to ask a million questions. But there was no way to be sure if the venom was gone, if I sweated things out enough to be free. Did I want to test myself now?

I opened my mouth as Svelte looked at me with forlorn eyes. "Did you come?"

"No," I said. "I wanted to stay hard so you could both finish."

"That's not fair!" Choker said, rolling on to her ass and crossing her legs like a showgirl. "That was groovy as fuck and you're left hanging? Brimstone, we need to make this right."

"Yeah," Svelte said, sliding off the bench. "If word got out that we can't make you pop, well, that would hurt our reputation, right Haley?"

"Rachel's right," Choker's said, one hand on my face, pulling me closer. I loved their stage names more than the ones I'd tossed into my frontal cortex, Rachel the Svelte, Haley the Choker. "We take pride in our work." Rachel stood before me while Haley hooked her nails into my hair, her big lips curling into a smile. "Now we're going to make you lose it." She drove her mouth onto mine in a deep, long kiss, a starved energy in her eyes as her left hand ran its nails across my chest. She pulled back. "I could fuck your mouth all day," she said. "But look at Rachel."

Rachel took one step forward and parted my legs.

Then she grabbed by cock, hands moist and strong. "It's only fair I get a ride, too."

She turned around and fed me into her pussy as Haley nibbled my ear and let filth drop from her thick lips. "You're going to think of me as she fucks you." Our mouths clasped as Rachel began slow, grinding stokes and Haley drove her tongue deeper, trying to devour me, then whispered.

A shadowy and slick part of me awakened. The James Brimstone I'm not proud of. The one who liked orgies, and sloppy partners, and hedonistic palaces of flesh. A lost soul who conquered women as a means to compensate for that which he lacked. A bastard who would charm someone for a night's plea-sure by tricking them into thinking they were in love. A hedo-nist who would die in a Roman bath house when he got old and frail, because he planned to burn out all the candles before he hit forty, a guiltless creature of lust and abuse and selfish desires who craved dominance over others far more than the pleasure of the intimate. That James Brimstone swam in my blood and whis-pered back between the thrusts. The one who ran wild after Izzy said no . . .

Take them. Make them beg. Make them worship you. Make them slaves to your desire. Make them puppets to dance at your tune, fuck them until they bore you, toss them into the pits and replace them when they age or displease you, find a new harem to eat out your ass, suck you to oblivion, for the dark waters that run through you are limitless, fill them all until . . .

I pierced the creeping darkness of my shadowy self with one image.

Izzy. Legs crossed, slit of her pencil skirt high, tanned knee bumpy, pink blouse and white coat, and a smirk on her face as if to say "In all of your conquests, you still pine for that which you cannot have?" She re-crossed her legs.

"Yes," I hissed, then hooked my lips deep onto Haley and gripped Rachel's hard ass and began to pound, sucking in one and drilling the other, the picture of Izzy shaking her head as she undid one button from her blouse.

"Fuck!" Rachel screamed. "Oh fucking God!"

Haley screamed in my mouth. Because we were still one siz-zling chain of bliss. And when I came, it was Izzy burning in every cylinder of my guts and soul. And my release was not short. Not a gun shot. It was a scream of blood, lust and sacrifice against an idol who ignored its worshippers. I blasted thick and tight and they did, too, until there was nothing left but contractions, shud-ders, and the trenches of our fingers deep in each other's skin.

I pulled out with an ache, and Haley yanked herself from my mouth and gasped. "Whatever the fuck that was," she said. "If you can get it on film, you'll be a rich man."

"Thanks," I said, Izzy still fresh in my mind. I hoped that was a once-in-a-lifetime event. But what of the venom? I coughed. "You were both amazing."

Rachel's spine curved up and back as she turned and stretched, body moist with sweat and mist. "You're really good at this." Her voice shifted between bedroom soft and business sharp. "If you're done turning tricks for Terra, you'd have a future in this business."

I smiled, then stood, edging myself towards my trouser and gun. "You're too kind, but this is a young man's game."

"Not today, Daddy," Rachel said, sliding on the bench next to Haley, who had taken a stoic position by leaning her elbow on her knee and gripping her rich hair. "We were called in by Octavia for a last minute shoot. She's desperate for talent."

Two replacements for Maxine and Nico. I'd just made the beast with three backs with the stunt doubles of the woman I had lost. My afterglow took on a very rusty hue. "Well, what's the story about?"

They started giggling. "It's a gas," Haley said. "It's about a Roman Queen who uses her daughters against her enemies. Wild sex and then a horror show."

"Like the Grand Guignol," Rachel said.

"Here comes the theater princess again," Haley said, with some actual disdain. "You already rode him like a bull, Rach, you don't need to impress him."

Rachel looked at the ceiling in disgust, allowing me to grab my trousers and shove the gun into the shadow. I hated to leave it after my tussle with TV and his pet, but it would bring me more problems hanging out my backside on a movie lot. "It's not my fault you're uncultured, Haley, try reading a play instead of *Tiger*

Beat." Haley pouted and Rachel's harder stare dropped on me. "They are setting up for the climax tonight. Her two best seducers are put in a flesh pit. The queen sends in lover after lover to saitiate them and the first one to quit will be killed by the Queen's henchman, a masked gladiator."

"Maximus!" Haley said. "But the original Maximus got sick, like the two leads. Some bad fish on set or something. I ate before I came here."

"She gets most of her protein on set anyway," Rachel said.

Haley snarled. "I'm not the only one. Anyway, they need a Maximus and all the guys on set, well, a lot of them are hung like a jury, but they're . . ."

"Thin. Athletic. But not manly." Rachel's tone dropped a few degrees and damn if it didn't warm me up again. "You look like a gladiator. Fit, tough, solid. You got scars in nice places. You're built for rough things."

"Well, not that pretty face," Haley said. "God, sad eyes just make me want to fuck, you know?"

"You also have daddy issues, Miss Freud," Rachel said.

"That makes two of us."

"Anyway, if you're interested, we could take you to the makeup room and get you ready. Bet she hasn't had time to get a real gladiator."

A masked man in a blue film . . . there was no better way to get near Octavia.

But I needed to test something first.

"Ladies, I'm flattered, believe me. But, before I say yes, I just need to tell you something."

They both looked at me like cats.

"My real name is Horace Pisker." The lie pinched my nerves, and sweat itched as the fake name found its way off my lips . . . but it died down into a dull throb and not a stake in the heart. "Is it okay if I use my professional name, James Brimstone?"

They covered their mouths and giggled. "Horace?" Rachel said. "Oh God, that's my Uncle's name. Yeah, your secret's safe with us."

I whistled joy as the lie was accepted and the venom's worst bite was diluted.

Haley gripped one hand, Rachel the other. "C'mon, handsome," Haley said. "Let's get back into makeup so Octavia doesn't fire us all."

CHAPTER 32

THE FUSE ON MY RUSE WAS BURNING DOWN AS WE WALKED through the hallway toward the bathroom and away from the pool area, heading back upstairs. The grunts of Vice and Octavia's staff had finished. And Terra would likely sleep until morning, but TV was tough enough to wake up soon, and then the jig would be up. But I wasn't concerned with them. The only other person who had seen my face was Octavia.

We took the stairs to the main floor and the AC blasted hard enough to turn Haley and Rachel's nipples to dark diamonds. Octavia probably paid more in a month to cool this mansion than Hefner's water bill for the grotto, and the dark wood of the main floor spoke volumes: this was her palace, and all palaces are reflections of the mind of the owner. Someone grew up in New England pining to be part of the power elite who saw such dark tones as signs of class: light-sucking walls that put a premium on power being generated. Rachel and Haley pulled me along into the east wing, away from the apartments and kitchen into a larger hall that filled with other sounds. Electricity buzzed. "This where they make the movies?" I asked with pig ignorance.

"The movies are made everywhere," Rachel said, who clearly liked being the authority. "The sets for the final scene are outside, of course. Most of the costumes are upstairs because they needed room for the new soundstage below. Editing is up here, too." She nodded at a door that had a giant roman X. "Never seen that door open."

"I've never seen the editor."

"That's because Fulton was editing it."

I stifled the grimace. "Who's that?" Lies hurt, but it was a flicker of suffering compared to when the venom was hot.

"The . . . assistant director. He was working on this picture, but he got sick, too."

"We worked with him and Octavia on their last picture."

"What was that?"

Haley giggled. "Their version of *Taming of the Shrew*, but it got turned into *Gonzo Girl Can't be Tamed*. Thank god for Roger Corman." And they told me how Corman was the godfather of all these wonderful directors pushing the boundaries of love and sex and violence, and how he loved to work with women because they were eager and cheap, and how Octavia funded some of his work and met Fulton on set. They hit it off, he the angry vet who didn't care about anything but his art, and she . . . a producer with money to burn.

We passed by a dining room table full of broken chairs and tables; the sawdust that lingered in the air smelt angry and stinging. "Hard to believe she makes such good money from the movies."

"Well, her real money came from . . . electronics," Rachel said.

Haley snorted. "Just a bunch a rumors, Rach."

Rachel shrugged. "She is an electronics wizard."

Wizard. It was slang. But in my work slang was often literal. My short and curlies itched as I thought of fighting a woman with the power of Zeus. And lightning was a proud symbol of the Nazis. Jagged lightning like the scars on Nico's face. "What rumors?" I asked.

"Octavia made the first modern vibrator. The kind you can only get from secret catalogues. Not a massager. Not a toy. Built to keep women from going crazy."

I smiled, impressed with Rachel's dirty knowledge. Running with Edgar, you read a lot about madness. Not just Poe and Dostoyevsky, but the hard stuff. Freud and Jung. Both those geniuses were obsessed with women and madness, and how it related to women's sexual bliss. Hell, most men didn't believe a woman could have an orgasm, as elusive to find as a unicorn in a coal mine, but I found out different. Reading those books I learned men didn't know piss about a woman, how they moved, how they thought, how they felt, unless it was through the lens of man's cock. They never understood them on their own terms. They listened, but they didn't hear. After Izzy left, I went on a bender for women, all women, any woman, and while I'm not proud of how easy it could be being gifted with a face that was easy on the eyes, I soon craved giving women bliss, making that inner thunder rock her back and forth until her nerves sparked. Any man who gets off without his lady going wild is a tool, an amateur, and a rube. You make a woman come, you're providing a service. Vibrators were meant to beat us to the punch because, as good as I am with mouth, tongue, fingers, and cock, I can't vibrate worth a damn.

Haley snorted, then rubbed my hip. "So librarians and spinsters never have to leave home. I hate robots. Bet they spark and set your cooch on fire. Give me manhood any day."

The room ended in a T-section and we headed left. The hall widened, as if it to accommodate not just more people but freight. A fifty-year-old guy in a tight red golf shirt who was trying to look twenty with a wispy beard and thick brown hair down to his shoulders pushed a dolly. On it sat a white statue, a poor man's

David missing its arms and nose, bird shit on its head, carved out of plaster judging by the easy way he shoved. "Where the fuck have you two been? Octavia's waiting outside. We're doing the final scene as soon as lighting is up so I need you two in costume in five."

"We found a new gladiator, Bob!" Haley. "So keep your shirt on."

Bob was clearly depressed at the news, then he looked me over like I was a slab of bison hanging from a hook. "Where did you pick up this piece of action?" I bit my tongue to keep the truth in, then was amazed at how offended I felt to be discussed as if I was not there. Fast jabs of words nearly shot out my mouth to teach this sucker a lesson, but the meek shall inherit the earth and, one hoped, a gladiator costume. Verbal boxing would only get me thrown out of the ring.

Thankfully, Haley spoke enough for the both of us. "He's Terra's boy toy, and he lays down a mean rod, so unless you have someone else this buff I say James is our hero."

"James, huh?" Bob crooked his head to one side so a gold chain with a pentagram dropped down and hung, then swung. "Look a little bit older than most gladiators."

"He's in better shape than you, Bob," Haley said.

"Guess you like our Peaches?"

I smiled. "Among other things."

His head righted itself and a grin crept through his thin beard. "Alright. Costumes. Now. Go." We strode off. "Nice to be working with you, James."

I nodded, then carried on as Bob pushed the cart away.

"No way you like Bob," Haley said.

"The way we like each other?" Rachel said, slipping one hand around my other hip. "Let's not be sexist."

"Ha! It's not sexist. It's just different with girls."

"You mean women?"

They both hugged me a bit closer as we approached a wide set of double doors. The powdery smell of foundation, blush, and the stinging aroma of glitter and hair products sizzled some as the doors opened. A row of dressing room mirrors and lights covered one end of the room, a series of dressing room racks full of costumes, clothes and props filled the left: swords, helmets, sandals, more plaster statues of cracked Roman and Greek design. Not a flicker of magic could be tasted in the room . . .

But my jaw clenched all the same.

In the far mirror on the left of the dressing room desk, I saw the reflection of one of the actors. He was sitting stiff and proper, being brushed by a makeup artist. He wore nothing but a loin cloth around his waist. His eyes were shut. But they opened before I could think of a plan.

There was the crooked actor who played the priest at a con job funeral. The one who saw me and Nico at the diner when we almost got shot. The only one in this place that knew who I really was.

Two women's lives were at stake, and holding their fate was Chip Toledo.

CHAPTER 33

"GEMMA! WE FOUND A GLADIATOR!"

Haley's siren voice made everyone turn as they pulled me to the chair next to Chip, whose eyes tracked me across the mirror like a ghost trapped in a portrait.

Gemma was a fifty-year-old woman who wore her close to three hundred pounds like a queen. A long black blouse with hanging sleeves revealed snow-white skin. Her hair was big, bleach blonde, her lipstick brighter than an H-bomb blast, and the pancake upon her visage was thick enough to stop a bullet. Some might view Gemma as garish, but having worked in burlesque houses and more since I'd run from Oakland, I found it both commanding and worthy of respect in a world that spat at women who dared to grow older and bolder as they headed toward the grave.

But I said nothing charming or kind as I sat and avoided Chip's glare in my own mirror.

"Nice find, ladies," Gemma said, voice nasally high. "His face is pretty swollen."

"Which makes me authentic," I said.

"You have a name, gladiator?"

"Maximus," I said. Gemma and the girls laughed.

"He's got the job!" Gemma said. "Rach, Hale, go get changed and bring him his costume. I need to work fast." She grabbed a can of High-C that looked tiny in her fist and sipped from a lipstick-stained straw until the hollow grind of the empty can made her gasp. "Damn it. I need to stay cool, back in a flash."

Gemma waddled away on sandals that flipped and flopped as she shuffled to the opposite end of the counter, where a rack of coolers sat stacked upon each other.

So it was just me and Chip.

"Hey," he said.

"Hey."

"You . . . following me?"

I hadn't even thought of that. "No." I flared my eyes so I had his attention and then spoke quietly without moving my mouth. "I'm working a case. The girl I was with? She's now missing. Those responsible are here."

Chip sighed. "That's a relief, man. I was worried you were still pissed at me. But this makes a lot more sense than you hunting me down at a stag flick." He laughed. "Those pants clash with the James Brimstone I know!" Gemma's slap-shuffle sandals harkened her return as we watched her make a wide turn and walk back toward us.

I flared my eyes again. "I'm undercover," said my soundless mouth.

"Ah, gotcha!" Chip said, then winked.

Gemma arrived before I could make it clear to my handsome and idiotic colleague that his life was likely in danger. Oh well.

Gemma cracked the next Hi-C, plunked in a new straw and gave it a kiss until her cheeks were full. "Ahh, better." She squinted down at Chip. "Your eyes are still too . . . simple." She gripped an eyeliner pencil from a mug with the face of Frankenstein's monster and then did two hard lines under each of Chip's eyes. The application was done with a combination of precision and *laissez-faire* mastery from years of stabbing people's skin with color. "Perfect," she purred. "Now go and hit your mark while I work over our Spartacus."

Chip stood up and his countenance shifted into what I can only call "performance mode," where Chip assumed a new character—which was Chip-plus-grimacing. "Thanks, Gemma. See what you can do about this guy's face. He looks old enough to play my dad!"

And I'll be damned if that snide comment wasn't the finest performance I'd ever seen from the one and only Chip Toledo.

"Don't listen to him, beautiful," Gemma said, grabbing a yellow sponge dabbed with flesh-toned color. "He'll be lucky to be half as handsome when he's your age."

"Flattery will get you everywhere," I said, and we both smiled as she began to daub my chest.

"My, your face has seen some trouble, huh? And your body has been to a few crash-up derbies, too."

"I've got a few hard miles on me," I said, scanning the rest of the room. Nothing. No taste of magic. No trace of Maxine, lost somewhere in this madhouse of sex and celluloid, and not a whiff of Nico.

"Any tattoos I should know about?" Gemma asked, smiling with a dark, arched eyebrow. "You know, down under?"

I smiled. "No identifying marks or ink." None that could be seen. The deepest scar Edgar drove into me, his gift for twenty years of service, was not visible to the naked eye. A hex on my heart. What was known to the Greeks as Aphrodite's Tear. *No spell, no hex, no sigil, and no potion will charm you to be that which you are not. Truth venom may hold you to its promise for a time, but it will fade. But no enchantment on your nature can force you to love, worship, serve other people's needs. Even my own.*

It would have been a sweeter gift if I hadn't been tortured in order to receive the tear through a hole Edgar ripped in my aura while I was lost in a nightmare dreamscape too hellish for my waking mind to conjure. Such torture remained invisible to all but me.

"He's back!"

A girl with blue bellbottoms had flown through the double doors, and Rachel and Haley approached wearing matching white and purple loincloths, holding leather straps and a grim, black metal mask in their hand.

"Who, Cheryl?" Haley said.

"Fulton! Fulton's back!"

CHAPTER 34

ELECTRICITY SEEMED TO INFUSE THE ROOM. BODIES MOVED WITH renewed precision and determination. Rachel and Haley plopped down their costumes and ran outside without turning back or saying goodbye. The only one who moved at regular speed was Gemma: because even my heart was racing knowing that berserker was now back in a contained space.

"So the captain returns to his ship," Gemma snorted, dabbing the last coat of skin-colored liquid that suffocated my flesh. "How courageous."

"What do you mean?"

Gemma shrugged, knowing she'd just talked outside of the coven. "When our stars took a powder, he gunned out of here like a madman behind the wheel of his Ferrari. Directors, what men. Am I right?"

I smiled. "I'm just glad for the work."

"All scabs are!" she said with a chuckle, then grabbed a mask. "Before I put the dark around your eyes, let's see how this fits. You have a pretty good-sized melon, so we may need a different model."

The thud of boots approached. Cheryl ran to the far door with a sign above saying "MAIN SET."

"Places! Everyone, places! Our hero has returned." Anyone who'd been in a war knew that all men can be soldiers, good or bad, but being a soldier never de facto made any man a hero.

Gemma handed the mask to me and it nearly broke my wrist. The sucker weighed more than a golden skull and smelled like old sweat and rust. Two big slits for the eyes, a circle of punctured holes for my mouth. Worn leather straps fastened it to the back of the head. As soon I brought it close I knew was too small.

In the mirror reflection of the double doors, Fulton popped into the room and I tasted the faint lash of magic like a leech falling off his catch as I sucked in my cheeks and shoved on the mask.

Breath whooshed around my face like a squall made of old meat and three women's tongues: smoky, sweet, and sour. I fastened the mask hard and fast and looked back in the mirror.

Nothing. But the leechy taste of his rage was a calling card.

"Who the *fuck* is this guy?

Behind Gemma, Fulton hissed breath with a low and nasal refrain. He hadn't said many words while he was pounding Izzy's door to shreds, so I was surprised his vocal chords wheezed and his voice was high. He filled the mirror. "I'd remember a body like this one."

Fulton looked like hammered shit. His wide face was ghost pale, the gold-rimmed sunglasses he wore matched his green army vest as hallmarks of his lost days in 'Nam. The muscles in his arms were hard, defined. His pallor was so corpselike I wondered if he'd sweated out all his liquid and replaced it with formaldehyde. But he looked smaller. Half of the juggernaut I'd tussled with in the vet's clinic. And yet, no taste of magic.

"Who the fuck are you?"

But still a first class asshole.

Fear cooled to an easy breeze in my guts as a theory was soon to be tested: I assumed Fulton's jacked-out attacks and creeping were about Nico. Some men, when charmed or enchanted, are given to heightened senses of smell and can track like a beast in the urban jungle. As soon as I said a name, any name, he'd pounce.

"A friend of Chip Toledo," I said. It wasn't so much a lie as an exaggeration of a fact.

"Do I fucking know who that is?" Fulton said. "Who are you and why do you think you can come on to my set, grab one of the most important roles of my film, and think you can get away with it?"

Gemma stood back, knowing well and good to leave this maniac to his mania.

"My name is James Summers," I said, unable to think of anything more clever than the last name of the author who drove me here. "I'm . . . I'm scab labor."

Fulton growled. "Scabs on my set." He gripped the back of my chair and it shook with his anger.

"Fulton!" Cheryl cried. "Lighting outside is perfect. We're ready for the gladiator scene!"

Shaking gave way to a tight calm. Fulton leaned down until his mutton chops scratched my mask with the sound of churning blades. "Summers, you make my day any worse than it is, and I will fill this mask with crazy glue and pound it on your face with a nine-pound hammer. Test me, kid. Test me and I'll read the riot act into your flesh. Now get off those idiot pants and get on set before I rip you a new one."

He shoved himself back so hard I was tossed into the makeup mirror, mask-first. A crack snapped across the mirror's skin like lightning. In the crackled reflection, Fulton stormed off without once looking back.

But I could taste it. Acrid, bitter, and twisted, but it was magic. A flicker of the rage-magic I'd tasted at Izzy's place.

Gemma's face crinkled. "Oh, God, you're a mess." She meant the dozen or so colors that had ruined the masterpiece of smooth-colored skin on my chest. Fulton's demonstration of dominance left me stained with makeup from the counter. "Better start from the top."

Gemma went back to work dabbing me to perfection, but my breathing was easy and sharp.

Fulton hadn't tracked me to Izzy's because of Nico's scent or presence on my skin. That would have led him to her first. Not me.

So, had Fulton had been looking for *me?*

Which means someone tipped him off that I was on the case. Me, James Brimstone. Someone turned this shell-shocked maniac into an ICBM looking for yours truly and then told him where to hunt. I keep my private life goddamn private, and my past is as locked up as Edgar's coffin.

Someone had seen me with Nico. The same someone who had dragged her away from the motel. Because it was hard to believe she vanished on her own.

Gemma gripped my face "Okay, handsome. He *was* right about those slacks."

Pants off, loincloth on, I was halfway into my last sandal when someone screamed. "Places!"

Then I followed the last of the set hands racing toward vast double-doors. They opened to the nightscape outside the mansion, to the backyard, heading toward the scene of the crime.

CHAPTER 35

THE WIND SMELLED OF OCTOBER, BUT THE HEAT WAS PURE L.A., AND being outside made me feel alive, vulnerable, and humble.

Octavia's back yard wasn't a backyard: it was an outdoor movie lot an inch smaller than a football field, covered in palm trees that cut the distant sound of the highway to a magnetic hum, and littered with tents, lights, and cameras in sections cut to look like Roman ruins and edifices: Now it was obvious why no one complained about the Porn Queen next door: she owned the block I'd drove up, put up houses, and had one massive back yard for filming in the Valley without having to go out for a shoot. Stadium lights blared down on the scene of the action, one house over.

Night air braced on the fistful of items that amounted to my costume, one without a gun, without cards, without an anting-anting. The mask echoed my breathing like a dirty masher practicing for a crank call as I hustled toward where the stadium lights burned down: a pit, surrounded by giant torches like it was a Tiki Party. Three cameras and dozens of stagehands circled the mouth. At the far end, a canopy had been built and painted black and silver. Inside upon a gaudy fool's gold throne sat Octavia. A producer starring in her own shows was the height of narcissism, but in terms of appeal I could see it. She possessed a regal bearing, was beautiful for her age, and imperial in her countenance. Her faux throne was about as Roman as a candle. Rachel and Haley flanked her in thin purple robes, two different kinds of beautiful heightened by touches of eyeliner, eye shadow, hair in curly waves.

A filthy taste of magic bristled in the night air. Metallic and sour, and something foul and fetid, magic twisted, turned, brutalized. The taste of ruin among these faux columns and artifacts. I tried to swallow and almost gagged.

Fulton's vested back was facing me as I walked toward the set, but his voice was loud. "We are *not* doing this all night. One take, one time, that's it." He pulled his head away and barked more instructions for how he wanted the light, how he wanted the shadows. "Where the fuck is my new gladiator?"

I jogged toward the pit, but one eye stayed on Octavia, who glared into the pit, head nodding as if approving some human chess match. She was flanked by pages and crew and younger makeup artists with dirty blonde hair. Getting to her would not be easy. "Here I am, sir," I said meekly.

Fulton pulled himself from the film camera's eye, grabbed my shoulder, then tossed me into the pit. "Then fall, idiot."

Tarzan Jane had warned me on how best to take a "bump" in a wrestling match: "It's physics, kiddo, just spread out your arms to spread out the impact. Land like you're on a cross."

The earth smacked my back as I shot my arms out. The thudding pain made me wonder if TJ was playing a gag, or just made of sterner stuff. I coughed, then shook off the pain from hitting clay and dirt.

"Nice crash landing, dummy. But if you're done playing Jesus," Fulton said, "get off your ass and take your mark."

As I pulled myself up like Frankenstein's monster, I realized he'd said "gladiator." Not gladiators. And traditionally, when gladiators weren't fighting each other, they fought . . .

Fulton growled. "Where the hell is my snake?"

Oh God.

"And where the fuck is TV? It's his damn pet."

Ah, shit.

I wiped dirt off as PAs scrambled and Fulton tore off his vest. "Fuck it. If that rodent can't be here, he can't dictate the script. His was the one that fucked us over this morning." A collective hush ran through the crew. "And unlike all of you fuckers, I fucking went out and looked for the fucking girls. They are gone and ain't fucking coming back." Meaning Fulton was either lying or didn't know that Maxine was somewhere on this set. But his hunting for Nico had led him to me, perhaps.

"They ain't coming back," he repeated, as if lost in thought. And a glazed countenance flashed over his face like being hit with splash of wax. It burned away with the scrunched anger that was his normal mug. "And it is my fucking movie. Somebody get me a helmet and a loincloth! And Greg? You're on camera one. Do not fuck up the exposure or I will tear off your arm and beat you with it." He tore off his boots and trousers. "Now listen up, here's the scene. Fuck the idea of them pining for one guy and the Queen sentencing him to death with the cobra. And fuck Terra for being late. Octavia's the queen now. Let's get this shit going." It was not a cobra that I had ripped the head off of, making it clear that Fulton was not a driving force behind the picture or this sorcery at play. "The two pussy princesses have picked different gladiators instead of fighting over the same one."

"Wasn't that originally going to be Riley?" said Greg at the camera.

"That dumb fuck?" Fulton screamed and Greg shivered. "He's a dick with a pulse and never seen combat. Now listen. One of the pussies likes the masked guy, the other likes me. We'll fight until the scab wins, the Queen calls for archers to kill, and the pussy sisters kill their mom and take their prize. Sound jake?" He looked around.

The crew grunted agreement to this Roman atrocity featuring sister incest instead of an Oedipal complex, but it made my shit itch. And calling women pussies was being a first-class shithook.

"Groovy."

A minute later, Fulton was in a mask, too. It had a bladed top, like a sideways metal Mohawk, with a visor instead of eyeholes, so he could see far better than I when it came to the periphery. There were no mouth holes, though, so he probably tasted metal instead of mud, sweat, and old spit. Fulton didn't ask anyone to shove him into the pit, but slid down the dirty side feet-first as if skiing down a dirty mountainside in sandals.

His presence began to leak more magic, primal and unnerving. He paced back and forth, riling up his own anger, his shadow long in the orange torchlight. The shadow pointed at me with a jagged finger. "Your job, scab, is to take a beating until the very end, when you get a lucky punch in and win. That's the story. David and Goliath. Simple as dirt. When I fall, raise your hands in victory, I yell cut, and then Riley the stunt cock can get to work with the cunt twins up there. Can you follow?"

I nodded, but hearing him use the C word turned my hands to stone.

Fulton barked orders about lights, camera gauges, and mics, and we became washed in a mix of tiki-flame illumination and modern blasts from the open-face and Fresnel lights. Shadows grew as I paced back and forth. "Whatever happens, Josh," Fulton screamed, "do not stop rolling. We are using everything in this scene. No second take. Only going forward. We don't have time for anything else. And the crowd, you better roar. You got that?"

"Yes, Fulton," came nervous young voices from up top.

"That didn't sound like a roar," he barked as if this was his first day as drill sergeant in boot camp. An agitated roar followed. "Let's finish it." He turned to look at me. "Once and for all. ACTION!"

CHAPTER 36

AND THEN HIS SHOULDER CHARGED INTO MY GUTS AS HE PLOWED ME into the mud wall.

Above me and below the night sky the whirl and sizzle of camera and light blended with the strange screeches of women and a handful of men. I stole a glance while breathing out the pain. Around the lip of the pit like rows of jagged teeth were beautiful women and men. They were punctuated by black cameras and stage lights like a jumble of blistering eyes and dark orbs, a monstrous spider gazing upon two flies in its web that fought each other knowing all victories were doomed.

At the crest stood Octavia, purple robe fluttering over the lip, legs as white as bone.

Dirt hugged my back, crumbling over my shoulders as Fulton pulled back for a haymaker. My knees dropped as his fist cut the air. A shower of dirt filled the eyeholes as he yanked out his fist. "Good!" he said. "Keep dodging until I say stop."

I smiled with dirt in my mouth. "My pleasure."

Fulton's boxing skills shut the lock on my smart-ass mouth. Army-trained, he was jabbing and holding his body to the side like a pro, exactly like a Thracian gladiator would not. He mixed up his combos to keep me on my toes, and I got tagged a few times in the ribs so hard it strained my lungs as I fought to get another breath. He was picking me apart and toying with me like a bully. I was thrilled it was being filmed for posterity.

Because I let him hit spots. Spots that were tough. My shoulder. My pec. He thought bruises were victories and was getting cocky. A left cross sliced toward me and I pulled back in time to smell the blood and dirt from his hand where he'd cut his knuckles on my bones and flesh, an invitation to sepsis courtesy of me.

"Good," he said, breathing ragged. "You dance like a faggot! Keep it up!"

Spasms of fists, knees, and swinging backhands revealed something else: he wasn't just a boxer. His stance changed, hugging the earth with his toes . . . and before I knew it Fulton was a blizzard of chops, kicks, knees . . . Karate time! A Chop Suey of martial arts that white guys seldom know.

"Now you're scared," he said as I pulled away from a claw against my masked face. "I can see it in your eyes. Good. It's on camera. Now I want you to fight, like your life depends on it."

Fulton lunged, clawing for my neck, and I side stepped and pinwheeled my forearm to keep his killing hands away. Momentum had him stagger in the pit and dive both hands into the wall of dirt. "Faggot," he said again, tearing himself from the wall and pointing at me. "Come and get what's coming to you!"

I desperately wanted to suggest that Fulton's ire at men who liked men was probably a deep-seated resentment against his own nature, as Oscar Wilde put it, and that if anyone should champion a Roman lifestyle and Greek view of love, it was him. Instead, I ran around the pit backwards while his rage grew with the chase.

"Stand still, fucker!"

Fulton launched himself like an angry football and crashed so hard into my guts I doubled over, but not before grasping him in a hug and spinning so when we crashed, it would be him on his back.

The impact knocked out his air and jutted his visor so all I saw was a slit full of darkness. "How's this?" I said, driving my knees on his shoulder.

"You're fucking with the wrong monster," he said, his voice gruff and low. "Get off of me."

I slapped him once, hard, shaking the mask like a gong. "I thought Davey was supposed to beat Goliath."

"Get off!" He flailed, so I patted his sternum with a baby punch that looked as lousy as a punch-drunk brawl in skid row, but it snapped pain through his nervous system and held him still.

"That's a nerve punch I learned from a man who could kill a gang of Green Berets before his morning soup. But don't worry, I'll keep up appearances." I gripped his wrists, then had his dead fist punch me to the side. I rolled him on top of me so we could keep fighting and have some alone time while Octavia oversaw the rising tide of her movie.

I smashed my mask against his and drove it down so I could see through the visor to his bloodshot eyes. "Where is Maxine?" I said.

His pupils dilated. "Who the fuck are you?"

"Answer my question, Fulton," I said, smashing his fists against my ribs as I mock groaned. "And Nico. Where are they? Tell me, and I'll let you walk out of this pit without a scratch."

His eyes went wide and loose with terror. "You . . . you're the detective . . ."

"I've been called worse by better. Now, tell me where they are. I know they're here. Where? And what did you do with Nico?"

Her name slapped him. "You have no idea what you're fucking with."

I drove an elbow into his ribs, hard enough to bruise with the promise to break if he laughed too hard. "Neither do you."

Above, the roar of the crowd was dying. "Fans are getting bored," I said. "Guess you better tell me now before I knock you out. Where are Maxine and Nico?"

At Nico's name, laughter came out of those eyes as his pupils twisted into red Cheerios. "You . . . you're fighting in your own grave! Ha! HAHAHAHAHA!"

That should have been a warning, but the movement was overwhelmed by the strip of magic touching my tongue: and in a hair-trigger second, I felt darkness ripple through Fulton like the first tremor of the End of Days.

Then his forearm wrenched itself from the earth and bashed me into the dirt. High above, lightning crackled against the black sky. A storm wasn't coming, it was being born. I thought all of this while on my back, seething from pain and holding ribs that I'd protected with my right arm—the right arm that currently felt stuffed with cotton drenched in Novocain.

Raindrops smacked me at strange intervals. A Morse code from above that clearly said "Well, Brimstone, this time you're fucked." Fulton seemed to gain mass as his arms raised, hands punching the sky, teeth thick and hungry for death.

"GRAAR!"

Ever see a strong man hit the high striker at the carnival? Shooting the puck right at the bell? Well, I was the puck, and the slippery dirt wall was the bell. Fulton dropped his arms and kicked me like an army sack of dirty laundry, and pain from every ounce of this godforsaken day snapped open: my cheeks, my chest, my hands, and worse.

I flew across the pit. I landed to find another kick crashing into my guts and propelling me towards the far mud wall. I'd need an encyclopedia to keep up with all the variety of shitty I felt when I hit the pit floor with rain on my back. Steps away, Fulton seethed, muscles rippling with a dark fury, and now the taste of magic was puke in my mouth. With both hands he grabbed his helmet and tore it apart. The face it revealed had analogues with Scottish warriors covered in woad, or berserkers high on blood-lust and belladonna. His body seemed to have gained at least fifty pounds of angry menace since I'd hit the pit.

Through the hazy pain, I managed to be grateful Fulton wasn't shooting his mouth off about who I was. Just in time for him to growl "BRIMSTONE," ruining my anonymity.

He sprang like a wolf with paws up. I sucked in pain and pulled my knees in tight before launching them at his descending solar plexus: right at the pit of his stomach.

My feet jammed in there, heels first, and hit muscle hard as an oak desk. Shock bolted through my shins, but the impact of his momentum and my force also jarred Fulton enough that he staggered back. Enough time for me to kip up . . . though not time to plan any more offense. Rain thickened as the situation soured.

Fulton's Karate Time fighting style was half Special Forces kill-centric move sets, all murder and no philosophy, plus the disposition of a bear after it was stung by a thousand wasps. Fury-fed punches and a flurry of ax kicks kept me bouncing around a pit that was turning into the chocolate milk of the grave beneath our feet, dodging as his berserker heart pumped him forward, the crowd roaring as if it was all part of the show. And he was winning.

Jabs stung my ribs and face, I blocked kicks with my fore-arms, and my bruises got bruises. Fulton cut like a butcher who had just started his day shift and had something to prove. My blocks sagged, my dodges cut too close, but his pace was still full rage. Normally a man would tire with all this exertion, but whatever magic was in him was like a perpetual motion machine. If I didn't attack, this pit would be my grave.

Thankfully, rage turns men stupid.

He clasped me in a bear hug, the dumbest offensive move in the history of violence, but Fulton's strength at crushing the wind out of me did a good job at trying to make it a contender.

Up close and personal, his face was all teeth and red Cheerio eyes. The same berserker who had crushed Izzy's office, who had probably torn Nico from her room, was back. All Hyde, no Jekyll. He roared with wide mouth and eyes, locking my arms at their side, lifting me from the ground, crushing my kidneys with my own arms and leaving his noggin exposed.

Jaw loose to absorb the impact, I drove my masked forehead into Fulton's. The first time, I grunted more than he did. The second time, he actually stretched my back out so that my spine wanted to shoot through my neck. For the third, I drove down and pressed hard until the roaring maniac's shit breath gargled some of the blood that was leaking into his mouth from his crunched nose.

His arms broke off their assault on my shaking rib cage long enough that my arms could slip out and my feet could touch terra firma before he wrenched me again. So I started feeding him enough elbow sandwiches to stuff a hippo. The last one caught him in the throat. Finally, those killing arms were off me, and his big mitts were around his throat. Gasping, trying to dislodge his maladjusted Adam's apple, Fulton stumbled back from me. His face was a half-chewed ham sandwich with too much ketchup.

Time for more offense.

I attacked from the side, jabbed three times. Each shot was knocked away by heavy hands, but they weren't meant to connect. Hit, run, making him move. Make him feel weak in his strong body. Fear sets in. Bad ideas form. Especially for a guy who was all about offense.

A killer straight right that would knock the earth off its axis came in like a telegraphed message of my own imminent death. I slid away from it, snaked my arm across his, and let his momentum carry him forward as I curled around his back and secured his neck in a blood choke. This little move was a home run. Pulling back, I wrapped my legs around his guts and sunk in my arms like a python. Rain smacked us both as I tried to crush the larynx of a madman. It was only a matter of time—until both meaty hands gripped my masked skull and started to squeeze. The world blotted out into a haze of red mosquitoes floating through my vision. The strength of those hands could have crushed God's balls. My ears popped, eyes crushed closer together, jaw about to snap. He was out-crushing me.

And I heard Edgar laugh.

Poor James! Such a softie now. A pretend gentleman who forgot what he learned on the streets of Oakland, where the first rule is: the street ain't fair.

My internal lights flickered against the encroaching abyss. There was Nico, Maxine. And I saw the dead . . . hungry eyes of darkness, awaiting my arrival.

Screams from the primordial goo of my brain surged forth. My hands clawed onto Fulton's face with malicious intent and accuracy, muscle memory from Fuji's training and the countless times I'd fought for my life in alleys, rail yards, and 'bo camps across this violent country, childhood memories etched in blood and horror, a skill set of maiming and mayhem unleashed.

The fingers of my right hand dove into the jelly of Fulton's left eye socket, pushing hard and going knuckle deep. Then, they clasped and yanked.

Lightning cascaded and thunder followed, as a shriek shot out of Fulton's mouth with shotgun impact. He dropped and I landed on my feet. I raised my hand to the crowd and showed them the eyeball, the strands of viscera wrapped around my bruised forearm. Fulton bucked like a bronco and tossed me against the dirt and mud walls that were covering my skin with layers of filth. He ran around the pit, hands over his face, screaming like a feral child until he collapsed on his knees. I picked myself up, unable to drop the eye, hand locked with violence.

Above, the ring of onlookers cast a disturbing pall. Their faces were pure deadpan. Even Haley and Rachel had the emotional reflection of two porcelain dolls. Even in the gore, rain, and mud, I could taste the foul magic.

And at the lip, arms crossed, face full of imperial indignity, stood Octavia.

"Where are Nico and Maxine?"

She grimaced. "Who *are* you?"

With a shaking left hand, I tore the laces off my mask. It smacked mud. Rain tagged the scraps, bruises and wounds on my raw face as I looked up, hand still in a fist, eye dangling. "My name is James Brimstone." Night silence held my name. "Private Eye. You will hand over both women to me. Now. Or I won't be responsible for what happens next." Of course, I was a half-naked man in a pit with an eyeball tied around two fingers, so my threat sounded better than reality would allow. But, when in doubt, posture. "And hurry up."

Octavia smiled, beautiful and vicious. "You desire to see our star?"

"Now."

"As you wish."

Octavia took a step back from the lip of the pit, casting her gaze like a rusty school marm made of disapproval and royal indignation.

The rains eased. The taste of magic vanished from my tongue like a blacked-out memory. I have loved that taste of absence for as long as I can remember. It was among the greatest flavors of my life, one that I was banking would get richer the further away I ran from Edgar.

Right now, the absence tasted of lesions, absences and openings that were not natural.

While Fulton quivered on the mud floor, I waited. And then I heard it. Soft sneakers on grass, coming close.

Under the set lights, a familiar hooded figure stood, first glimpsed leaning upon my office door, last seen at a motel.

Two thin hands pulled back the hood.

Nico, face full of scars, glared down. "James."

"Nico? Are you okay?"

I've seen more horrors in my time than most grindhouse theaters combined, but nothing prepared me for what dropped next.

Her scars rippled, and then undid themselves as if they were zippers closing upon themselves. "My name is Tabitha Vance."

The last name punched me like a comet. Fulton's eye slid down and dropped from my fist.

"Daughter of Edgar. The man you murdered."

My jaw hung like a rube watching a geek show, so I barely registered as Nico . . . Tabitha . . . hexed the air with a finger. Fulton pulled himself out of the fetal position like a Jack in the Box. His haymaker hit my temple with the force of God, and I could not take my eyes off the woman whose hands danced in the air with magic I couldn't taste, playing Fulton like a heavyweight puppet until the punch landed and I went crashing into the dark.

CHAPTER 37

ONCE UPON A TIME, BEING KNOCKED OUT WAS A RELIEF. A PAUSE ON the world. A space in between the land of the living and the great unknown. If I were more of a transcendentalist poet, I'd romanticize this gutter as something darkly fascinating, a seductive caress of night before morning broke, the swoon of gothic romance. Live long enough, though, and the swoon was pregnant with shits, critters, and kin of your dirty past, clawing at you, mouths of acid eating a path through the darkness to sup on your guts and more.

I won't tell you what hid in my swoon, but rest assured it was no land of milk and honey or peace and tranquility, but a blighted planet of horrors and screams.

When water smacked my face and tore me away, I wasn't just relived. I was grateful. Grateful that I wasn't swooning, and grateful it wasn't Nazi ice water. "Thank you," I muttered, half-delirious. Spit and water dribbled down my sore chin. One drip later, a hand cracked against my face, and the spray followed my face as it cracked to the side. Burning torches and rain made my nose itch as I pulled my head up . . . and felt my hands high above me.

"Awake, James Brimstone."

My hands were tied tight above me, my heels taking almost all the pressure of my weight, burlap rope burning my wrists and ankle. I was tied to some kind of metal stake, painfully straight and with no give. I was elevated, a few heads taller than the crowd of onlookers. About ten yards away was the pit, the mansion a black hole down the back yard. Everyone's look was glazed and hard, even the one-eyed beast Fulton, who wore a red bandana over his gaping eye socket.

Minus the two before me. Ice blue and bright. Nico . . . Tabitha was floating, or so it seemed. Her face shorn of the violent mauling that had hooked my sympathies. Without the scars, it would be safe to say she was among the most beautiful things I'd seen walk the earth, a rare beauty that held breaths and possibilities as it walked by, neither virgin nor slut, neither farm girl nor city posh, as if you could see what you wanted in that beauty . . . without her scars, she was a reflective pool of desire.

"Nico," I said.

Another crack of her hand and fresh blood and sweat slapped me to my left.

"Tabitha Vance," she said, with a burr in her voice, still floating eye level. "And don't you forget it."

Pain shimmered as I opened my eyes, staring to my left.

Hanging from another pole was the object of my failed quest. Her frail and beautiful body was covered with a thin green sash, ankles and wrists tied like mine, a mane of red hair covering the face I'd seen on a box of detergent.

"Maxine," I whispered.

Tabitha cackled and slapped me even harder with the palm of her hand and I swear my molars shook two inches away from my gums before snapping back in place. "Yes. Your *cherchez la femme* is finally over, Brimstone. You win, you fucking loser." I winced, tucking my chin. She laughed with enough malice to make a sadist cry. I looked down . . . she wasn't floating. Her sandaled feet stood upon someone's back. Judging by the purple gown and black heels shining in the torchlight, it was Octavia. Just in case it wasn't clear who was really running this show.

Her finger stabbed me under the chin and brought my eyes back to her level. "Uh-uh, can't have you fading into the darkness just yet. I want you to bear witness to my victory—or, should I say my triumph? Do you like that better, Octavia?" she said to her human footstool. "A triumph?"

"Yes, Tabitha," the older woman said, voice waving with the stress of keeping her master balanced. "It's lovely."

"And fitting," Tabitha said, craning her head and regarding me as one would a crippled bird. "Just like you, playing into my hands. The old fashioned way." Mock concern stretched across her face. "Aww. Is the little detective having troubling piecing together the clues? Honestly, Brimstone, everything about you is sad. Which makes you being the heir to father's fortune even more insulting."

Her words were typewriting on my skull, and my winces were general, hiding the reflexive facial ticks you'd ascribe to someone realizing a hard truth that was in the air . . . She claimed to be Edgar's daughter. And she thought Edgar was dead. "Heir?"

Her small hand vice-gripped my cheeks like talons. "Don't play coy, don't play stupid, and don't play ignorant. Or I will rip your jaw off and feed you to my brood."

". . . Tabitha, I don't know what you're talking about."

She shoved my head away. "Of course you don't. You don't understand anything. Which is why father's . . . investment in you is vexing."

That made two of us. Edgar *never*, and I mean, *never* said he had any children. I assumed he had none, and figured picking me as an apprentice was some sorta last ditch chance at having a family, albeit a family of master and slave. And yet, here was a twenty-year-old creature of his lineage. Or, at least a creature of his who looked twenty.

Her disdained countenance hardened. "He never told you about me at all, did he? Oh God, don't give me that look, James. I'm reading your pretty face, not your third-rate-mind. Father kept you ignorant so you would do his bidding without questions. Just like me. How fucking droll." Lightning crackled against a ink-black sky. "Time for the climax, James." She stabbed her heel into Octavia, and the old vibrator millionaire started a slow march toward Maxine, tied to the post beside me. "I should thank you, though. You danced so well on my string."

My wrists grooved in small circles to gauge the thickness of my bindings

"I'd heard father had made you . . . immune to most charms. Aphrodite's Tear, I suspect. A powerful gift for an idiot."

The bindings bit hard and sent rivulets of blood down my forearm. Unless I wanted to lose both hands, this was a no go.

"Wasting his time on some carnival rube," she said, approaching Maxine, voice smooth and frustrated. "A mark from Oakland, pulled by his cock to save a wittle girl with wittle scars on her wittle face. Like some dime novel hero." She spat on Octavia's back. "Pathetic."

Dime novel? Shit, I was older than her apparent age by two decades, but I'd never read dime novels. How old WAS she? I dug my fingers into the rope and started to pinch with my nails. The strength in my digits was greater than most, but even for me, this would need time that was draining out by the second. "Nico . . . *Tabitha*, listen, please. What you're messing with is big. Bigger than Edgar. This isn't even magic, but an abomination."

"Fulton?" she said. "Make it hard for him to talk."

The one-eyed monster stalked over. I sucked in a deep breath and braced myself to exhale the impact and avoid what Edgar called Houdini's fate. Instead of a gut shot, I got a straight right into my groin. White pain flashed across my eyes. Bowels loosened. Guts became a typhoon. Agony ate its way up my spine like a school of piranhas, and a return to Blackout, USA seemed in the cards until I exhaled hard. The sharp edges dulled but I knew I wouldn't be telling any Cock and Bull stories for a long time, unless it was about Hemingway's Jake Barnes, whose plight I felt in my numb nuts. My chin stabbed my chest, breath seething with spit.

"What I am doing is my family's true business," Tabitha said. "A business you tried to steal."

I shook my head but no words came, fingers still digging into the rope.

She stood before Maxine, green dress wet and clinging to her breasts with desperation. Tabitha's hands forked into Maxine's red hair and lifted it from what I gathered was drugged exhaustion. Her eyes were glassy, hollow, and her forearms were covered in stinging scars: sigils cut into the flesh . . . blurry still, but I knew their intent: to control. "When father died," she said, "I was ready to reclaim the House of Vance for myself. I had charmed all of these . . . dolls . . . these puppets of desperation on the edge of Hollywood. I brought them here to be tendrils of my will so that I could birth a creature that would let my influence grow." She caressed Maxine's face. "You were to be my vessel for the creature . . . but I wasn't strong enough to birth it alone. Oh, Maxine. I'm so sorry." She pressed her lips to Maxine's gaping mouth and plunged in a corkscrew kiss that made fresh agony down below. She pulled back while suckling Maxine's tongue. "And you ran, pretty thing."

Tabitha slapped Maxine's face hard enough her drugged eyes opened. "After scarring me." Another slap. "As if you had the right to hurt your master." Another one and Maxine whimpered, eyes now open but dull as a caveman's art. "But those scars were inspiring, too." She rubbed Maxine's sex and the poor girl went rigid and Tabitha licked her teeth. "I could use my father's idiot servant to get what I wanted. But he'd need a story. A sad one.

Because James Brimstone is a rube for the pathetic things of this world, and you'd made me one." Her hand rubbed faster, hard, and Maxine's jaw clenched and Tabitha's lips trembled. "Ugly. Spoiled. Ruined. He would follow me into the nether regions, looking as I did. Then I sent Fulton out to cause havoc, to give our idiot hero something to follow and feel smart about. Because I knew where you'd be, with that idiot suitcase pimp's Auntie's house." Two fingers entered Maxine who whelped. "Your sanctuary. So while the world's worst private eye stumbled along to where I would need him, I collected you. Had fun with you. And made sure they both watched until I no longer needed witnesses."

Maxine screamed with her mouth shut as Tabitha removed her hand from inside her, sniffed her fingers, and wiped them over Maxine's face. "And it all worked, pretty. I've done it. I've found the book that will anchor my daemon and give me what I need."

Book? "Oh hell."

Tabitha's laughter jabbed at my ears, as she played with Maxine's head. "Yes, the rare tome of Montague Summers you had in your pathetic car? There are few on this earth. Father had one, but his estate has more charms than even I can handle. You were supposed to go straight to the estate like a good little errand boy and get me the book. Instead you traveled across half the city chasing after who-knows-what, like an incompetent buffoon. I had to send Fulton after you." She plunged into Maxine's mouth, holding both sides of her face as if a Ming vase. She pulled back, baring her teeth. "But eventually, the incompetent carney-kid father had chosen over me finally managed to get me my book. All I had to do was return and gather everyone back into the strands of my sigils." She caressed Maxine's face "and nurse you back to the Abyss, my beautiful womb." Maxine shivered. "This time, you will release that which I've seeded in you. An abomination that will allow my sigils to burn from film to eyes, to make me worshipped like a goddess who will have every man and woman who sees my visage bend to my will to become my thrall."

My fingers bled from the friction of severing ties of rope one strand at a time, but if I kept her talking I had some kind of chance instead of a certain death.

"No," I said, despite knowing one-eyed Fulton was ready for another round of speed bags on my low hanging fruit. "What you're raising? It can't be controlled. Not by humans. I saw its true form when I fell into the nowhere spaces when I was almost in a pain coma. It is not a servant, Tabitha. It's a beast . . . the tower for a darker king. Edgar couldn't rule it, even with Aphrodite's Tears. So what chance does some runaway starlet think they have?"

"Ah!" she said, but her eyes were still on Maxine. "Do you hear the dead man talking? He thinks I'm going to make the same mistake twice. But we know better. That's why he's tied beside you. You see, my darling, you will surrogate my familiar." Maxine shook and Tabitha shh'd her and cooed as if talking to a baby. "No, no. It won't lash out. Not this time. You see, according to my book, it was angry for food. It needed to be fed. And not just any milk would do."

Her head turned so that I got full charge of her withering gaze. "It needed someone touched by magic."

CHAPTER 38

MY FINGERS GROUND AWAY WHILE TABITHA HEEL-KICKED OCTAVIA and walked back to her throng. "I thought you'd go to father's estate to help me, James. To take one of his many artifacts. Why did you avoid it?"

"I'm not an heir," I said, face still singing echoes of agony from Fulton's right hand. "The only thing Edgar left me was funeral debt. That's why I took your case."

Tabitha considered me very carefully, and my fingers froze in bloody submission. "Yes. I learned that while you were running around the city. As part of my ruse, I sent Fulton to Vance Manor."

Edgar had a home in West Hollywood where he'd teach me, a bungalow filled with memorabilia but never any real magic, unless he brought it himself. Vance Manor was forbidden to me. Only die-hard magicians knew where it was. The one time I'd decided to hunt for it, the clues led me to storage unit. Inside was a dead cat and a note from Edgar that not only had I failed to find his "moving" mansion, I'd been so slow that this cat had starved to death. Worse, it had been pregnant. My curiosity had literally killed a cat. I got the message and kept to my studies.

"And how'd that go?" I said, looking at one-eyed Fulton.

Tabitha sighed. "Poor Fulton was . . . redirected."

"And sent back to find me?"

Octavia led Tabitha through the throng. "Fulton is good at many things. Killing gooks, making awful films, and hunting people." The people parted so she could caress his cheek. "But contending with the magic of Vance Manor . . ." She stroked his hair. "Father loved his privacy more than anything," Tabitha said as she rode back to me. "Certainly more than me. Do you even know where Manor House is, James?"

"I gave up trying to find it a long time ago."

"Giving up," she said with disgust. "Isn't that the story of your life?"

I said nothing.

She smiled and heeled Octavia to bring her toward me. "You didn't even know I existed. Yet I know you. I never gave up trying to find every ounce I could about father's little pet project, the throw-away from the rails of Oakland, the runaway who joined the circus, then ran away to war when your heart got broken. How sad, dull, and pathetic. I see why father wanted you: broken, desperate, willing to take orders."

I smiled. Because everything she said was right.

Until this morning. I don't take orders. "You know what Edgar said about his amazing daughter?" I said. It was there, the barest of flickers, a slice of vulnerability so thin it would melt on your tongue. "Zilch. You weren't even a ghost. It was as if you'd never been—"

She curled her fingers into her palm. The knots around my wrists and ankles bit into me, and nearly tore through my fingers.

"Don't speak to me of being born. Of legacy. I am my father's daughter. But where he played an old man's game, I am going to rule the new horizon. You're not even chosen, Brimstone. You're a thrall without a master. Your story is *over*. And the last good thing you will do in this world is usher in a new one." She held out her hand. Fulton reached into his vest and pulled out something dark and familiar.

The book by Montague Summers.

"I recently discovered there are only two first editions in existence," she said. "One in father's library. And this one." She gripped it with both hands as if it were her very first Big Mac. "It's charming to me that the one good thing you did on your first day as a detective will be the thing that births my new age."

"What age is that?" My fingers moved at a glacial pace, but the tightening of the binds had snapped some of the fibers. I needed to egg her on. "The age of daughters with daddy issues?"

Another hex in the air and the binding bit harder . . . and while blood ran down my forearms, more fibers snapped. I seethed in the pain.

She smelled the pages of the book with a deep, erotic inhalation. Those blue eyes closed. "Of idol worship. And one idol above all. The last one. The only one." Her eyes opened. "Me."

A flutter of movement came from the glazed crowd, as if a dog were sniffing his way through the legs of the charmed and chosen. Not a single note of worry came from Tabitha, who seemed high from the book's pages. "Ah, now we are all here."

Cutting through the legs, TV arrived, still puffing away. He had a first-class shiner from where I popped him in the eye. His left hand held my pistol as if it weighed a ton, but he'd rolled down his sleeves where I'd plunged the snakehead . . . and where I'd wrapped the anting-anting. Which meant there was a good chance that he was no longer charmed. My fingers worked the rope as Tabitha patted him on the head.

"How is my little hammer?"

TV grunted. "Found da guy's cannon." He gripped the nose of the pistol and handed it to Tabitha. She placed it snug inside her black belt.

"Well done, my first conquest." She turned away, kicked Octavia again, who led her to stand between me and the barely conscious Maxine. TV grimaced, face ashen minus my shiner, and looked at me. That beady little eye was the only thing uncharmed in this land of rot and beauty.

"Tonight!" Tabitha said, voice strong as a dagger in the heart. "Tonight, my pretty things, we will watch the birth of a new age. An age of beauty and rapture, where all who watch my visage shall fall under my spell and worship my majesty until the eons break against the shores of time."

"Please," Maxine said, ghostly fragile. "Please . . . Nico, don't."

Tabitha raised her chin. "You were honored, Maxine. Don't forget the ecstasy when I put that Kraken's eye inside you. The bliss. The blood. The wonder. The kind you only feel when you resist before you surrender." Nausea at the thought of brutal sex magic almost tore me from my mission. "And no," she said. "You will succeed where we last failed. You will call forth your progeny. I will tame it with words from a sacred tome. It shall feed upon James Brimstone. And its favors will be all mine."

"Last positions, everyone!" Tabitha glared and snarled at me. "Last positions, all!"

CHAPTER 39

LIGHTS BLARED AT TABITHA'S BACK, SENDING A SHADOW BESIDE Maxine, whose head slowly crept up from resting on her ample bosom. Cameras craned their necks, took us all in: the siren, the breeder, and the snack.

"Action!" Tabitha screamed, and my raw, bloody fingers worked overtime as I looked upon my day: it started in a graveyard, and it will end with my death.

My fingers dug deeper, fingers flexing at the frayed bits, the nausea from Fulton's ball-killer punch still shivering through my body.

Tabitha raised the book above her head as thunder rolled in dead clouds. Her voice rang out in a hodgepodge of German and Japanese. *"I call upon the spirit of the butchered Kraken, rapine lover of the sea, seducer of wives and killer of men. Hear me! I call you from your slumber."*

Maxine's head rolled up, jaw dropped, eyes as dead white as Little Orphan Annie. A sound rippled out of that beautiful mouth the color of lost nightmares, her lips baring teeth, a hiss that painted the air green.

"You are angry, my pet," Tabitha said in English. "You fear I will play with you, but not care for you."

Maxine's neck craned from side to side, body riding waves of supernatural horror.

"Taste the air."

Maxine's tongue craned out.

"Taste the essence of power I have brought for you to sup."

Maxine's tongue darted to her left and those dead eyes were reckoning with mine.

"Be born! Be mine! Anchor your power on this earth to my will!" She raised the book above her head. English vanished as she returned to the twisted tongue of German and Japanese, a language of corruption and hate.

Lighting struck Tabitha before thunder crackled. The heat wave and sparks sent a shockwave across the crowd and yanked me so hard the rope started to fray. I pulled until bone touched rope.

Tabitha threw down the burning book at Maxine's feet. "Come! *Now!*"

My arms snapped down, free at last, as Maxine screamed to the skies. From her mouth shot out a crimson baseball mitt, or so it seemed . . . something that could not be regurgitated and yet was forcing its way out.

The air was fetid with flecks of misery and pain. The creature was red and black, the color of fresh blood and twilight, and grew as its body voided from her mouth, vomiting a demon too big for its incubator. My fingers tore at the rope around my legs as the creature craned in the air, hovering before Tabitha. Its eyes were brackish and brown and full of tendrils that swam in the air like cancerous tumors hunting for a fresh host. The mouth opened. Razor-sharp teeth better fit in a great white shark lined the mouth, and then came the tongue . . . a smaller version of the demon snake, thick as a horse cock and staring Tabitha in the face.

"You lashed out at me out of hunger and fear," she said. "I forgive you. Now go and eat your fill, and in return, you will give me your eyes!"

She pointed at me, just as the last strand of rope flung off my ankles. "No!" she said. Someone, get hold of him!"

I dropped the ground, spread my legs wide, wondering how on earth you fought a crowd of slave-minded porn actors and a demon snake from the Axis. Fulton lurched forward, but was shoved aside by a punch to the knee. "Dis bastid is mine."

"Hold him, you miserable dwarf!" she said as TV sprang at me like cannon fire. He cracked against my chest and the wet ground slipped beside me. He dropped a hammer-fist next to my head instead of on top, his hand going five inches deep.

"Play along, idjit," he grunted low, then winked at the ant-ing-anting that was under his shirt, covered in puffs of smoke. "Or we're both dead." TV smacked me hard enough that it was echoing across the wind, but not as hard as it sounded. I feigned being knocked out.

TV tore my neck from the ground so that I was sitting up, brought my arms back, then took the anting-anting off his arm and wrapped it loose around my hands. "He's tame," he grunted.

"Stand him up," Tabitha said. "And back away. I would hate for my pet to eat a munchkin by accident."

TV muttered to himself, then mumbled, "Make it count, yewz bastid."

The demon slithered through the air as if swimming, half of its body zigzagging from Maxine's gaping mouth.

I had one shot. If the creature was still in Maxine when I used the charm, it would kill them both. I had to get its body all the way out . . . and because I am a rough and tumble carney kid at heart, there was just one way.

The demonhead crawled through the air until it was before me, pulsating tubular eye-strands a horror that ate my courage until all that was left was instinct, courage, and a gentleman's agreement to save a girl in trouble.

"Howdy," I said. And the creature recoiled the slightest, as if sensing something was off. "Wanna dance?"

Its mouth cracked open wide. Hell awaited in that gullet as it darted. I sidestepped its dagger strike to my head. It tasted the earth for a hot second, and I dove onto its back and held on for dear life while my arms tried to strangle a demon snake from hell.

"No!" Tabitha screamed. "Let go! You're ruining it! *You're ruining it!* Someone, get him off!"

The crowd circled the demon that bronco'd me around. They were knocked back on their asses like tenpins as it thrashed like a scythe. Bodies flew into the gladiatorial pit as the snake squealed. Fulton got in one punch before the wiggling beast crashed me into him, shooting the soldier over the pit and into the camera.

Tabitha's voice was a siren of hate. "No! You can't do this!"

I held and squeezed as the creature tried to pull me off. We drove further from Maxine, swimming the night air. It was trying to run away, because there was no turning back. I was pleased with myself until it began to whip its head against the ground, rolling in the mud to scrape me off. Blood filled my wounds, then mouth, but I held on. For Maxine. For myself. And to make sure Tabitha's nightmare never came true.

"Drown him, my beast! Drown him in mud!" The creature flung itself on its back and hammered me into muddy ground. The weight on my chest was crushing. Breath cracked out of my lungs, but I couldn't draw another.

Black flies swarmed my eyes. My spine felt feathery. My iron grip was starting to weaken. Mud stained every gulp of air. Poisons filled my blood. Sepsis. Infections. Sickness. Death.

The creature yanked itself into the air and my grip slipped. I clasped the rope of the anting-anting but it wasn't enough.

My back hit the ground. The demon serpent reared. Death was knocking. I blinked away the blood and agony as lightning flashed. Upon the pole I saw Maxine gasp a gurgle of blood as the tail of the creature emerged.

She was free.

"Kill him!"

The deathhead of the demon unhinged its jaws, and the snake tongue inside did the same.

"Now!"

It descended in a wordless scream.

Tears flushed my eyes as my right hand's bloody, raw fingers tore themselves from the mud-sucking ground and launched the anting-anting into the beast's maw. The eye tendrils buzzed like hornets in all directions, as if it sensed what magic was heading its way, but the mouth snapped shut out of reflex, cutting the air before my fingers. It swallowed the anting-anting. A charm against harm in the belly of a monster.

The demon shook as my lungs came back to life, smacking mud over me as it crashed to the ground. It writhed, shimmied, and jived to make itself free from the charm burning havoc in its guts.

I dragged myself back as its head moved like a clothesline and cut down all that were standing, shoving them into the gladiatorial pit. Whipping back, it twisted until it was on its back.

"You can't die! Not now!" Tabitha's face was manic as she launched off Octavia's back and ran toward her beast. "You are mine! You must do as I say! Kill what's killing you!" She pointed at me. "Kill him!"

The words wrenched the demon to right itself. Gasping just out of its reach, I had no plan B. If it wanted a piece, it would have it.

The snake head reared up, three stories tall, then arched its spine and descended behind itself. It wasn't heading for me. It headed for its tail. The damn thing was going to eat itself.

"I command you!" Tabitha said, pointing at the sky. "Stop!"

It dove to earth and bit its tail, spinning mud as it charged into itself, turning and twisting and consuming.

"Stop!"

The beast tried to eat what was killing it and spun itself further and further, the circle of consumption getting smaller and smaller, until the heat crept upon its own neck, and it was a whirling dervish of tendrils and fangs—

And then it was gone.

Gasping, I pushed my body out of the mud's pull, and across the field of battle there stood one soul . . . the most beautiful creature I've ever known, face a blanched wound of shock and horror.

My pistol was in Tabitha's right hand.

CHAPTER 40

"STAY DOWN," SHE SAID, LIFTING THE HAND-CANNON. "YOU'LL BE back in the earth soon enough."

At the lip of the pit, TV's hands gripped a cable plugged into a knocked-over TV camera that weighed as much as a Rolls. If he was my ally, I had to keep alive. For just a bit longer. "Then get it over with," I said.

That shocked her, almost as much as me.

"You dare speak to me—"

"Oh, I dare. I dare to tell you to shut up and do it already. I'm tired of your shit, Nico, Tabitha, whoever the hell you are. I'm tired, and I don't care. Plug me if you've got the guts. But just remember that I won."

She seethed. "You won nothing."

"The hell I didn't." I smiled. "How much blood and treasure did you spill for this hokey show? Seducing the porn people, getting them to be your slaves to your siren charms . . . and you failed. You failed twice. You got scared, then you got beat. No wonder Edgar tossed you aside." TV was slithering across the ground with an awkward grace, until he was behind her.

She raised the gun. "Shut up! You know nothing about my father."

"I know he didn't mention you once in thirty years. What were you doing, Tabs? Selling Avon door to door?"

TV crept behind her. Perfect spot to kick out her knees. "You're a dead man, Brimstone."

"Aren't we all?"

TV charged, but there was nothing to grab. Tabitha side-stepped his approach. TV hit the ground with his guts and then she lowered the gun.

"NO!" I said, springing to my feet against the rivers of pain through my body.

The shot was a sonic mule kick to my body, sharper than lightning. A black hole bloomed in TV's back. The little man had saved us all, and now he was dead, facedown in the mud. Tabitha's glee was manic in her beautiful smile. "A hack writer, a hack thrall, and a hack Judas." She leveled her eyes at me, smile big and bright. "And so too goes the prodigal son."

I ran. Toward Tabitha. Anger flushed my mind red. Three words chugging through my rage like pistons of a hot rod about to crash at Mach speed.

Glee gripped her face as she pulled the trigger.

Tyger, Tyger, burning bright.

The blast was slow, the flash like a candle being lit and then blown out with a kiss. Blood ran through all of my wounds and I felt every single one like gaping bird mouths in need of food and closure.

Tyger, Tyger, burning bright.

The first bullet passed by my thigh, and I was grateful for her bad aim as I slipped into Joyride mode . . .

. . . Blood ran down my nose as fast as spilled milk over a table's edge. Another blast, and the bullet came like a fastball for my gut. I twisted out of the way as another shot fired and I gritted against the pain as I moved out of the way . . . until what mojo I had for the Joyride drained . . . the real world rushed back, and the shock on Tabitha's face grew. All I had left was anger at her pretty, evil face.

"Tyger, Tyger, burning bright!"

A fifth bullet blasted toward my chest. No way to dodge, so I thrust out my hands, trying to catch a burning piece of metal like a firefly.

Sizzling agony ate my palms as if holding a coal from hell, but I cupped the bullet, hands stretching outward, as I tried something no magician had ever done. I pivoted on one foot, spun on my heel, and swung the damn bullet like a shot from a sling.

It tore itself from my hands as I slipped out of my Joyride and collapsed to my knees while Tabitha prepared her next shot. The bullet tore through the air as she aimed again. It crashed into her skull so hard it knocked her back and the piece flew from her tiny hand.

My hands hit the ground a second before Tabitha tripped over TV.

Shaking on all fours like a beaten mutt, I tore my hands from the ground and looked at my palms. Bloody pulp looked back, like a poor man's stigmata. On willpower alone, I rose.

I was the only critter on two feet that wasn't tied to a stake. I shambled over to Tabitha and pulled her off TV. Black blood leaked out of his chest like a Texas oil strike. "Why?" I said. "Why . . . help me?"

He coughed ink across his broad chest. "Youz . . . helped me be free. In any world, dat's a debt to be repaid before da lights go dark. Ain't no such thing as a free . . ." he grimaced, then smiled. "See ya around, bastid."

TV went silent.

Slowly, I crept toward the staked woman, Maxine. She was awake, gasping, blood dribbling from her lips thanks to the expulsion of a demon seed. "Who . . ." she said. "Who are you?"

I bowed and my eyes swam with darkness. "James Brim-stone," I stammered. "Private Investigator. I'll have you cut down in a jiffy. Just need to not . . . black . . . out."

I fell back into gravity's embrace, but was caught.

I looked up into a one-eyed face. "Ffffulton," I mumbled. I tossed a weak red punch that failed to connect before I said "pow." Then all the lights went out on set.

CHAPTER 41

I WOKE IN A BATHROOM, STILL DRESSED IN TATTERED AND MUDDY gladiator clothes, with Fulton barking orders to people coming in and out of the bathroom and waving smelling salts under my nose. "Yeah, he's awake, but we all have jobs to do. Now scat before I lose my shit."

My hands had been wrapped in gauze; wrists, too. The white bandages had dark centers, most of my leaking cuts were covered with band-aids, and my head and guts were filled with a million tiny sacks of pain . . . but I was alive. At Fulton's knee was an Army med kit, complete with vials of morphine and penicillin. "Welcome back, asshole."

"Thanks for . . . bringing me back."

He nodded. "Thanks for waking me up."

"You mean you're not mad about . . ."

"I'm mad about being drafted, and fighting a war we can't win, and for being seduced by that woman into being a monster . . . and yeah, I'm holding back about ten days of beatings for what you did to me." Hot red anger flushed his face, but he breathed out hard. "But not today. Because you broke whatever spell that had me . . ." He shook his head. "I'm sorry. I don't remember all of what I did, but I'm sorry."

I lifted my hands. "I'd say we're jake, Fulton."

He grinned. "You up for a visitor?"

"Given the dope in my system, I could also slow dance if she's pretty."

He snickered, stood, then left.

Octavia walked in, her regal appearance in tatters, but the strength in her eyes present, if distant. "Mr. Brimstone."

"Call me James."

"James. I can't say I . . . understand everything that just happened." Which was probably for the best. "But you saved my family. That's what Nero Pictures is. A family. With one very black sheep."

"More like a wolf, I'd say."

A practiced smile emerged. "Well said. I want you to know that we will take care of any fallout. The Los Angeles Police Department are good friends of ours, so I want you to know that there will be no . . . ripples of tonight's events that will reach you. This is my responsibility. And I take that seriously."

I gave a big morphine smile. "Lovely. Thank you. I liked . . . meeting your family."

She raised an eyebrow. "And they liked meeting you as well. But there's one in particular that wanted a meeting. Come in," she said to the open door.

Red hair on a green dress made my blood sing even through the dope. Maxine strode in, face clean and pure, red hair hanging to one side, covering part of her face. Her thin fingers covered her bottom lip as she spoke. "How are you?"

I took a long, dumb inhale. "Holes plugged, still breathing, I'd say that's a glass half-full. More important, how are you?"

Fingers tapped her lip. "Better, I think. It's such a haze, so much of it dark. What she did to me, to us." Her eyes squinted as fresh tears ran down a face that had already seen too much horror.

I braced a wounded hand on the sink counter and stood, amazed that gravity didn't drag me back to the cool floor. "And she can't do it again. Any of it."

"I just feel so stupid, and weak."

"She had that effect on all of us. You hear me? Tabitha was . . . born to manipulate, to control, and she was very good at it. Even charmed me without having any charms . . ." I shook my head, talking too much about myself. "Don't be hard on yourself. She promised you your dreams coming true, and made it look possible. People have fallen harder for much less."

"We spoke once," she said, dreamily. "Though we hadn't met, I think."

I nodded. "The soap box. Your image was on it, back in the laundry. Hell of a trick. Probably had something to do with Tabitha's magic. She wanted . . . control of people through images. And that box is as popular as beans at a hobo camp. And, Maxine, you're one hell of an image."

"We shared something. Like being in the same dream. I was drugged, trapped, but I could . . . taste something warm, a presence that was coming to me"

Even though she was talking New Age mumbo jumbo, I smiled. "Few people reach out to each other like that, through an image to a . . . presence.

Her lips were very wet. "I could sense something beautiful and strong."

I shrugged. "Must be my aftershave. Just promise me, if you ever use soap box magic to contact me again, don't do it while I'm getting groceries? I'm liable to have a heartache in the detergent aisle."

My clever banter was killed by a hug that made every wound pucker, but I let her shake me like a willow, head buried in my chest as she cried "thank you" and "sorry" and more. She pulled herself back, looking up to my eyes. "Is there anything I can do to repay you?" She bit her bottom lip. "Anything."

There wasn't enough dope to keep me from wanting her—

Then, the rest of my life crashed like angry waves against my skull. I had rent. I had a car with no windshield that I had to drive home. It would have been so easy to slip into the fantasy world of Nero Mansion, but it would stop the onslaught of realities that awaited me. "There is, actually."

We kissed, I made a request, and the rest was bliss that vanished as soon as it began.

Ten minutes later, I was dressed in my ratty blue suit that smelled like a homeless graveyard burning with dry sweat. I made dopey goodbyes to everyone. Terra seemed the saddest to see me go, though Rachel and Haley were a close second. The door closed behind me as I walked into the moonlit street toward Lilith.

I sat, keys in my hand, then froze. A shadow breathed in the back seat.

"James, you look awful."

In the rearview mirror, arched eyebrows glared back. What was left of my courage died.

"Edgar."

CHAPTER 42

"DON'T SOIL YOURSELF, JAMES. I WON'T BE HERE LONG."

I remembered to breathe. "What do you want?"

"Two things. First, thank you for dispatching Tabitha."

"You're thanking me for killing your kid? Jesus, Edgar."

He sighed. In the mirror, he was looking past me and into the night. "You broke her some, dear apprentice. But kill? My blood is stronger than a bullet. Though, I must applaud you for not becoming a casualty yourself using that old standby. Catching a bullet, how low. Still, she'll be . . . unable to cause much of a fuss for a bit. Cheers."

I ran the key's jagged teeth across my index finger. "The funeral. That was to flush her out. That's why you agreed to my terms. To be free of you."

He grunted. "The morphine is making you simple. Have I ever done anything for just one reason?"

"Never. You always have a dozen angles."

"You exaggerate. But that brings me back to the second thing. With Tabitha gone, for now, and my death established, I'd like to renegotiate my offer."

"No."

"Don't be hasty."

"No."

"What are you going to do, James? Waltz back to that whore-house?"

"Burlesque show, Edgar. I live at a Burlesque show."

"And scrounge for coins in the sad cases of the poor. You escaped those roots, my dear apprentice. You hated them in Oakland, and this running back to poverty is tired and old as a saint's chopped finger. I opened you to worlds unknown, James. To powers that could thrill you, make you far more powerful than a taster of magic and catcher of bullets. I made you capable of great things. Thus, I am offering you a better deal. Come with me as I—"

"No."

"You haven't heard the best part—"

"No."

"Stop acting like a child."

My anger ripped through the drugs. "No. The answer is no. It is always no. You don't care about the peasants of the world? Great, terrific, boy-howdy. But I do. You don't give a shit what happens to the little guy and gal? Fantastic and resplendent. I do. You want to fight other aristocrats and elites to save the universe or for your own ego, have fun, but I don't give a shit. Someone has to fight for the underclass, Edgar, the folks who come where I come from. Might as well be me. I don't want to be your apprentice, your heir, or your goddamn sidekick or prodigy. I said no, I mean no. It will be no until the end of time when death eats its own skull. We made a deal, Edgar. I would give the world your death, and you would give me my freedom. Or is your word as full of shit as you are?"

Silence held us for about three heartbeats, and I felt the ground slip away from my ass. The starlight sharpened like daggers and Lilith melted away while red eyes glared in the rearview mirror that evaporated. "You dare speak to me like that? I could eat your spine for dinner if I wanted. I could rape that Filipino *cunt* who spurned you before your very eyes and make her beg for more while you watched and applauded my efforts. I could tear down the walls of reality in your mind until all that was left was the drooling mouth of a dying soul, hanging from a puppet string made from his urethra until I killed it and resurrected it so that it could learn fresh suffering again. You are awaking a dragon with a toothpick. Press further, little puppet, and you will burn."

The world snapped back to normal, though Edgar's voice was a whisper. "You will come back to me, James. You'll see. You'll need me. And when you do, the price will be oh so very high. Face it, apprentice, no matter where you go, you're *mine*."

I exhaled, then looked behind me.

Shards of broken glass and the echo of his words in my ears were all that I found.

I awoke Lilith's engine and stared at L.A. through her broken eye.

The drive home was quick, that burp between the late shift and the early birds that let me travel at good speed. The morphine wouldn't last, so I stabbed the accelerator and roared through the city of angels. The wind through the open windshield tried to push the past away. It felt good, if useless.

I pulled into the Thump & Grind parking lot. Only one car left. Bee's Wagoneer.

I walked through the backdoor. Bee's office light was on, down the hall from my place. The locks were still on my door.

Bee stepped into the hall, then hit the light. I covered my eyes.

"Brimstone?" A sawed off shotgun was leveled at me. Her eyes calculated the amount of damage my face and body had taken since this morning. "What happened to you?"

"My client . . . turned out to be the problem." I stumbled toward my office door. "I'll get the rest of my rent tomorrow. I just need to rest my eyes for a minute." I was on the floor, back against my door, muttering, "Just a minute," when sleep blanketed me hard.

MUSIC WOKE ME. FROM OUTSIDE MY OFFICE DOOR, BASS AND FUZZY guitars were filling my head as the MC said "Dee Dee Lightful to the main stage! Dee Dee Lightful, your life is calling!"

I was on my couch. Moonlight cut through the shades and made the world black and white. A thick and fluffy pillow rested under my head, and a wool blanket was draped across my chest. Two things I didn't own. Each smelled like Bee: Pall Malls and Chanel No. Zero, the knockoff you get in Tijuana. My little rolling desk had a note taped to the agenda that was currently empty. I stood slow and moved slower.

The bar fridge opened with supreme effort, but I scoffed out two ice cubs and plunked them into a highball glass. From the top of an empty filing cabinet that came with the room I grabbed the Dubonnet with both gauzed hands and poured myself the tall, dark treat that had been denied me all day.

Like a baby with its bottle, I sipped the cool sweetness and tasted every wound as it cried through my dank clothing. The booze gave me enough strength to sit at my desk and read the note.

It was stuck on what I presumed was today's date, forty-eight hours after I'd buried Edgar and discovered Nico. Bee's immaculate script was a delight to the eyes.

We're good this month. Burn this after reading. And get pretty again. Ugly is bad for business. QB

I lit a match from a stray pack and sent the note to Ashville. I sipped my baby glass and enjoyed the dirty guitars coming through the stage, too tired to put on something better like Django or Dorsey or Ellington.

The phone rang and I dropped the glass across my lap, pain squeezing my sore balls like a nutcracker. Fear prickled my nerves as I reached for the receiver. "The Odd Job Squad," I grunted, pulling the wet glass from my lap. "Want the best? We're up to the test!"

"Hi . . . my name is Mandy. I'm a friend of Maxine's?"

"Is there anything I can do," Maxine had asked.

"She said you help people. Help people with . . . weird problems? Because, well, my boyfriend's in trouble, but not bad trouble, just weird trouble, you know? But . . . oh God, I can't even say. This is so weird."

"Yes," you'd said. "There is."

I licked the sweetness from my fingers until they were clean, then grabbed a ballpoint pen from a tin cup. "My dear," I said. "Weird is my specialty."

ABOUT THE AUTHOR

JASON RIDLER is a writer, improv actor, historian, and author of the Brimstone Files for Night Shade Books. He's written numerous crime and horror novels, including *A Triumph for Sakura, Blood and Sawdust,* and the Spar Battersea Thrillers. He has published over sixty-five stories in venues such as *The Big Click, Beneath Ceaseless Skies, Out of the Gutter,* and writes the column FXXK WRITING! for Flash Fiction Online. He also writes and performs sketch comedy and improv in the San Francisco Bay Area. A former punk rock musician and cemetery groundskeeper, Mr. Ridler holds a Ph.D. in War Studies from the Royal Military College of Canada.